NECROMUNDA
SALVATION

FAME OR DEATH.
OR POSSIBLY BOTH...

ZEFER TYRANUS IS an inquisitive man and an able administrator. His family has been in the service of the Noble House Ko'iron for generations, acting as curators, record keepers and occasionally spies for the famed scholars and poets of that glorious house. His position affords him residence in an exclusive zone of the Spire, enveloped in luxury, and very close to the walls of the ruling House Helmawr.

However, Zefer's comfortable world is turned upside-down when he hears tales of an ancient artefact that could possibly link House Ko'iron to the founding fathers of the Spire itself. Sent out on a dangerous mission to retrieve it, Zefer must learn the hard way that the Underhive is no place for a simple curator!

NECROMUNDA
SALVATION

C S GOTO

For the Reverend and his faith (in me).

A BLACK LIBRARY PUBLICATION

First published in Great Britain in 2005 by
BL Publishing,
Games Workshop Ltd.,
Willow Road, Nottingham,
NG7 2WS, UK.

10 9 8 7 6 5 4 3 2 1

Cover illustration by Clint Langley.

A CIP record for this book is available from the British Library.

ISBN 10: 1 84416 189 7
ISBN 13: 978 1 84416 189 8

Distributed in the US by Simon & Schuster
1230 Avenue of the Americas, New York, NY 10020, US.

Printed and bound in Great Britain by
Bookmarque, Surrey, UK.

See the Black Library on the Internet at
www.blacklibrary.com

Find out more about Games Workshop
www.games-workshop.com

In order to even begin to understand the blasted world of Necromunda you must first understand the hive cities. These man-made mountains of plasteel, ceramite and rockrete have accreted over centuries to protect their inhabitants from a hostile environment, so very much like the termite mounds they resemble. The Necromundan hive cities have populations in the billions and are intensely industrialised, each one commanding the manufacturing potential of an entire planet or colony system compacted into a few hundred square kilometres.

The internal stratification of the hive cities is also illuminating to observe. The entire hive structure replicates the social status of its inhabitants in a vertical plane. At the top are the nobility, below them are the workers, and below the workers are dregs of society, the outcasts. Hive Primus, seat of the planetary governor Lord Helmawr of Necromunda, illustrates this in the starkest terms. The nobles – Houses Helmawr, Cattalus, Ty, Ulanti, Greim, Ran Lo and Ko'Iron – live in 'The Spire', and seldom set foot below 'The Wall' that exists between themselves and the great forges and hab zones of the hive city proper.

Below the hive city is the 'Underhive', foundation layers of habitation domes, industrial zones and tunnels which have been abandoned in prior generations, only to be re-occupied by those with nowhere else to go.

But... humans are not insects. They do not hive together well. Necessity may force it, but the hive cities of Necromunda remain internally divided to the point of brutalisation and outright violence being an everyday fact of life. The Underhive, meanwhile, is a thoroughly lawless place, beset by gangs and renegades, where only the strongest or the most cunning survive. The Goliaths who believe firmly that might is right; the matriarchal, man-hating Escher; the industrial Orlocks; the technologically minded Van Saar; the Delaque whose very existence depends on their espionage network; the firey zealots of the Cawdor. All striving for the advantage that will elevate them, no matter how briefly, above the other houses and gangs of the Underhive.

Most fascinating of all is when individuals attempt to cross the monumental physical and social divides of the hive to start new lives. Given social conditions, ascension through the hive is nigh on impossible, but descent is an altogether easier, albeit altogether less appealing, possibility.

excerpted from Xonariarius the Younger's
Nobilite Pax Imperator – the Triumph
of Aristocracy over Democracy.

1: THE SPIRE

Everything is built on something else –
What shoulders the burden of elsething?
Glory rests wholly on the Undying Emperor
(or elsewhere only if strictly necessary).
Praise the Emperor for the heights of Ko'iron.
For it is better to be well defined at the top
Than lost in the paradoxes of foundations –
unless it isn't.

From *Paradoxes of the Spire*

ANYTHING COULD HAVE happened and he wouldn't have noticed. He was not an observant man at the best of times, even when his nose was not pressed deeply into the glue-cracked spine of an ancient tome. He read with his whole being, always sniffing each page before he read it, hunching over his desk and pushing his face close to the parchment, as though certain that he could inhale some of the original intent that the author had been unable to transliterate into the orderly etchings of script. When his lungs rattled with the forgotten damp of the paper, he would raise his head and sigh, nodding slightly in appreciation. Smoothing the pages flat with his pale hands, he would begin to read, before commencing the ritual again on the next page.

Zefer's desk was tucked away on the seventy-third floor of the Ko'iron librarium. He called it his desk because he sat at it every night and read for three hours exactly. In the four and three-quarter years that he had been permitted access to the higher levels of the librarium, he had never once seen another curator sitting at that desk. Hence, he reasoned, it was as good as his. Every ninth evening, he would carefully place his stylus into an ostensibly careless position on the desk and leave it there overnight. On those nights he would not be able to sleep, and he would sit on the edge of his bed wringing his hands in anxious excitement. Nothing could match his sense of satisfaction and relief when he saw it there, unmoved, the next day. It was *his* desk.

In his most audacious moments, Zefer might even refer to the seventy-third floor as *his* floor, since he was invariably the only person there. He never actually said those words out loud: *my floor.* But they echoed around his head in the hours of late afternoon, before he was released from his duties in the lower levels of the librarium. Once, caught up in the euphoric regression of whispers in his mind, Zefer had even moved his desk to the end of another book stack, feeling his power over the floor growing with each scrape of the table leg on the flagstones. In the end, his resolve had cracked and he had run back to the librarium in the middle of the night and replaced the desk in its original position, cleaning the scratches off the floor with saliva and the cuffs of his robe.

The book smelt like cold vegetable soup, and its pages were slightly damp with his breath in the frosty night air. Zefer traced his finger along each line of text as he read, letting its slender, flickering shadow dance in the candlelight, nodding slightly at points that made sense to him and screwing up his forehead when things made no sense at all. It was the *Paradoxes of the Spire*, so his face was a perpetual lattice of cracked ice.

Over the last few months, Zefer had made it nearly halfway through the ancient tome. As far as he knew, this was the furthest that anyone in his generation had managed to get. The text was tortuously convoluted and riddled with mysterious allusions that were wasted on the normal reader. It was not exactly a heavy book – indeed the poetic style was faintly ridiculous – but it was dense and deceptively impenetrable. It was the opposite of a labyrinth: impossible to get into, but easy to get out of. Most people simply gave up on it after its famous introduction:

> *In the beginning they lay the end into the ground,*
> *And the finale was buried beneath the foundations,*
> *As though expecting the sky to fall into the abyss*
> *In the days of Ko'iron's salvation to come.*

The book stacks of level seventy-three were overflowing with commentaries written by renowned scholars, many of them focussed exclusively on those first four lines. Zefer had read them all and, on reflection, it seemed fairly clear that even the most erudite and wise of House Ko'iron had not made it beyond those muddy introductory lines. Zefer had read all of the commentaries before he even picked up the *Paradoxes*, thinking that he should approach the original text with as much rhetorical ammunition as possible. That was why it had taken four years before he had even opened the hallowed book itself, and why he had read the first four lines over and over again every day for three months, experimenting with various interpretations and test-driving the theories of the past masters.

He was not sure that he had produced any great or innovative insights, but he had made careful note of his thoughts in a little book of his own, *his book*. Sometimes, on his long, lonely walk home through the gently twisting streets of the Spire, Zefer would fantasise that his son would stumble across *his book* at the end of stack 4.73.2176b. There were one or two things that needed to be done before this particular fantasy could come true: Zefer needed to write the book, and he needed to have a son. He wasn't confident that either condition would be satisfied in the near future.

After he had got through the complicated web of the first four lines, progress had been much smoother. Indeed, he had covered more than five hundred lines in just over two months. He was relatively sure that the speed was because he wasn't paying as much attention, but part of him remained confident that he had gained an important foothold in the text in the first few lines, and that the rest built logically upon those foundations. In fact, those first lines made more and more sense as he read further and further into the book.

Turning the page deliberately, Zefer ducked his nose down into the exposed inner-spine and inhaled deeply. Sighing, he pressed the new pages flat and started to read. Then he stopped. He flicked back to the previous page and read the last line again.

Though it may be lost, salvation is always found

Turning back to the new page, he read the first line.

When you look up, there is nothing but the sky.

He sniffed again, picking the book off the surface of his desk and squashing it against his face. The new page smelt different, as though the chef had forgotten to add salt to the soup.

Stretching out his arms, he held the book in front of him, balancing it precariously on the palm of his left hand. With his right, he turned the problematic page backwards and forwards in front of the candlelight, feeling its pendulous shadow swinging across his face as he squinted at the movement of the parchment. He pressed down slightly on the edge of the paper with his right index-finger and the shadow split into two vertical stripes, with the candlelight burning brightly straight through the middle.

In shock and excitement, Zefer snatched his hands back and the book clattered down to the desk, its heavy leather covers snapping shut. Pushing his seat back from the desk, Zefer jumped to his feet and took a couple of paces towards the exit. Almost immediately, he stopped, changing his mind, and turned back to the desk, wringing his hands with indecisive anxiety. The *Paradoxes of the Spire* lay solidly on the small writing-desk, unmoving and unconcerned by all the commotion. Zefer stared at it.

Slowly and hesitantly, as though stalking a terrible enemy, Zefer shuffled back towards the book, fixing his eyes on the faded gold lettering on its atrophied leather binding. The yellow candle light burst into periodic reflections, luring him back to the desk with the flickering promise of riches and wisdom.

He picked his chair off the ground, standing it back onto its legs in front of the desk, and sat down, breathing evenly to calm his nerves. The book seemed to look back at him, implacable with the confidence of unspoken ages, and he shivered slightly as though caught in the glance of a ghost.

Taking a deep breath and exhaling loudly, Zefer
flipped open the front cover to the frontispiece with its
elegant illumination of Hive Primus – the capital of
Necromunda. Never having been outside of the huge
hive city, Zefer always paused in wonderment at this
picture. He looked at the contorted and vaguely coni-
cal structure, pushing up from the crumpled remains
of the Underhive. It rose erratically from the barren
wastelands of the surrounding planes to a height of
about ten miles, slicing through the permanent layer of
lethally poisonous, yellowing and noxious undercloud
at about three miles, created by the continuously vom-
iting factories of Necromunda. Then, at the five mile
mark, there was the layer of natural cloud, thick and
billowing, as the heavier toxins rained down into the
underlayer leaving only the relatively clean, acidic
water vapour congealing into a thick cumulus belt.
And high above that, aspiring to the heavens, was the
majestic spire of House Helmawr – the hereditary lords
of Hive Primus and guardians of all Necromunda. The
hive was surprisingly beautiful, thought Zefer, each
time he looked at it.

Out of habit, Zefer glanced over his shoulder
towards the reinforced window cut into the thick
exterior walls of the librarium. At night, he could see
nothing out there at all, except for the faint glow of
millions of lights refracted through the thick vapour.
During the day, the view was only slightly better:
swirling and eddying cloud sweeping past the glass
and smudging it with moisture.

He shook his head at the marvel of the structure in
which in sat, and at the glory of Ko'iron that it represented. The great Ko'iron librarium was a tower of
more than one hundred levels; at unbelievable
expense, it had been built on one of the exterior

walls of Hive Primus, five-point-two miles from the Underhive. The founders of the great House had insisted that its curators should be granted the extraordinary privilege of natural light by which to study the history and glory of Ko'iron over the generations to come. Hence, the librarium protruded like a thorn from the side of the Spire, the windows of three sides pointing out into Necromunda's vaporous atmosphere and the fourth connected by a web of bridges and walkways back into the Spire itself.

In fact, the Ko'iron curators enjoyed almost no natural light at all. The House Ko'iron architects had overlooked the fact that this altitude was perpetually enshrouded by the natural cloud belt. When the local star was at its peak, just after noon, a thin yellow light filtered through the thick clouds, but it was certainly not enough to read by. In any case, most of the curators would be on their lunch-breaks at that time. Unfortunately, the architects had been so stubborn about the potential wonders of natural light that they had neglected to install sufficient interior lighting – thus, like the other curators in the librarium, Zefer had to carry a supply of candles with him at all times. Rather than producing the most magnificent librarium in the Spire, bathed in the splendour of natural light, House Ko'iron actually boasted the darkest and dingiest librarium out of all the Spire's great Houses.

As usual, Zefer ran his finger over the cloud line etched into the frontispiece, tracing the contours of the voluminous vapour trail. He knew that the librarium was hidden behind that layer, but it was the first paradox of the *Paradoxes of the Spire* that the Ko'iron librarium was hidden from view in the frontispiece of one of its own most famous tomes.

He flicked through the pages of the ancient book, searching for the lines that had caused him such consternation. Finally, after a few minutes of flicking and sniffing, Zefer found the page: '...*though it may be lost, salvation is always found*'

It didn't even end with a full-stop. And the first line on the next page was a clear non-sequitur: '*When you look up, there is nothing but the sky*.' For a few more moments Zefer wondered whether this was really a non-sequitur, or whether it was simply a characteristic, stylistic device. In the end, it was the missing full-stop and the odd smell of the following page that proved decisive. He held the book up to the light once more, flipping the page in question vertically against the candle. He delicately pressed the page with his index finger until it buckled and split into two. He pushed his finger in between the pages and tugged it up against the top edge, but the pages were still uncut and thus connected together as a single, folded sheet.

This time Zefer was ready for the wave of excitement that gushed over him as he realised what he had found, and he laid the book carefully back onto his desk. He looked nervously over each shoulder, as though suspicious that this would be the first night in nearly five years that there would be someone else on the seventy-third floor, watching him. He couldn't see anyone, but it was almost completely dark beyond the reach of the candlelight, so there might have been an entire troop of Delaque spies waiting in the shadows for all he knew.

Picking up his stylus, he slipped it between the uncut pages and tugged gently, watching the folded edge separate and tear a fraction. He checked back over his shoulders again, paranoia trickling down his spine like a droplet of icy water. Another slight flick with his stylus and the crease ripped nearly halfway along, revealing the lost pages where the missing full-stop suggested that they would be. With a final, nervous thrust, he sliced the pages open and instantly stuffed his nose down into the new pages, inhaling deeply. They smelt unlike any pages he had ever smelt before; they smelt… untouched.

Zefer pressed the hidden pages flat with his hands and sighed loudly, letting the intoxicating scent of the unblemished paper escape from his lungs at last. Nobody had ever read these pages before. Nobody. Not since the book was written, thousands of years before, had anyone seen these words. Zefer was so excited that he could hardly bring himself to lower his eyes to the page. Instead, he glanced down at the timepiece on his wrist and realised that he had been at his desk for three hours and seven minutes. Seven whole minutes more than usual, his routine he had kept for five years shattered by a few moments of lost concentration. In mild panic, he checked back over both shoulders once again, suddenly fretting that somebody might be witness to his incompetent time-keeping.

Snapping shut the *Paradoxes of the Spire*, Zefer placed his stylus carefully onto its cover, diagonally across the top left-hand corner, and then he hurried out of the librarium, flustered and conscious that his routine had been broken.

THE GOGGLES BLINKED and whirred, chiming quietly when they clicked into focus and then buzzing when the image fuzzed again. They were an old and unreliable technology, with a blind spot right in the middle of the lens where the tiny pixels on the little image intensifier had burnt out, but they were all that Krelyn had been left with after House Delaque's Red Snake gang had cut her off. She bobbed her head slightly, like a mongoose taunting a cobra, trying to trick the goggles into focussing on the speck of reality hidden behind the digital blind spot, but it was no use. The faulty pixels where precisely those used for focussing, so the little machine had no hope.

Clicking the goggles to manual, Krelyn estimated the distance between her rooftop perch and the circular access tunnel set into the wall on the other side of the street. It was an unusual tunnel, employed by only a very few of the Ko'iron curators who stayed in the librarium late into the night, after the more orthodox exits had been sealed. The tunnel emerged about eleven metres above the surface of the street, presumably because of a miscalculation on the part of the librarium's architects, or perhaps because of subsidence in the street itself. This part of the Spire was more unstable than most, and small hive-quakes were not unheard of.

About three hundred metres, thought Krelyn, thumbing the dial on the side of the goggles and watching the image leap into focus. She was concerned that she had missed him – it was already more than five minutes past his usual time. By now she would have expected to have seen a steady stream of spies spilling out of the tunnel, springing from its lip onto the nearby rooftops and then vanishing into the shadows. But there had been nobody, unless it had all happened in that cursed blind spot.

There he was. Shuffling and sleepy, tripping occasionally on the uneven floor of the tunnel and staggering to a halt just before the edge dropped eleven metres down to the flagstones on the street below. He looked nervous, thought Krelyn, even more nervous than usual.

The curator paused for a moment, letting his heavy, dark over-robe flutter in the breeze that funnelled through the passageway. His hands were clutched anxiously together, and he was wringing them, as though trying to squeeze water out of them. A candle flickered precariously in his grasp. Hunching his shoulders into the suggestion of a cringe, he looked back behind him, perhaps concerned that he was being followed.

Krelyn watched the figure blow out his candle and crouch down to the ground, sitting onto the floor and swinging his legs over the edge of the tunnel mouth. He sat for a moment, apparently mustering the courage for the short drop down to the ledge that protruded from the wall a couple of metres below him. He didn't look very confident, and Krelyn found herself scoffing inwardly at the frailty of the man. Too much time in that librarium, she thought.

Finally, he twisted himself around and caught hold of the rock edge with his fingers, sliding his body down the wall until he was dangling from his hands. From her position on the other side of the street, Krelyn could see that the man's feet hung only a few centimetres from the ledge below, but he was kicking his legs frantically, as he struggled to find something solid to put them on. She could see the knuckles of his hands gradually whitening as his grip locked and then faltered. One hand slipped and the man swung momentarily, like a hooked fish, before the strength of the other hand failed and he tumbled into a heap on the ledge below.

Just like last night, thought Krelyn, shaking her head behind the goggles. Just like every night.

Uncrumpling himself, the man smoothed out his over-robe with his hands and set off along the ledge towards the narrow stone steps that led down to street-level. But once he was out of the tunnel, he was no longer Krelyn's concern. She was supposed to ensure that the librarium was emptied each night, and to monitor the movements of those employees who kept unsociable hours. For the last few years, the bumbling Curator Tyranus had been the last Ko'iron servant out of the great librarium, and tonight appeared to be no exception.

Krelyn lifted her goggles back to the tunnel mouth and waited. It usually took another couple of minutes before the spies started to appear. There were invariably five of them; Krelyn presumed that one was in the employ of each of the other Noble Houses of the Spire. She wasn't sure why they would want to spy on the Ko'iron librarium, but she was aware that Ko'iron also sent spies into the librariums of a couple of the other Houses, especially Ulanti and Catallus. Indeed, she had served for a time as a spy in the upper levels of the Ulanti librarium, keeping tabs on the discoveries of the curators who were researching the history of that ancient House. Nobody ever found anything new – all of the oldest books had been read and reread hundreds of times. There was not a page unturned and not a word unanalysed.

Nothing happened for nearly ten minutes, and Krelyn shifted her weight uneasily on the tiled rooftop. If they didn't appear in the next sixty seconds, she would have to go in after them. What in the world could they be doing in there – it was only a librarium – and Krelyn didn't savour the thought of putting her life on the line for a few stacks of paper and twine.

Still nothing. Krelyn dropped the goggles from her face, tucking them into her belt as she stood. Her long black cloak fluttered out behind her like a shadowy banner, and she paused for a moment, balanced perfectly on the apex of the roof, with the building dropping fifty metres down to the sparsely peopled street under her toes.

The light in this sector was always dim, and hardly a single ray found its way up to the roofline when the streetlight-gargoyles were dimmed to encourage the residents to sleep. Despite her dramatic pose, Krelyn was confident that she would be almost invisible from the ground – her cloak was made of a special, unreflective fabric that actually drew light into it, soaking it up from the surrounding air like a sponge, producing a blurry phase-field that cast the wearer into a perpetual dusk. Wearing the cloak was like having tinted glass windows on your transporter, but without the transporter.

She turned away from the edge and took a couple of steps further onto the roof, letting her cloak swirl into an arc behind her, before turning again and taking a long, slow breath, preparing herself for the jump. With a burst of motion, she dashed forward, kicking off the apex of the roof and bicycling her legs as she flew across the street. Her cloak spread out like an air-sail in her wake, keeping her buoyed up. After a couple of seconds her feet touched down lightly on the tiles of another roof, lower than the first and about fifty metres away from it. She kicked off as soon as she landed, peddling her legs and letting her cloak give her wings.

Halfway to the next rooftop, Krelyn stole a glance towards the mouth of the tunnel. There was a faint flicker of deep blue in the shadows, and Krelyn cursed under her breath. She dropped down onto the next tiled roof, landing a little heavily, and pushing herself into a roll to ease the impact. As she turned over her shoulder, she pulled the goggles out of her belt and brought them up to her face, already focussed on two hundred metres by the time she was back up on one knee at the very rim of the rooftop.

A hooded figure was pressed up against the deeply shadowed inner wall of the tunnel, almost invisible in his trademark Delaque over-cape – it was the kind used by all the Delaque gangs, and it made them almost indistinguishable from each other to out-siders. Slashed across his face was a visor of midnight blue – an optical enhancer used by Delaque spies in particularly bad light to heighten their already sharp vision, or in intense light to pro-tect their sensitive eyes. A tiny reflective burst from the visor had given him away, and Krelyn could see him clearly. Besides, she knew what she was looking for, having been trained by the same spymasters as the hooded man.

The man was looking nervously back down the tunnel, as though fearful that he was being followed, or hunted. Of course, he *was*, just like every night. But tonight there was a new quality to his anxiety, and Krelyn was suspicious that he was not simply going through the motions this time. He waited just slightly too long in the shadows at the end of the tunnel, and he stared back into the darkness with just a little too much intensity. When he sprung down from the tunnel mouth, his cloak ballooning out behind him to slow his elongated descent onto a low rooftop nearby, he was just a fraction too hur-ried. The man had something to report to his masters, and Krelyn needed to know what it was.

After another moment, another figure appeared in the mouth of the tunnel. He was virtually indistin-guishable from the first, and his manner was equally agitated. Then another and another, until the usual five had finally emerged from the darkness and fled the Ko'iron librarium on their way back to make the most important routine report of their lives.

Krelyn watched them go one by one, crouching behind the castellated perimeter of the Quake Tavern's elaborately tiled roof. The curdling smell of roasting meat seeped up through the building beneath her, teasing her senses with the idea of dinner. She inhaled involuntarily, savouring the flavours absently while her brain raced to keep abreast of the night's developments.

More than anything else, she needed to know what had waylaid the curator and the spies – their routines had become so regular over the last few years that they were almost rituals, and this kind of variation suggested that something profound was amiss. However, she could not simply approach the curator and ask him what he had found, since House Ko'iron had a well know policy of trust in its hereditary servants, and it would not be fitting for one such trusted servant to discover that his movements were being tracked by an in-house spy. Conversely, there would be nothing gained from following one of the other spies and trying to prise the information out of them – Krelyn was well aware of the pycho-conditioning undergone by all Delaque agents and she still had the scars on the base of her neck to prove it. Besides, her masters in House Ko'iron would not look favourably on the creation of the kind of major diplomatic incident that would arise if she damaged the servant of another House, even if that servant had been spying on Ko'iron's famous librarium. Some open secrets were best left in the shadows, where they belonged. Politics.

Placing one hand onto the fortified eaves, Krelyn swung her legs up and over the edge of the roof, dropping in a flurry of cloak down onto a narrow balcony.

There was only one thing for it, she thought as she peered through the window into one of the ostentatious suites in the upper floor of the Quake Tavern: she would have to go into the librarium herself and find out what all the fuss was about.

She slipped the latch on the window and climbed through into a bedroom suite that momentarily took her breath away. The walls were covered in lush, purple velvet, and the carpet on the floor was so deep that footprints had been left in it by the last people to enter. The centrepiece was a huge, antique bed, surrounded by drapes and tapestries. Judging by the muffled sounds coming from the other side of the curtains, the bed was already occupied.

Without ceremony, Krelyn swept through the room and clicked open the door on the far side of the bed. Letting the door swing shut behind her, she headed straight down the stairs, through the bustling bar and out into the street below, paying no attention to the commotion in the Quake Tavern or the whispered conversations about an incredibly courageous curator. She was in no mood for the petty rumours of the effete clientele of the Quake and was entirely focussed on getting across to the mouth of the librarium's entrance tunnel.

ZEFER COULDN'T SLEEP. He hadn't even gone home. Instead, he had walked around the winding, undulating streets of Gwentria's Fringe – an affluent sector of the Ko'iron domain that lay up against the edge of the exterior wall of the Spire itself – muttering to himself and wringing his hands. He couldn't get the book out of his head.

Before he knew where he was, he found himself propping up the bar in the Quake Tavern with a frothing tankard in his hand. The place was bustling with people, just as it was every night. The locals were chattering boisterously about money and trade, and small pockets of strangers were huddled around tables in the darkened corners, talking conspiratorially about their adventures in the lower reaches of Hive Primus. Zefer had once found himself in the middle of such a group, since it had descended upon his table as he sat quietly next to the fire nursing his drink. One of the men had claimed to be from Hive City, on the other side of the great Wall that separated the unsanitary masses from the civilised people of the Spire. He had told some remarkable stories about his adventures in the Underhive, where he claimed to have found ancient archeotech from the time of the Emperor himself. Zefer had assumed that it was all nonsense, but he had subsequently seen the man in the Ko'iron librarium, evidently in the employ of the Acquisitions Section.

Zefer surveyed the scene absently-mindedly, wondering vaguely whether he should go and find a seat somewhere. As he turned to face the room, a dark-hooded figure brushed past him, jolting his arm and sending his drink flying. The man gave no apology and seemed not even to have noticed, leaving Zefer standing forlornly in a puddle of mead, with his arm still outstretched, clutching nothing.

As the hooded man approached the bar, the jostling patrons almost fell over as they pushed each other aside to make space for him. The man behind the bar came rushing over at once, leaving a drink half-poured on the counter in front of a fetching young woman in a distractingly revealing red shirt. For a second, Zefer and the woman shared a glance of annoyance at all the fuss being made of the Delaque venator, but Zefer dropped his eyes quickly, suddenly searching the ground for something that he hadn't dropped.

It's no good, thought Zefer as his glance jumped around the room in agitation and the mead soaked slowly into his cloth boots, there are too many distractions in here. He needed a place to think.

There was a sign above the bar that read: *Simple rooms – comfortable beds.* Somebody had scribbled a broad smile and an exclamation mark onto the sign in a childish or drunken hand, but Zefer didn't care about the innuendo tonight. He lent over the shoulder of the hooded figure at the bar and slapped a fistful of money onto the counter. The barman stared at him in something approaching awe as Zefer rested one hand on the shoulder of the venator to push himself back away from the bar again. The hooded agent paused momentarily, with his drink just licking at his lips. With an eerie slowness, the venator turned his head to face Zefer, and the Quake Tavern fell into silence. Their faces were so close together that Zefer could clearly see the little red snake tattooed under the venator's left eye.

To the barman, it seemed that the venator affected a slight double-take when he saw the exhausted features of Zefer next to him. There was only a fraction of a second of hesitation before the venator turned his gaze back to his mead and took a deep draw on the foaming liquid.

Zefer hardly seemed to notice the minor miracle of his continued existence, as he dragged himself up the tavern stairs towards one of the guestrooms, he just wanted to rest but the rest of the Quake immediately broke into urgently whispered gossip. The woman in the red shirt watched him go in admiration, wondering whether all the bravado had been for her benefit.

At the top of the stairs, Zefer just pushed open the first door that he came to and stumbled into the room. He trudged through the incredibly deep pile carpet and flopped onto the bed, letting the curtains around the bed-frame close in around him. For a few minutes he lay on the edge of sleep, as nervous exhaustion fought with nervous energy for control of his consciousness. He rolled fitfully, and moaned, clutching at his head with his hands, as though trying to bring his racing thoughts under control with sheer physical pressure.

The click of a latch being released brought him back to his senses and he froze. Although Zefer could see nothing through the heavy drapes around the bed, he was certain that somebody had entered the room. They were light on their feet, but Zefer could just about hear the deep carpet compressing as they walked carefully around the edge of the bed. After a few seconds, the intruder made it to the other side of the room and there was the sound of another latch clicking, and then the clunk of a closing door.

Zefer pulled back the curtains around the bed and hastened over to the door, sliding home the intricate series of bolts and locks that peppered its surface. Then he rushed over to the window on the other side of the room, tripping slightly in the heavy carpet, and clicked its lock into place. He had been through enough today already, and really couldn't cope with any more excitement. He just wanted to sleep.

THE TUNNEL WAS dark and damp, and the floor was an uneven patchwork of cracked rock. Through the optical enhancers built into her visor, Krelyn could see the hazardous passageway clearly. She could even see the glaring structural weaknesses that would cause the corridor to rupture and collapse if there was ever another sizeable hive-quake in the area. As she stepped carefully over the cracks and ducked under the splinters of stone that stabbed down from the ceiling, she thought about the five miles of open air that lay beneath the weathered passageway under her feet. She walked a bit faster, keen to get across the invisible drop and into the firmer structure of the Ko'iron librarium on the other side. Like the vast majority of people in Hive Primus, Krelyn had never been outside the immense edifice, and any reminder that there was an outside made her slightly nauseous. Like most people on Necromunda, she was intensely agoraphobic, and the thought of five miles of open space beneath her feet made her eyes bulge as she dashed through the last few metres of the tunnel.

Once inside, Krelyn found herself on a dim landing, with a wide, spiralling, stone staircase twisting off to her left into the upper-levels and down to her right. The mouth of the tunnel itself was perfectly in line with the landing – so the architects clearly had known what was going on inside in the librarium, even if they had not been not so sure about the structures in the Spire itself – but it was hidden behind a large hanging tapestry. As Krelyn looked back from the landing, she winced slightly when she caught sight of the giant, embroidered face of Hredriea, an old, long-dead matriarch of House Ko'iron, flapping slightly in the breeze from the tunnel behind it.

Where to begin? Krelyn peered through the darkness of the unlit librarium, looking for some sign of where the curator might have been working. Sitting outside on the rooftop, night after night, Krelyn had not really appreciated how huge this place actually was. She had

imagined a pokey little tower with a few curators at
rickety old desks. But the tower from her imagination
would have fitted easily into this huge landing, the
vaulted ceiling of which disappeared into the shadows
far above her head. A little sign on the wall showed the
number sixty-five next to an arrow pointing to the
right, and Krelyn shook her head in disbelief.

Clicking to infra-red on her visor, Krelyn studied the
marble steps. The stone showed no trace of footsteps –
it was an incredible heat-conductor and thus a tracker's
nightmare. However, there was a thin strip of carpet
that ran up the middle of the stairs, and Krelyn could
just about make out the telltale pink of human
thermo-prints heading up into the upper levels. Five
nimble spies and a heavy-footed curator left just about
enough of a heat trail, even after half an hour.

Springing up the steps two at a time, but keeping her
eyes trained on the ground to keep track of the thermal
images, Krelyn rapidly ascended into the upper levels
of the librarium. Had she looked up, she would have
noticed a distinct change in the decoration after level
seventy, marking the beginning of the restricted-access
collections, open to only the most trusted of curators.
These levels lacked the overbearing grandeur of the
fifties and sixties; they were austere, dusty and undeco-
rated, but the carpet was deeper and less worn. Krelyn
could actually see physical footprints in the pile, just as
she had noticed in the decadence of the Quake Tavern.

The footprints stopped ascending and shuffled off
into one of the reading rooms. Krelyn looked up and
made a mental note of the number on the grubby little
sign that indicated the librarium level – seventy-three.
She stared long and hard at the staircase that ran up to
seventy-four, even running her hand lightly over the
surface of the carpet. There was no sign that even a

single foot had compressed that pile in recent days, or
even recent years, reflected Krelyn.

The prints led directly to the fourth reading room on
level seventy-three, and Krelyn began to detect more
agitation in the gait of the curator who had left them.
As soon as she entered the reading room itself, the
prints of the associated spies broke away from the main
track, spraying out into different parts of the room as
though scattered by an orderly explosion. Krelyn smiled
at the neat organisation, as she realised that each of the
spies had taken a different direction automatically,
clearly fully aware of where the others would be and
unwilling to tread on anyone's toes. This kind of pattern suggested that there was a regular routine at work
– after all, she herself had been watching Curator
Tyranus for over four years, and the spies had been
around for at least that long, presumably without
bumping into each other.

The curator's wooden desk was still glowing with an
excited pink imprint, suggesting that the man had been
pretty agitated by something before he left it. There
were hand prints all over the place – not all of them
from the same hands. However, glowing brightest of all
was the book on the desk, its paper having absorbed the
sweaty attentions of all six of the night's protagonists.

Krelyn carefully picked up the stylus that had been
laid across the cover of the book, placing it onto the
desk with a faint clink. Then she picked up the book
itself, turning it slowly in her hands in case there was
something physically special about the tome. It felt like
a normal book to her. Perhaps slightly heavier than a
comparably sized volume made in recent years, but she
was willing to believe that older technologies were
heavier than modern ones. *Paradoxes of the Spire* looked
older than most.

The thermal prints on the pages stopped about half way through the text, so Krelyn was confident that nobody had read beyond that point. The first line on the last page to have been read caught her imagination: *When you look up, there is nothing but the sky.* In her mind's eyes, this was the privileged view of House Helmawr – the only House in the spire without anything built above their glorious domain. To her, it sounded very boring up there.

A noise made her start and turn her head back towards the stairs. Had she been followed? She froze, straining to hear. In her ear, she could just about discern the faint whirring of the aural implant that amplified and filtered sound; it was slightly faulty now and the whine of the device seemed to obliterate every other sound in the silence of the dark librarium.

There were heavy, dragged footfalls, and she could also hear some wheezing. Whoever it was, they were not very fit. It was very unlikely that this was a dangerous pursuer, but it seemed equally unlikely that it would be some kind of menial, up here in the upper levels of the librarium.

Krelyn closed the book quietly and returned it to the desk. She took a couple of steps towards the heavy darkness between two of the dustiest and least consulted-looking book stacks but then stopped. She hopped back to the desk and snatched up the stylus, placing it carefully across the cover of the book, just as she had found it.

By the time Zefer staggered up to his desk and slouched down into his seat, Krelyn had retreated into the shadows to watch him, with her cloak wrapped around her like a death-shroud.

HE HADN'T BEEN able to sleep. At first, the thought of the stealthy intruder had kept him awake, hidden behind the thick drapes around the bed waiting for silent death to come upon him. But his mind was a mess of activity, and he wouldn't have been able to sleep anyway. He had just laid there, twisting his body under the covers with each convoluted contortion of his brain, working himself into a fever and bringing on the prefigurings of a migraine.

The words of the book had swum in and out of his mind, taunting him with their nonsense and goading him with the fact of his astonishing discovery. He might be the only curator of his generation to have discovered a new piece of authentic historical text. Its authenticity was beyond question, of course, since it was contained within the very pages of one of the most lauded volumes in the Ko'iron collection.

And there was also the question of the stylus. Zefer had been torturing himself about having left the little device on top of the book. If there was anything that was going to draw people's attention to that particular tome, he thought, it would be the unexpected and inexplicable appearance of a wayward stylus on its cover.

He had thought that his careful positioning of the stylus would permit him to work out whether anyone tampered with the book whilst he was away – in much the same way as he had often left it sitting on *his desk* in the past. However, it gradually dawned on him that he didn't want to know whether anyone else had tampered with the book, he simply wanted to make sure that nobody else looked at it at all.

That was the realisation that had finally got Zefer Tyranus out of bed and stumbling urgently down the stairs of the Quake Tavern toward the librarium. As he entered *his floor*, he was breathing heavily and muttering to himself, rehearsing the now-obvious non-sequitur over and over again in his head: '*Though it may be lost, salvation is always found… When you look up, there is nothing but the sky.'*

As he sat down at his desk and snatched up the stylus from the cover the book, Zefer wondered about that last sentence – the one that followed the newly discovered pages. As far as he could tell, it must be referring to one of two places. It was either a spatial reference to the House of Helmawr – since the only thing higher than the House of the Lord Guardians was the sky itself. Or, alternatively, it could be a temporal reference to a time before the hive had even existed – at such a time, there would be no hive to look up to, so when you looked up there would be nothing but sky, no matter who you were.

Flipping through the pages to find the rough edges of the freshly torn paper that he had sliced earlier that night, Zefer found himself trembling with excitement about the possibilities contained in two entire sides of new, unread lines of the *Paradoxes*.

He found the page and stuffed his nose down into it instantly, savouring the unusual smell of discovery. He recoiled slightly from the scent, snapping his head up out of the book and scrunching up his nose in appalled confusion. He paused for a moment and then sniffed again, just to make sure. There was no doubt: someone had touched the page since he was last there.

Of course, he realised suddenly, casting his mind back to the moment when he had slumped back into his chair, the stylus had moved too. He had very deliberately left it diagonally across the top left-hand corner. When he had returned to the desk, it had been laying perpendicular to that corner – close to where he had left it, but not exactly in place.

Zefer looked nervously over his shoulders and peered into the almost featureless darkness around

him. He screwed up his eyes, looking for some variations in the shades of black, but it was hopeless. There
was nothing. Whoever had been spying on him was
probably long gone by now. In any case, Zefer was too
excited to worry about anybody else watching him –
the most important thing was that he had the book
and that he could spend the whole night poring over it.
Whoever else had touched these secret pages, they
could not have understood their significance or the
meaning of these lines. Zefer had spent years of his life
without even daring to dream that this night would
come.

2: FRESH AIR

It HAD ALL been a bit of an anti-climax. He had written up his report two weeks ago, rolling it into a perfect tube and shooting it down one of the funnels into the intricate system of pressurised pipes that served as a communication system in the librarium. The valve had hissed open and sucked down the message, and then clicked shut with a satisfied clunk. The passage of the paper tube could just be discerned as it hissed and thumped through a series of other hidden valves in the complicated pipe network until it vanished into the invisible depths of the system. After a few seconds, a scrap of paper had been spat out of the little slot next to the funnel. It was his receipt, completed with the printed signature of Princess Gwentria herself, together with a friendly note telling him that he would have a response as soon as possible, if a response was considered necessary.

Zefer was absolutely sure that his report justified a response. He had never been so certain about anything in his whole life. How often did his superiors in the Historical Research Section receive genuinely innovative reports based on newly discovered primary sources? If they were ever going to receive a paper tube that required a response, it would be this one.

But nothing seemed to happen. For the first few days, Zefer had been so excited about the prospect of the response that he had been completely unable to work. He had simply sat at his seat, staring at the message funnel, smiling fixedly and waiting for the little chime to sound and for the slot to hiss open. But nothing had happened and Zefer had pretended to go about his business in a disinterested manner, finding any number of excuses to pause and stare at the message funnel, as though only casually interested in whether anything popped out of it or not.

After a week, he was getting a little frantic. One night, after everyone else had gone home, Zefer abandoned his usual trip to the seventy-third floor and crept back to his daily work-station. He prodded and probed the message funnel, holding the valve open with his stylus whilst peering into the dark recesses within. The following morning, he sent a tube off down to the maintenance department to request that somebody should be sent to check that his message funnel was functioning properly. A couple of hours later, the valve had hissed open and a dirty brown roll of paper was ejected into the receptacle. Picking it up and sniffing at it gingerly, Zefer was fairly sure that this was not the response that he had been waiting for. When he unrolled it, he saw that it contained only four poorly penned words: *Seems to work fine*.

Finally, after three more days, Zefer looked up from his work at the delicate sound of a chime. The funnel hissed disgruntledly and out popped a pristine white tube sporting the little blue crest of the Ko'iron on the seal that held it together. It was of the kind used only by officials and curators of the Historical Research Section.

Zefer just stared at it, hardly believing his eyes and not daring to let his arm reach out and take the message. He pretended not to be interested for a few minutes. Instead of rushing over to open the message, he shuffled some papers around his desk and moved his stylus from one position to another, pretending to check which was the most efficient arrangement.

When he could contain himself no longer, he half stumbled and half tripped over to the message intake and reverently lifted out the little white tube. Checking over both of his shoulders to ensure that he wasn't being observed, he carefully secreted it into the loose sleeve of his shapeless grey jacket.

That evening, he virtually ran up the winding staircase to the privacy of the seventy-third floor, where he leapt into his chair and tugged the little tube out of his sleeve in a single, smooth movement. He slid his fingers under the seal and opened the roll, closing his eyes and pressing his nose down against the paper as he smoothed it out with his hands.

It smelt strangely familiar. With his nose still only millimetres above the paper, he opened one eye and peered at the text in trepidation. The eye bulged as it registered what was written on the page and Zefer threw back his head in a fit of vented disbelief.

It wasn't a response at all.

THE GROUP IN the corner were beyond blind drunk. They had gone through blind and come out the other side with big, bold splashes of colour all over their field of vision. They were colourfully drunk and irritatingly loud. And they were not making friends.

By far the loudest of the group was sitting confidently on the back of a chair with her feet on its seat and her back to the wall. Her dirty blue dreadlocks thrashed around her intricately tattooed head like a storm of snakes as she yelled and laughed at the story of an older woman seated opposite her. The older woman's back was facing the interior of the room, so Triar could only catch glimpses of the wrinkled skin of her studded and pierced face as she turned her head to include the rest of the group in her narrative.

From his place at the bar, Triar counted fourteen other Escher gang members in the saloon of *The Breath of Fresh Air*. They were from a local branch-gang of House Escher called The Coven – named after the unapologetic witch by whom it was led. Only six of them were at the table with the raucous group, but the others were as easy to spot as hellfire in a dark room. Triar had marked them as soon as he had walked in the door, making a mental note of their number and position, just in case there was trouble later. There was always trouble later.

He was watching the corner-table through the mirror over the bar, taking occasional glances up from his drink and peering out from under the folds of his heavy hood. He was pretty sure that the drunken women had no idea that they were being watched – or, at least, no idea that he wasn't just another man gawping at their immodesty. Enveloped in his bright blue cloak, even with his back to them, it would not take a genius to work out that he was a Cawdor ganger, but the ladies were drunk beyond such colour-recognition. Given his location in this part of Hive City, they should also have realised that he was from House Cawdor's evangelical local gang, The Salvationists.

'That's them,' said the man standing next to him, sloshing the remains of his pungent drink around in the bottom of a cup.

'Really?' questioned Triar sarcastically, turning his tarnished silver mask to the black-cloaked agent at the bar. 'I would never have guessed.'

'You pay me for information,' hissed the informant, his visor glinting slightly with a hint of blue in the inconstant light. A little red snake tattooed under one eye twitched irritably. 'I am merely providing it.' The man nodded his head into a vague bow and then turned to leave. There was obvious false-modesty in his manner.

The Delaque may be the finest spies in all Hive Primus, thought Triar as he watched the black cape slip between the jostle of other patrons and out of the door, but they are not noted for their wit.

Following the figure of the retreating spy in the mirror, Triar noted the spread of blue hoods throughout the *Fresh Air* with satisfaction. Here and there the metals of their masks glinted with understated menace, and Triar knew that he had manoeuvred well this evening. The neutrals in the bar were also beginning to realise that something was going down, and one or two had stopped drinking and were starting to look from one blue cape to the next and then at the women in the corner, doing the sums. The wiser amongst them were already finishing their drinks and quietly filing out of the door.

The Breath of Fresh Air was an unusual establishment. At first glance it looked like a genius-stroke of planning. Outside its main doors was a huge, four-bladed fan in the junction of three enormous ventilation shafts. It was the only fan in this area of Hive City, and thus the only source of even remotely fresh air, which made it an extremely valuable site. The *Fresh Air* was full all day and all night, with half of its patrons more excited about drinking in the fresh air than the crude liquor.

However, the genius of the site also bordered on insanity. The fan was the biggest point of contention between three separate gangs that held territory along each of the ventilation pipes that fed it. Gangers from all three would frequent the *Fresh Air*, which brought in a great deal of money. But with the gangers came tension, broken bottles and occasional skirmishes, which cost a great deal of money.

The proprietor was a tiny man, not more than a metre tall. He only had one eye, but never wore a patch – he liked to watch people staring into the open socket with his other eye. He told everyone that his growth was stunted by the potency of the liquor that he distilled in the smoky backrooms of the *Fresh Air*. For some strange reason, this seemed to make people want to drink even more of it, so Squatz prided himself on his rare psychological insight.

Perhaps Squatz's real insight was the realisation that the Hive City gangers would drink in *The Breath of Fresh Air* rather than in the safer, gang-owned establishments inside their own territories. Squatz knew that the most important thing for all the gangs was to be seen to be unafraid of each of the others. His bar was the perfect, neutral venue for such posturing, and the strategic importance of its location gave everyone the excuse they needed to be there. The money he made more than compensated for the occasional damages. Besides, most of the real violence took place outside in the public space in front of the great fan so that everyone could watch the fun. In the end, Squatz had realised that the three-way competition over the site was a better guarantee of its security than the patronage of any single gang might have been. He was one of a very small number of genuinely inter-gang institutions.

'Take it outside,' said Squatz, walking along the counter of the bar to refill Triar's cup from a grubby

looking bottle. Standing on the bar, he could look lev-
elly into Triar's masked face.

'I'm sure that I don't know what you mean,' replied
Triar, smiling invisibly behind the shimmering silver
mask that twisted around his face like a metallic skin.

'You know what I mean,' retorted Squatz, the opaque
bottle poised to pour as the ugly little man waited for
some sign of acknowledgement from Triar. But the silver
mask just stared implacably back into his face, and
Squatz decided to pour the drink anyway.

'Why do you let them in here? They're... unclean,' said
Triar, tilting his head slightly to one side to indicate his
curiosity.

'Their money's as good as yours,' replied the short man
on the counter, lifting the steaming bottle neck away
from Triar's cup.

'No it isn't. It's unclean. It may look the same, but it
will rot your soul while you sleep.'

'That's my problem then, not yours,' countered Squatz,
trying to placate the Cawdor without being forced to
convert. He had never understood the appeal of the Cult
of Redemption, nor the strange devotion of many of the
Cawdor gangers. In fact, Triar was such a devotee that he
had named his own gang The Salvationists, and he made
it his business to prosecute the cause of righteousness as
though he were himself the leader of a Redemptionist
crusade. Not all of his gangers shared his passion for the
cult, but they were all in awe of their boss's sense of duty.

Triar gazed at Squatz for a moment, holding his cloudy
green eyes for a number of seconds, his face-mask seem-
ing to glow with compassion. 'That's where you're
wrong. Souls are my concern, Squatz. You know that.'

The tiny barman shook his head in a sudden fit,
shaking the image of Triar's startling blue eyes off his
retina. Squatz had been in business a long time, and he

was not about to let this fanatic's cheap conjuring tricks derail him now. Triar was one of the most charming of his patrons, but sometimes it seemed to Squatz that he was a little too charming. His eyes were occasionally a little too bright. Triar himself would dismiss his curiosity, saying that his manner was touched by the glory of the Undying Emperor himself, but Squatz suspected that there was something wyrd in Triar's ways. He was certain that the adherents outside Triar's own little gang of Salvationists would not appreciate his secrets.

'Do you know what they are saying under your roof, little man?' asked Triar, keeping his gaze level and his tone low. 'They,' he continued, flicking his head towards the group in the corner, 'are talking about an archeotech finding that "proves" the Undying Emperor visited Necromunda and that – listen well to this part, little *man* – he was a *she.*'

'Oh, you know that I never listen to the private conversations of my patrons, sir,' mumbled Squatz, trying to sound deferential. 'Present company excepted, of course,' he added just in time.

Triar had just slugged back his shot of Squatz's house special and slammed the cup down onto the bar. He eyes were beginning to burn and Squatz could see the 'righteous anger' building under the so-called Redemptionist's hood. He wondered for a moment how the young gang leader could be so righteous if he also engaged in so many sins: he was a heavy drinker, a constant profaner, and at least an occasional fornicator. In the same thought, Squatz found himself wondering about Triar's wyrdness, but that might be a crucial step too far for a Cawdor firebrand, especially for one who called himself the Salvationist. In any case, reasoned Squatz pragmatically, a little sin was good for business.

'Of course,' replied Triar, his voice set into a hard edge as he turned his back to Squatz and the bar. The blue hoods throughout the room turned in his direction, and he raised an open hand to signal his own readiness. From behind him, Triar could hear the whispered pleas of Squatz: 'Please, outside.' And the remaining neutrals in the room fell over each other trying to get out of the door. Only the drunken women seemed oblivious.

In a sudden movement, Triar clenched his hand into a fist and then pulled it down to his waist. A fraction later and *The Breath of Fresh Air* erupted into turmoil as the Salvationist gangers pushed and barged their way towards the Escher women of The Coven at the corner table, fighting their way through the fleeing throng of neutrals. Meanwhile, Squatz jumped down behind the bar, not for the first time thankful that he was short enough to be completely shielded by its heavy metal structure.

THINGS HAD NOT been quite the same since that fateful night a few weeks before, and Krelyn's routine had been shot to pieces by the suddenly erratic behaviour of that cursed curator. For nearly five years she had been able to rely on his routine. Most importantly, he would leave the Ko'iron librarium through the minor exit tunnel precisely three hours after he clocked off work. Krelyn had been able to make plans for the rest of the night based upon his movements. There were a great many distractions in the luxury of the Spire for a bored venator, and Krelyn relied on them to keep her mind off the life she had lost when House Delaque had cut her off. But her well timetabled displacement activities were no more.

Over the last few weeks, Curator Tyranus had been leaving at irregular times. Sometimes later than normal and sometimes earlier – once or twice he was not even the last person to leave the building. On three occasions, he had left so early that he hadn't even used the little exit tunnel opposite the Quake Tavern. Instead, together with the other curators and pledge-workers of the Ko'iron librarium, he had filed out of the great gates that opened into spacious expanse of Hredriea's Plaza. Krelyn had only been there by chance, taking an unusually circuitous route to her rooftop perch, when she saw the man shuffling along with the others. As she had struggled to confirm that it was him, Krelyn had stifled a chuckle when she saw the clutch of other venators pushing through the crowd and peering over shoulders, checking the same thing. That curator was causing more trouble than he was worth.

The sudden shift in her mark's behaviour had made a new series of demands on Krelyn – demands that she had not been required to meet for years. She was not entirely sure that her equipment still functioned well enough to enable her to perform these functions. Most of it, like her goggles, was old and decrepit – it had not been replaced since her masters in House Delaque lost the lucrative Ko'iron Contract nearly ten years before. The collapse of this ancient commercial agreement between one of the houses of Hive City and one of the Spire's Noble Houses had left Krelyn stranded in the service of the Ko'iron, since she had already given her oath of loyalty to the great Noble House, despite the fact that she could trace her bloodline directly back through the Delaque family itself. She was one of the very few Delaque agents entitled to use the Delaque name. This lineage, at least, did not atrophy with time, even if her equipment did. She would always be Krelyn

Delaque. However, a fancy name was not enough, and the venator masters of House Delaque had severed all contacts with House Ko'iron, which also meant cutting off all communication with one of their favourite daughters. Since then, Krelyn had been on her own amongst the ritual and pompous splendour of the Spire, struggling to service her own equipment and to fulfil her obligations to her adopted masters. She wondered whether her brethren in Hive City had forgotten her already.

The only things that hadn't fallen apart were her blades, since she had very little use for them in her recent line of work – spying on librarium curators for their own employers. She kept an elaborate array of bladed weapons in a state of highly polished perfection, sharpening them and purifying them every night in her chambers. Each morning, she would fix them against her skin with straps, securing them under specially made slits in her fatigues, so that she could access them quickly if needed.

Her firearms were a completely different story. She was trained to use them, not to maintain them. A glorious example of a pilfered Van Saar laspistol, perhaps the finest weapon that Krelyn had ever had the good fortune to steal, was displayed in a wrack above her bed. Before she was posted up in the Spire, she had even had the audacity to take it to a House Van Saar weaponsmith to have it customised to her requirements – the butt was extended into a shoulder-brace for better stability on ranged shots, almost transforming it into a rifle. As it was, she could wear it hanging vertically at her side, with a simple strap securing the stock under her armpit. Her cape neatly covered the whole thing. Of course, it didn't work any more. It had seized up years ago and now it just glimmered like a finely polished ornament in her immaculate and unfashionably sparse chambers.

When she had first entered the service of the Ko'iron, the young Prince Jurod had been just about to embark on his first hunting jaunt into the Underhive as part of a Spyrer team. Although he was unaware of it, Krelyn had accompanied the young prince, hidden in the shadows, to ensure that no real harm could come to the patriarchal heir apparent. During those months in the slovenly underworld of Hive Primus, Krelyn had silently offered prayers of thanks to the Undying Emperor for her laspistol and her blades. However, as his little sister, Princess Gwentria, had grown up, Jurod had changed his ways and hardly ever ventured onto the other side of the great adamantium Wall that separated the stately abode of the Spire from the vast bulk of the working hive below. And when he did go down, he no longer needed a chaperone. Hence, now, Krelyn's weapons were little more than memory crutches of a more glorious time.

She tutted and shook her head, as she crouched in readiness on the rooftop across from the mouth of the librarium's exit tunnel. Most people in Hive City spend their lives wondering what it would be like to get through the great wall and into the mysterious world of the Spire on the other side. Krelyn would have given anything to trade places with one of those aspiring weaklings. Hive City might be dirty, diseased, chaotic and dangerous, but at least it was alive. The Spire was… she searched for the right word in her head. The Spire was *boring*.

A line from that ridiculous book seeped back into her mind: '*When you look up, there is nothing but the sky.*' It wasn't true of the Spire and, even if it was, she would hate it.

Swaying her head to shift the blind spot in her goggles, Krelyn saw the shuffling figure of her curator stooping to sit down at the end of the tunnel, dropping his legs over the edge as he had done hundreds of times before. He was about an hour early, and he looked decidedly agitated. Instead of twisting his body round to lower himself awkwardly to the ledge, he simply sat for a moment before pushing off with his hands and kicking out with his feet, sending himself flying forward and down towards the ledge. Krelyn could swear that she had seen a flash of anger cross the bookish face an instant before he jumped.

Curator Tyranus hit the ledge hard and stumbled forward before falling flat on his face against the rock. He lay where he had fallen for a few seconds, and Krelyn found herself worrying that the stupid man may have hurt himself in that moment of bravado. But, after a while, he pushed himself back up onto his feet and limped off toward the stairs that led down to street level.

BEFORE ZEFER EVEN knew where he was going, he found himself sitting on the marble steps of the Matriarch's Shrine, picking at his fingernails in the half-light and mumbling incoherently. A thin trickle of blood was working its way down from the corner of his mouth, and his leg was burning with pain. He couldn't remember walking past the Quake Tavern, but he must have done in order to get to the shrine.

Behind him, the towering statue of Hredriea, the maternal grandmother of Gwentria, the current Ko'iron matriarch, loomed regally over the plaza. The shrine had been built two hundred years before as a testament to the power of the female line of the Ko'iron family. The history books in aisle 2.81.4527c of the librarium told of how the shrine had been commissioned by Hredriea herself, following a huge hive-quake that had destroyed much of what is now Gwentria's Fringe. Evidently, all of the construction work had been done by the female pledged-workers of House Ko'iron itself. Hredriea's idea had been to build a monument to the glory of the Undying Emperor that tied her family intimately to his patronage. So, she herself stood as the guardian to the shrine, and her immense statue at the crest of the steps dwarfed the pale stone of the Emperor's image in the temple building itself.

Zefer often came to sit on these magnificent steps, usually in the middle of the day, when the plaza would be bustling with merchants and the vibrancy characteristic of this affluent district. The square was flanked on three sides by shimmering white marble buildings, each with intricately castellated rooflines, sprinklings of potent gargoyles, and gloriously soaring arches. This district had found its wealth under the protection of Hredriea and it had thenceforth maintained its association with the Ko'iron women, just as it had maintained its reputation as one of the most affluent quarters under House Ko'iron's control. It was, in any case, unusual because of the natural light that seeped in during the day through the huge stained glass windows set into the thick exterior wall of the Spire that curved slightly around the back of the shrine. Of course, the cloud belt took the edge off the sunlight, and the torches in the streetlights burned all through the day to ensure that there was enough light, but the glow of the sky outside gave the stained glass an eerie radiance found nowhere else in the Spire. At night, the ancient and colourful windows were floodlit from giant spotlights set into the marble steps. Zefer sat between them, with their beams criss-crossing into a web behind him.

A group of chattering youths bumped and stumbled through the plaza, supporting themselves on each others shoulders as they sang wordless songs in a jumbled chorus. The noise made Zefer look up out of his bitter reverie and he realised that what he really needed was a drink.

ELRIA BIT DOWN on the zip-tab, cracking its membrane and flooding her system with an eclectic collection of stimulants. They kicked her metabolism into overdrive just as the group of Salvationist gangers reached the table. She threw her head forward, thrashing her blue dreads down between her knees and reaching up into the thick hair with her hands. As she flicked her head back, the dreads rushed back into place revealing vicious, gleaming blades in Elria's hands.

She was on her feet in an instant, standing on the seat of her chair with her arms outstretched to her sides, pointing the blades menacingly at the blue-cloaked gangers who were trying to flank the table.

As she moved, the rest of the women at the table leapt to their feet, crunching their tabs and spinning on their heels to face the approaching blue hoods. Their drunken abandon was instantly replaced by lethal focus, and their readiness startled the advancing gangers.

Seeing his men stall, Triar leapt up onto the bar and pulled the long-bladed dagger out of his boot, flourishing it ostentatiously from hand to hand. He pointed its gleaming tip at the flamboyant figure of Elria, standing dramatically on her chair in the corner.

'This witch is sowing decay into the souls of the weak and the helpless! Is it not enough that she blasphemes against the divine form by outlawing men from her House? Now, it seems, she blasphemes against the Undying Emperor himself – concocting and disseminating apocryphal stories that he was a woman!'

'This *man*,' countered Elria, her head turned to the side as she surveyed the scene out of the corner of her eyes through a curtain of blue hair, 'would have you surrender your thoughts to the soulless idol of a best forgotten faith. He is simply the deluded representative of an anachronistic, patriarchal system. Why not believe that the Emperor was a woman, if that will bring liberty to your life?'

In his hiding place behind the bar, Squatz slapped himself in the head. Why did they always spurt such nonsense at each other? If they were going to fight, why not just get on with it? And why wouldn't they go outside? He was pleased, at least, that they appeared to have honoured their vows not to bring guns into the *Fresh Air*.

'If you have proof of your heresy, bring it forth and show us the error of our "deluded" ways,' taunted Triar, dropping the tip of his blade into a mocking shrug, appealing to the crowd in this piece of amateur theatre.

'We have as much proof that she was a woman as you have that he was a man,' retorted Elria, still watching out of the corner of her eye and hardly moving at all. Around her, the Escher women remained completely stationary, perfectly focussed and unphased by their plight.

'There are centuries of records that support our position, Elria Escher, and none at all in support of yours.' Triar was laughing behind his mask, and his blade tip was now pointing at his feet. 'You will not find a curator in all of Necromunda who would take you seriously. And,' he added, snapping his blade back out towards her, 'you will not find a Redemptionist who would not take your head for heresy.'

'Your records mean nothing to me, Triar Cawdor, and your faith in the metal of the Redemptionists is pathetically misplaced… as you are about to discover, again.' Elria added the last word with some venom, turning her eyes to face the ganger directly as though to reinforce her point. Her red eyes shone unnaturally for a fraction of a second, and then the bar on which Triar was standing burst into flames.

'I DON'T UNDERSTAND,' said Zefer, throwing the message tube down on the official's desk. It was early in the new working day, and Zefer had hardly slept the previous night.

'It's very simple,' replied the senioris, unrolling the paper and inspecting the text in a dismissive and cursory manner. 'This is your response.'

'But it's not a response at all!' cried Zefer, nearly shouting.

'It may not be the response you wanted, but it is still a response,' replied the senioris with irritating and implacable calm.

'But… but it's just the report that I sent to them. They haven't even stamped it to show that it has been read,' continued Zefer, refusing to believe that this was really the end of the story.

'It should be of no concern to you whether it has been read or not, curator…' The official scanned the report for a name. 'Curator Zefer Tyranus. Is it not enough to know that you have done your duty by submitting the report in the first place?' The senioris looked up from his desk for the first time and stared at Zefer. He did an obvious and startled double-take. 'What happened to you?'

Zefer glared down at the officious man, seated so comfortably behind his protocols. There wasn't even a name plate on the desk, just a little plaque with the words 'Duty Senioris,' etched into it. This was certainly the longest conversation that he had ever had with a senior official in the librarium, and it was not going quite as he had imagined that it might.

'I fell,' said Zefer, immediately aware that this explanation sounded like a lie. 'It was a rough night,' he continued, without really clarifying anything.

'So it seems.' The senioris had decided that he didn't want to know anything more. The curator's face was animated with hysteria and a crusty line of dried blood was drawn down from his swollen lip. His grey eyes were gaunt and heavily shadowed, as though sunken into his head after weeks of sleeplessness. His smock was dirty and soiled with what looked like vomit. The cloth over one leg appeared to be stained with blood from the inside, and the senioris noticed for the first time that the curator was standing lopsidedly, with all of his weight on the other leg. He reeked of drink and the kind of inhaled-toxins that clung to your clothes no matter how many times you washed them, not that there seemed much danger of that.

'If you are not satisfied, then you will have to take the matter up with the Office of Princess Gwentria herself. She is the final authority over issues of historical research. I must warn you, however, that she will not tolerate a filthy curator wasting her time – if she has already not read your report once, she will be considerably angered by being forced to not read it a second time.'

The senioris looked back down at the report and skimmed his eyes over the lines of neat text that covered it. He had no idea what it was about, and he didn't really care. None of these reports ever had even the faintest significance to his life, and he didn't get to where he was today by paying any attention to them. Much better to hand it along the bureaucracy until the author got so fed up with trying to find somebody who would read it that they simply gave up.

Rolling the report back into a neat little tube, the senioris stamped his seal onto it and handed it back to Zefer, who took it dejectedly. Then, without looking up, the official stamped another sheet of paper three times and squiggled his signature at the bottom, before handing the completed sector-pass to Zefer.

'This should get you into Princess Gwentria's offices… eventually,' he said, lifting his eyes at the end, as though the last word had some particular significance.

Zefer took the piece of paper and studied it. He always read every note, report and memorandum, and he was not about to break that habit now. It certainly looked like a sector-pass into the highest levels of the Ko'iron precinct. This piece of paper would grant him admittance to the dizzying heights of the Spire, higher even than the cloud layer that inconveniently enshrouded the librarium – it could take him right up to the hallowed doors of House Helmawr itself, nearly two miles higher than he had ever been in his life.

Turning away from the senioris and limping down the long corridor towards his own desk, Zefer silently cursed himself for stupidly throwing himself out of the librarium's exit tunnel and then getting so drunk the night before. He knew that he was a mess today, but he hadn't cared when he had burst (he liked to think that he had burst, but really he had limped and shuffled) into the senioris's office and demanded (okay: quietly asked) why he had received no response to his groundbreaking report.

If he had known that the result of this dramatic confrontation would be a sector-pass to one of the most exclusive parts of the Spire, he would at least have cleaned the vomit off his smock.

As he limped down through the passageway, Zefer studied the pass. There were three stamps. One of them appeared to be the seal of the Historical Research Section: an intricate and slightly fuzzy image of an explorer with a torch brandished before him, presumably spreading the light of knowledge, or something. One of the stamps seemed to register the time at which the pass was issued. But the other was less obvious – it was some kind of reference number or code: CC9FB2. It meant nothing to Zefer, and that troubled him slightly.

THE EXPLOSION OF flame left Triar standing in a block of fire on the bar counter. The Salvationist gangers hesitated for a crucial moment, unsure of whether to help their leader or plough into his attacker. At least a few of them had never seen a wyrd in action before, and the spontaneous combustion of the metal bar had shocked them into indecision.

Triar resolved the dilemma for them, breaking into a run down the bar and then vaulting through the flames at its end. He cleared the short space between the bar and the corner table in less than a second, swinging his blade in a horizontal arc as he flew towards Elria, flames rippling along his blue cloak.

But she was faster. As her companions launched themselves away from the table, laying into the Salvationist gangers who had finally found their direction, Elria stamped down on the table-edge and jumped back onto the seat of her chair. The table pivoted on its legs and then flipped up into the air, directly into

Triar's path. Immediately, Triar smashed into the table, his blade piercing the surface and stabbing out the other side towards Elria's face. She neither flinched nor moved, and the blade lost its momentum about a centimetre in front of her nose.

Before Triar and the table even hit the plate-metal ground, Elria flashed out her leg and kicked them both. They slid across the room, scattering furniture as they went. When they came to rest, Triar was still trying to remove his blade from the tabletop, and Elria's eyes flashed again. The table erupted into flame and Triar kicked it away from him, abandoning his blade and scrambling to his feet.

The other blue-cloaks clustered around their leader, beaten back from the far corner all the way to the door, each brandishing a blade uncertainly. Triar clambered to his feet in their midst, staggering back against the heavy, riveted door as he struggled to maintain his balance after the shock of his fall.

'This is not the end, Escher witch–' started Triar, but he lost his footing and fell back against the door, barging it open under his weight. A blast of fresh air from the giant fan outside breathed into the bar, whipping the flames into renewed ferocity. Triar caught his fall and propped open the door with his arm, trying to capitalise on the dramatic blossom of fire.

'Your blasphemies and heresies will not go unpunished. The Undying Emperor suffers not the heretic to live.' The pronouncement was mostly for the benefit of the crowd that had hurriedly assembled outside the *Fresh Air*, hoping to see the fight spill out into the square in front of the huge ventilation pipes.

Standing in the middle of the still-flaming bar, her blue hair bathed in flickering golden light, Elria offered no response, but Triar was neither expecting nor waiting for one. He turned on his heel, letting his cloak whip up into a whirl as he spun, and swept out of the *Fresh Air* with his gangers hustling and jostling in his wake, their masks hiding their embarrassment. As they emerged from the tavern, a hail of cheers descended on them from the Cawdor gangers of The Salvationists who had collected on top of the battered ventilation pipe on the left. The sound poured eerily down from the mouthless, metallic faces. To the right, lounging casually atop the other horizontal pipe, was a small group of women from The Coven who simply smiled down at the retreating blue-cloaks, patronising them with their silence. They had seen Elria trounce Triar's gangers before, and they enjoyed the humiliation that their quiet amusement caused.

As Triar looked up, a flash of black just above the great fan caught his attention, and he wondered who else was taking an interest in his affairs. With another flourish of his cloak, he turned off to the left, heading back into secure Salvationist territory. As he left, the smug women sprang down from their perches and sauntered over towards the *Breath of Fresh Air*, claiming it for the The Coven, at least for tonight.

'CC9FB2?' ASKED THE admittor at the desk in front of the huge doors. He was a tiny man, dwarfed by the highly polished metal table behind which he sat. Zefer suspected that his feet didn't touch the ground, but he dared not peer under the table to check.

Towering over the little official were two inhumanly huge guards. Their feet were firmly and heavily set on the shiny silver of the floor and their reflections seemed to stretch right up to Zefer's toes. They had bright green hair, shaved on both sides of their heads to leave only a strip along the middle standing vertically on end. Both of them had the Ko'iron crest crudely branded onto their massive upper arms. In one of the books in aisle 3.70.1141a, Zefer had once read about a group of unsavoury people called Goliaths. They were supposed to be colossal barbarians from the Underhive, but he had never met anyone who had actually seen one. For a moment, he wondered whether these two guards might fit the profile.

Slightly anxious now, Zefer rechecked the stamp on the pass that the senioris had given him. 'Yes, CC9FB2,' he confirmed.

The admittor snorted slightly as he nodded and started to flick through the pages of the insanely thick book that was barely supported by the elegant curves of the table. Zefer noticed that the man did not start his flicking at the beginning of the book, but rather flopped the tome open about three quarters of the way through and started to flick from there. To be frank, Zefer was surprised that the admittor had enough strength to turn the bound covers himself; behind the book and desk, next to the huge sentries, and in front of the great doors, the little admittor looked comically small.

'Ah yes, here we are,' he said, licking the end of his stylus and preparing to make some sort of mark in the book. 'You are in luck. CC9FB1 has cancelled, so you are not as far down the queue as you may fear.'

'Queue?' asked Zefer as the significance of the number started to sink in for the first time.

'But of course,' replied the little man, looking up from his writing with a smirk creased into his face. 'Princess Gwentria is a very important person. You didn't think that you were the only one who wanted to see her, did you?'

'But… but I have very important news for the princess. I have information that she must be made aware of,' said Zefer, vaguely hopeful that he might be able to impress the importance of his discoveries onto this bookish man.

'Of course you do,' smiled the admittor, his smirk gradually fixing into a sinister sneer. 'That is why you are here. Nobody comes to the princess's gates if they do not. People have been coming for years – there is a great deal that the princess needs to know, it seems.'

'And where are you up to in the queue?' asked Zefer, sighing audibly and resigning himself to a wait.

'Oh, we're moving through it at quite a rate now. Oh yes, much faster than when we first started. Of course, some of the people have cancelled and some others simply forgot their place in the queue, and one or two have died – ah yes, like poor old CC9FB1 – but things are moving much faster.'

'Excellent,' replied Zefer, encouraging the man to continue. 'So, where are you up to now?'

'We are at CC9FB,' replied the admittor proudly.

'Should I take a seat?' asked Zefer wearily, waving his hand towards the empty row of red velvet seats that led along the silver wall away from the desk.

'By all means,' said the little man, excitedly jumping to his feet. 'I don't think that we have had anyone actually *wait* for their appointment for years!' The admittor sprang off his chair, and Zefer actually lost sight of him behind the desk for a moment. When he finally reappeared, he was even shorter than Zefer had imagined.

'What do people usually do?' asked Zefer, a little taken aback.

'Why, they go home, of course or they get back on with their lives. But, to actually *wait*. Well, that really is dedication. I congratulate you, Curator Tyranus,' said the little man as he ushered Zefer over towards the first of the velvet chairs.

'Thank you,' said Zefer, increasingly unsure about what was going on. 'Let me make sure that I understand this correctly. You have reached CC9FB. I am CC9FB2 and CC9FB1 has cancelled.'

'Well, yes, or rather died. But the effect is much the same, as far as the queue is concerned,' nodded the admittor enthusiastically.

'So I will be next.'

The little admittor stopped nodding and his smile disappeared instantly. 'Sir, do you take me for a fool? Is this some kind of test?' he asked, looking around suspiciously. 'You and I know perfectly well that you are not next. There are still BFD5B7 people before you… give or take those who have given up, forgotten or died.'

Zefer stared at the little man and tried to understand what he was saying. 'What do you mean, CBF5C7?'

'No, no, don't be ridiculous. There are not nearly that many. I said BFD5BF.'

'Okay,' said Zefer slowly, feeling like the little man was somewhat missing the point. 'So, what does that mean?'

The admittor returned the frustrated gaze for a few moments, screwing up his eyes as though it was impossible to imagine what could be so difficult for the curator to understand. Finally, the crease crept back onto his face, and he smirked.

'Oh, I see what has happened. BFD5BF is a number. After the first few years, the queue grew so large that it became increasingly inconvenient to employ numbers in base-ten. Hence, we shifted to base-sixteen, which obviously required the use of a few letters. Actually, the new system is working very well indeed. Take your own number, for example. Had that been written in base-ten it would barely have fitted on the pass!'

Zefer stared at the jubilant admittor and smiled weakly. 'What?'

'Yes,' continued the little man, climbing up onto one of the velvet chairs as his mouth muttered in calculation. 'If I'm not very much mistaken, you are number thirteen million, four hundred and ten thousand, two hundred and twenty six, as you would say in conventional decimal terms. CC9FB2, as we would say, more correctly, in hexidecimal.'

Slumping down into the seat next to the admittor, Zefer sunk his head into his hands. 'And what number are you up to the queue?'

'CC9FB,' replied the little man cheerfully. 'Eight hundred and thirty eight thousand, one hundred and thirty nine.'

'Which means that there are...' Zefer's mind was racing with numbers that it could only just contain. 'There are more than twelve and a half million people ahead of me in the list...' His voice plunged into silence.

'BFD5B7,' chirped the admittor cheerfully. 'Twelve million, five hundred and seventy two thousand, and eighty seven,' he added helpfully. 'Give or take a few here and there–'

'–who might have died while they waited–'

'–exactly!' flourished the admittor, as though a great breakthrough had been made. 'Can I get you something to drink while you wait?'

ZEFER SAT ON the velvet seat and stared into the shimmering silver floor, watching the colourful reflections of the ceiling fresco as though in a giant mirror. His mouth was working silently, as though a stream of words were rolling across his tongue without ever finding a sound. Every now and again he shook his head vaguely, in mesmerised disbelief. He was in shock.

It had taken six years to get through eight hundred thousand places on the queue. Six years. And that was partly because hardly anyone had actually turned up for their appointments. Zefer couldn't even do the maths. He had no idea how long it would take to get through another twelve and half million people. Come to that, he had had no idea that there were even that many people in the Spire, let alone in House Ko'iron or in the Historical Research Section. This was all too much for him, and he was glad that the vast, ornate waiting hall contained such comfortable chairs.

Other than the little admittor and his two huge Goliath guards, Zefer was alone in the cavernous hall. His loneliness was somehow consoling, since it permitted him to sustain his delusions that he was a significant actor in the affairs of the great house – a delusion challenged profoundly by recent news that he was only one of more than thirteen million people in a queue to see the boss.

Yet even the immaculate silver hall conspired against him. He gazed across the open space towards the polished wall on the far side, and saw a scruffy looking man hunched into a red velvet chair. The man was motionless and dejected, staring back at Zefer with the same expression of desperate resignation on his face. It was like looking in a mirror.

After a few moments, Zefer thought that it would be impolite not to acknowledge the man, so he nodded a brotherly greeting. The man nodded back again. No, thought Zefer, he's not returning my signal, he's doing it at the same time. Zefer raised a hand and waved, and the man did the same thing.

It was his reflection after all. Staring hard at the far wall, Zefer could clearly see that it was him. Even worse, he could faintly see the reflection of him staring at himself staring at himself staring at himself. An infinite regression of increasingly tiny Zefers disappearing into infinity, like a queue of millions of Zefers, all sitting on comfortable red chairs in a shining hall. He looked at the infinite line for some time, trying to work out which of the images actually corresponded to his place in the queue to see Princess Gwentria, but he couldn't see that far.

He shook his head again, violently this time, trying to clear it of befuddlement. How could the queue have become so long? He didn't believe for a moment that the other people had reports as significant as his own. Why could the seniorises not deal with the other problems, rather than passing them along the line to the end, blocking his way forward?

Casting his mind back to the officious senioris from whom he had received his pass, Zefer shivered at the realisation that he was not a man who would choose to deal with a problem if he could possibly avoid it. The bureaucratic structure existed precisely so that such men could pass anomalies up the chain of authority towards the top, thus relieving themselves of any sense of responsibility. Zefer clenched his fists in frustration as he realised that he had actually been intimidated by that snivelling man.

Thinking back on the conversation, Zefer could still remember the smug satisfaction with which the senioris had used the word 'eventually.' He had handed over the pass and said: 'This should get you into Princess Gwentria's offices… eventually.' So, he had known! The senioris had been fully aware that Zefer would have to join the queue – he had even stamped the pass with his position in the queue: CC9FB2.

If only someone would read the report, thought Zefer, then they wouldn't keep him waiting in an infinite queue forever. No wonder nothing ever got done, if the whole of the Historical Research Section was held in a infinite queue to see the only person who couldn't pass the problem along to somebody else.

A delicate bell chimed, echoing around the silver hall with metallic beauty, and Zefer looked over to the desk, where the admittor sat, half-hidden behind the huge log-book. A bright red light was glowing above the great doors behind the sentries, and the admittor was excitedly leafing through the pages of the book.

Clearing his throat and looking hopefully around the vast, empty hall, the admittor spoke. 'Uh um, CC9FC, please.'

He waited a few seconds, but there was no response. 'CC9FC?' he repeated, lifting himself onto his elbows and peering up and down the cavernous hall.

'CC9FD, please,' said the admittor, crossing something out of the log book and shaking his head in disgust. As he spoke, the great doors creaked open, slowly swinging back to reveal a dust-riddled darkness beyond. Slowly emerging from the shadows shuffled an old woman, leaning heavily on a stick that clinked against the polished silver of the floor. Her hair was wiry and white, and her limbs seemed to tremble as she moved, her head shaking involuntarily despite the faint smile of achievement that graced her withered lips.

Zefer watched the old woman struggle across the highly polished floor of the hall as he listened to the admittor mumbling angrily under his breath.

'CC9FE? No? Honestly, I don't know why these people bother joining the queue if they are not going to turn up... CC9FF? By the Emperor, this is pathetic.

CCA00?' The admittor appeared neither to notice nor
to care about the woman.

As Zefer watched, the old woman stopped shuffling
and swayed tremulously. She had reached the middle of
the hall and seemed unsure about where to go next.
Then, quite suddenly, she collapsed to the ground, her
walking stick clattering and ricocheting on the metal.
Zefer jumped to his feet and ran across to her, skidding
down onto his knees. He slid to a halt next to her head
and peered down into the glazed eyes. Lying on her
back, the woman smiled faintly and opened her mouth,
straining to tell him something. Zefer waited, but no
noise came, and then he realised that she was dead.

'CCA01?'

'She's dead!' cried Zefer, climbing to his feet and turning to face the admittor.

'What? Oh, really?' The admittor pulled a brass lever
and the red light above the open doors changed to
green. 'That is inconvenient.' A few seconds later, a couple of servants came rushing out of the darkness with a
large, cloth sack. They hurried up to the old woman,
pushing Zefer aside, and bundled her into the bag,
before rushing back through the doors, dragging the
dead-weight behind them.

'CCA02?' asked the admittor hopefully, looking up
and down the length of the hall, as though expecting to
see somebody waiting who had not been there mere
seconds before.

Zefer watched the old woman being towed away and
listened to the admittor reeling off the numbers. He
looked at the two huge Goliath sentries standing massively and immovably next to the great doors. And he
made a decision.

'Admittor, sir,' he said as he strode back towards the
desk. 'Why not let me in instead of CCA02? He or she

is clearly not here – they may be dead for all we know. In any case, they probably made their appointment years ago and are likely to have forgotten about it by now.'

'You must wait your turn like everyone else, CC9FB2,' replied the admittor, crossing out a name from the log. 'CCA03?,' he called, looking past Zefer into the empty hall.

'But there is nobody else here!' cried Zefer, starting to get angry. 'Don't you see, you are going to have to read out every number between CCA03 and CC9FB2 before anyone will answer you. And do you know how long that will take?' asked Zefer, doing some arithmetic in his head. 'If you read out one number each minute, it would take you nearly twenty four years to get to me, and you are not going at even nearly that speed. I am reasonably certain that I will have died of old age or boredom before you get to me, so then nobody will ever answer your call. Don't you wish that, just once, you could actually let somebody in?'

The admittor looked up at Zefer with guilty excitement written on his face. 'Yes, I do wish that,' he said. 'Nobody has been admitted since I started here,' he confessed, almost sadly. 'Perhaps we could move you forward a little.'

3: THE HEIGHTS

'So, you are CCA04?' asked the permittor in the next corridor.

For a few moments, Zefer said nothing. He was still struggling to take in the scale of Gwentria's palace. This corridor was the smallest that he had been in since entering the palace nearly three hours earlier, and it was huge. The ceiling was domed and decorated with brightly coloured frescoes depicting the past glories of House Ko'iron. At regular intervals along its length hung magnificent chandeliers, bristling with crystals and glowing orbs of light. And both the long walls were studded with paintings and portraits, showing the great and good of the family. He had never seen anything like it – it made the grandeur of the librarium seem pedestrian and shabby.

'Well?' prompted the permittor again.

'Oh, er, sorry. Yes, yes I am… that's me. Yes,' said Zefer, fumbling his words because he was new to the art of lying.

The strangely elongated man peered at Zefer over his spectacles. 'Are you quite sure?'

'Yes, of course.' Zefer wracked his brain trying to think of something persuasive to say, or at least something that would persuade the odd looking stick-man standing in front of him with a clip-board. 'How else would I have got through to see you?' Excellent, thought Zefer, that would do it.

'True,' said the permittor, apparently satisfied with this procedural logic. 'You may go in. The princess is expect-ing you. Do please endeavour not to try her patience, she has had a long day and it is about time for her nap.'

'Of course,' replied Zefer, feigning sympathy. 'I will be as succinct as I possibly can be.'

With that, Zefer stepped past the permittor and reached out to push what he hoped would be the last set of doors lying between him and Princess Gwentria. As his hand approached the shimmering gold metal, the doors gave way in front of him, opening out to reveal a narrow, brightly lit and gloriously decorated corridor. At the other end, Zefer could quite clearly see that there was no door and no permittor laying in wait. Instead, the corridor led straight into a large, airy chamber, from which Zefer could hear the magical sound of girlish laughter.

The constricted passageway was gleaming with light, although Zefer could not see its source. The pearlescent white floor seemed to glisten and the immaculately sil-ver walls reflected the light back in on itself, rendering the corridor into a blaze of light. Zefer squinted as he stepped forward, feeling the golden doors seal quickly behind him.

Hesitantly, he started to walk towards the laughter, as though drawn by the thought of happiness. The por-traits on the walls seemed to follow him with their eyes as he glanced furtively from one side to the other, fear-ing that the walls might close in on him or that another palace official was going to leap out of a hidden door and explode his lie.

As he neared the middle of the passageway, Zefer paused. There was a huge fresco on the wall, depicting Jurod the Humane – Princess Gwentria's elder brother. He was seated bestride a bizarre looking machine, brandishing an elegantly curving blade in one hand and a heavy looking firearm in the other. The machine had two fat wheels, front and back, and vicious looking spikes arrayed around a forked ram that protruded from its nose. A great cloud of black smoke plumed out of the exhaust cluster at the rear, billowing around the flood of midnight blue that was Jurod's cape.

Cowering before the charging figure of Jurod were a crowd of snivelling creatures that might have been men, or might have been animals. It was hard to tell. They were crouched close to the ground with fur coverings tied tightly to their bodies, like second skins, but human hands and feet were visible underneath the bestial visage. One of these man-creatures was at the epicentre of the scene, trapped between the charging figure of Jurod on one side and the seething mass of his brethren on the other. The figure stood upright with his head thrown back in a scream and his arms cast out wide in supplication; the ram of Jurod's machine was just beginning to puncture his finely muscled stomach.

In the books of the librarium, Zefer had come across tales of the exploits of the most senior members of House Ko'iron during their periods of Spyrering. He had read descriptions of scenes like this before, but he had never thought to see one, and certainly not in such a glorious place as Gwentria's palace. His nose scrunched in revulsion at the thought of the most hallowed members of his house descending into the inglorious abyss of the Underhive.

'Praise the Emperor for the heights of Ko'iron,' he recalled from the *Paradoxes of the Spire*, 'for it is better to be well defined at the top than lost in the paradoxes of foundations. Unless it isn't,' thought Zefer, letting the meaning of those last three words impress upon him as though for the first time, as he stared up at the dramatic and bloody scene. Unless it isn't: there was something perversely attractive about the grotesquely heroic images.

Jurod's eyes seemed to blink involuntarily, as though they had been open too long in the dry air. Zefer caught the motion out of the corner of his eye and performed a startled double-take.

'That's my brother!' came a delighted shriek from the chamber ahead of him, making him snap his head round to find the source of the voice. Then he remembered where he was and he dropped to his knees, lowering his eyes into the pearly white of the floor.

'Your excellency,' he muttered, fumbling around in his brain for the correct mode of address.

'Doesn't he look wonderful? He killed them all, you know. All of them in one night. Mummy had said that he couldn't return to the Spire until he had killed forty ratskins, thinking that he would be gone for months. But he did it in one night, all by himself. Without a gang. Isn't he wonderful?' The voice bounced off the walls of the narrow corridor, echoing and repeating itself until it became a breathless tirade.

'Most impressive, your excellency,' acknowledged Zefer quietly, still stooped in deference.

'Isn't that echo fantastic? Sometimes I like to stand at this end of the corridor and shout things, just to hear my voice wobble and repeat like that. It is fun, don't you think? Do you like echoes?' Again, the high pitched voice ricocheted around Zefer, and he was convinced that it all came from a single breath.

'Yes, echoes are lovely, excellency,' replied Zefer, not quite sure what to say. His voice was soft and low, and hardly echoed at all.

'I can hardly hear you. Mummy says that it's rude to mumble, so don't do it. Why don't you come over here where I can hear you properly, then we can both make echoes together.' For a moment there was the irritated edge of chastisement in the voice, but it quickly gave way to playfulness once again.

This was not going quite in the manner that Zefer had anticipated, but he nodded and pulled himself up to his feet. 'Yes, your excellency, of course.'

'What? I can't hear you,' came the voice again, this time in a mocking sing-song tone.

Zefer finally raised his eyes and looked along the corridor. When he saw the figure standing in the chamber at the end, his jaw dropped and his eyes widened just a little too much. Princess Gwentria was not at all as he had imagined.

'WHAT? WHAT ARE you staring at? Are you going to come and make echoes or not?' asked the princess, stamping her feet in irritation.

Zefer stared at the little girl, completely lost for words. She must have been about fourteen. Her red hair was bunched into pig-tails on either side of her head, and her freckled skin was paler than the marble floor. She was surrounded by piles of toy animals that Zefer could not identify, and scattered over the floor were a whole array of bleeping and flashing devices that must also have been toys of some kind.

'Oh, erm, nothing,' managed Zefer, endeavouring to compose himself. 'I am not staring at all. I was just struck by... your beauty, your excellency.'

The little girl clutched her hands together and swayed her shoulders shyly. 'Oh, well… stop staring!' she shouted to overcome her embarrassment.

'Your excellency,' said Zefer, trying to move the conversation into a more comfortable area as he approached the princess. 'I have business to discuss with you.'

'Oh, not you too,' grumped the girl, stamping her foot again and turning away from him. 'That old woman also wanted to talk about some kind of book or something. That's not why you're here, is it? I'm bored of books. I want to go adventuring, like Jurod did. Did you see the picture of him? Isn't it wonderful?'

'The picture is magnificent, excellency,' replied Zefer, trying to bring the conversation back round to his report, 'but I really must ask for your opinion on another matter.'

'Will it lead to adventure and excitement?' asked Gwentria, slumping into a giant, amorphous blob of a chair, which moulded around her as her weight sunk in.

'Quite possibly,' said Zefer, suddenly realising that it might indeed. He had already had the most exciting few weeks of his life; after all, here he was talking with Princess Gwentria. Admittedly, she was not quite what he had been led to expect, but that was merely a small detail. For a moment he found himself wondering whether he should have waited for his proper place in the queue, by which time the young Gwentria may have been a little more… princess-like.

'Oh goody, then do tell,' she said, dumping her elbows onto her knees and leaning forward attentively.

'Oh, well, I'm not really sure where to start,' began Zefer, realising that it was true as he said it.

'At the beginning, dummy. Everyone knows that,' she giggled.

'Of course. In my spare hours after work, I have been reading one of the greatest works in your librarium, excellency: *The Paradoxes of the Spire*. I'm sure that you've heard of it.' Zefer waited for some indication that she was following, but she had started to play with one of her pig-tails and offered him nothing.

'Anyway, it is a very famous book. It has been read and reread over the course of centuries, with nobody ever reaching a truly satisfactory understanding of its meaning. It is alleged that it was written in the distant past, when House Ko'iron was little older than you, excellency.' Gwentria twitched a little as the story pointed towards her personally.

'Is it a good story?' she asked.

'It is undoubtedly a confusing story, excellency, written in very cumbersome and convoluted terms. However, there is certainly a good story behind it, and that it why I am here. You have undoubtedly heard rumours from your servants and from other visitors about the strange and mysterious things that can be found in the Underhive?'

Gwentria's eyes widened with interest. 'Yes. And my brother, Jurod, he's actually *been* there!'

'Indeed, excellency. Well, I discovered a missing page in the book that sheds new light on the famous opening lines.'

'Tell me the lines,' said the princess, pouting, almost instantly bored at the mention of books again.

'Very well. These are the first lines of the book: "*In the beginning they lay the end into the ground, and the finale was buried beneath the foundations, as though expecting the* sky to fall into the abyss in the days of Ko'iron's salvation to come,"' recited Zefer carefully.

'I don't understand.' Gwentria scrunched up her face in displeasure.

'No, nobody ever has,' explained Zefer, 'until now. But the missing pages tell of a time before Hive Primus was the huge structure that we know today. It was a time when this world was new, and House Ko'iron was just beginning to take shape. This was the time when the ancients started to construct Hive Primus, under the guidance of the Undying Emperor himself.

'If you had been there at that time, Princess Gwentria, and you had looked up from the ground, you would not have seen the towering edifice of the hive. When you looked up, there would have been nothing but the sky.'

'How lovely,' answered Gwentria, her imagination caught by the image. 'I once visited the Palace of Helmawr, right at the very peak of the Spire, and from there I could see nothing but the sky when I looked out of the windows.'

'Yes, my princess. And you have cleverly hit upon exactly my point,' coaxed Zefer, keeping the girl's interest.

'I have?'

'Yes. You see, House Helmawr has its place at the very top of the Spire because of a long historical claim that ties it to the founding of the hive itself. *The Paradoxes of the Spire*, suggests on the contrary, that it is House Ko'iron that should claim this heritage. Don't you see, it's impenetrable language must have been a code to protect the author from the Helmawr,' said Zefer excitedly, 'but now the meaning is clear: "Though it may be lost, salvation is always found buried in the depths of space and time, where Ko'iron first planted her roots." It was the Ko'iron matriarch, not the Helmawr patriarch who stood shoulder by shoulder with the Emperor!'

Gwentria was playing with her pig-tails again. 'I don't really understand,' she said, puffing out her cheeks. 'Are you saying that there is something down at the bottom of the hive that belongs to me?'

'Yes, yes, I suppose I am suggesting that,' admitted Zefer, somewhat shocked that the little girl had seen straight through to the most material implications of his story.

'And, you have come here to tell me that you are going to get it for me?' she asked, smiling sweetly.

'Oh, um, no. No, that's not quite why I'm here, I don't think,' replied Zefer, suddenly confused about what he expected to happen as a result of this meeting.

'But, if you don't go and get it, why should anybody believe what you are saying. It's just a story for children, isn't it?' explained Gwentria wisely. 'So, I think that you should go,' she concluded with a firm nod.

With that, there was a loud clunk and a hiss, and the wall behind the huge, squishy seat in which Gwentria was enthroned drew up into the ceiling. In the space behind was revealed a group of scribes, each feverishly scribbling onto clipboards, presumably recording the details of the conversation, thought Zefer. The strange, stick-like permittor from the other side of the brightly lit corridor was also there. He looked up as the wall vanished into the ceiling, making a few last marks on his clipboard.

'CCA04, this is the end of your audience. Please come with me,' said the permittor as he strode through the chamber towards Zefer, picking his way naturally over the mess of toys on the floor. 'It is time for her excellency's nap now.'

'Oh, do let me know how you get on!' said Gwentria happily. 'Perhaps, next time, we can make some echoes?'

'Yes, thank you,' said Zefer in some confusion, as the permittor took him by the arm and led him back down the bright corridor, past the epic fresco of Jurod towards the heavy golden doors at the end. 'I'll do my best, your excellency,' he called over his shoulder.

There was a giggle behind him. 'Yes, that's it. That echoed!'

KRELYN HADN'T SEEN the Wall for years, not since she last passed through it to take up her position in House Ko'iron under the auspices of the now defunct Delaque-Ko'iron Contract. At that time, she had slipped through the Tunnel of the Red Snakes – one of the secret Delaque gateways – avoiding the entanglement of the authorities around the great Spiral Gates themselves, which were kept securely guarded at all times. Traffic through the Wall was tightly controlled; the people of the Spire guarded their privileges jealously, and the people of Hive City below were unscrupulous in their attempts to gatecrash the party.

Pulling her cloak more carefully around her body, Krelyn stepped out of the shadows of the little alleyway, quietly thrilled that her new mission would take her through the Wall once again. In front of her, the huge, immovable shape of the Wall loomed massively, making her want to gasp. The air quality shifted as she drew nearer, as though it were condensed or cowering before the monstrous barrier. Krelyn had never actually been in a storm, but she thought that this was what the air would feel like before one struck.

The Wall ploughed unstoppably through this border district, sometimes cutting straight through buildings and structures that had once been buildings. It stretched about fifty metres into the air before burying itself into the substructure of the Spire above, forming an impregnable adamantium barrier. There was no way to climb over it, since there was no open space above it – it was jammed in between two levels of the Spire, and the upper level had had its floor reinforced with adamantium to prevent smugglers and slavers from drilling through from above.

In this district, the buildings of the Spire pressed right up against the surface of the Wall, leaving only a narrow alley that ran along next to it, overhung with balconies and studded with structures that had bored into the admantium to provide extra support for their unusual or aspirational shapes. The sheer sides cast the alley into deep shadow, and reduced the hubbub of the busier neighbouring sectors to faint murmurs.

Krelyn reached out and pressed her fingers against the cold rivets in the adamantium. They were damp with condensation, and Krelyn's touch sent little streams of water cascading down to the ground. She moved her hand slightly and pressed against the metal plate, leaning her weight against it. Just as she thought that she had misremembered, there was a quiet crack and a hiss of steam. The panel sank back into the Wall revealing a small, almost perfectly cylindrical tunnel.

Something made her hesitate before stepping into the passage. She paused at the entrance and scanned the shadows of the narrow alley that ran alongside the Wall. The air was heavy and damp, but there was something else lingering in the darkness that Krelyn couldn't quite sense. It was something just on the edge of perception, leaving only enough of an impression to betray its presence, but not quite enough to identify it.

A faint noise, like a knife dropping into sand, made her freeze. Whatever it was, it was now directly behind her. Instinctively, her right hand dropped to the trigger of the modified laspistol that hung from her shoulder under her cloak, and her left slipped inside the fatigues of her leg, clasping the hilt of a blade strapped to her thigh. She inhaled silently, bracing her body for the inevitable.

'Are you going in, or not?' slithered a sibilant voice into her ear.

Krelyn held her breath, unsure of how to proceed.

'If you're not going to go through, please stand aside,' hissed the voice with impatient but polished politeness.

'I am in no hurry,' hazarded Krelyn, stepping to one side without turning around. 'Please, go ahead of me if you are.'

'I am, thank you,' came the reply, as a damp cloak rushed past Krelyn's cheek. Even from this intimate distance, she could only just make out the shape of a stooped man hurrying down the tunnel. His cloak was long and impossibly dark, just like her own, and it shielded him from the attentions of the already dim light.

She watched the man take a few steps and then vanish in the darkness. She clicked her visor onto infra-red, but the thermal balancing of the Delaque cloak meant that she could only see him for another step or two before he was utterly invisible. Nonetheless, Krelyn continued to stare, checking the tunnel for signs of anything suspicious. There was nothing. Just darkness and hints of shadows.

Then suddenly there was a face, bright and blaring with heat immediately in front of her. Krelyn gasped and jumped backwards, clicking her visor back to normal and staring straight into the face of the venator emerging from the tunnel, a red snake seemed to writhe under his eyes. As she flew backwards she smashed into something heavy behind her and felt it collapse under her weight. She stumbled on whatever it was and then fell back on top of it.

'Get off,' cried an annoyed, feminine voice from below her, and a pair of small hands shoved her to one side, rolling her unceremoniously onto her belly.

Before Krelyn could spring back onto her feet, the source of the voice had already vanished into the tunnel with her cloak fluttering dramatically in her wake, and the owner of the face that had made her jump had similarly vanished into the streets of the Spire.

Brushing herself down, Krelyn realised with a mixture of disappointment and relish that she had gotten rusty in the Spire, but that her next few steps would take her back to her spiritual home. She had no idea how the Delaque gangs of Hive City would react to her return, especially the Red Snakes themselves, and she knew that even House Ko'iron's new allies would be unlikely to welcome her with open arms, but she ducked her head and dashed forward into the tunnel through the Wall.

IT DIDN'T MATTER how many times he looked at it, his desk was completely empty. There were no document pouches waiting for him, and no requisition papers for him to use to equip himself for his journey. For the second time in as many weeks, Zefer was utterly crestfallen. He had been certain as he had walked out between the great, shimmering doors of Gwentria's Palace the previous night that the urgency of his mission had been understood. He had thought that, at the very least, his mission papers would be waiting for him when he turned up at work the next day or, more likely, that a representative from the Provisions Office would be dispatched to ask what he required.

Instead, Zefer slumped into his little booth and everything looked much as it had the previous day, and the day before that. The only difference being that Zefer himself was dejected and annoyed. He deliberately placed his stylus on the desk with the tip pointing in the wrong direction, and then sneered at it as though he had made an important point. Then he stood up irritably, looking around the huge librarium reading room across the tops of the hundreds of little work-booths. He grunted audibly and sat down again.

After a few agitated minutes, he pushed his chair back and stormed off towards the desk of the senioris with whom he had talked the day before.

'UM,' HE STARTED, conscious that the conversation had probably been derailed already by that opening. 'Um, I was wondering whether you had received any…' He trailed off, realising that he was not quite sure what he expected to have arrived. 'That is, have you received anything for me? Anything from the Office of Princess Gwentria, I mean. I saw her yesterday… you may remember. You stamped my pass. Erm, I spoke to you.'

The senioris didn't even look up from his desk, but the top of his head managed to emanate condescension. 'What are you talking about, Curator Tyranus?'

Zefer realised that it had all come out backwards, but he was sure that the official was just being deliberately obstreperous. The senioris had probably never even met the princess, and would certainly not have expected to have seen Zefer back from her offices so quickly. He probably hoped never to see Zefer again.

'I thought that I had dealt with you yesterday, Tyranus. I certainly didn't expect to see you again so soon. Are you sure that you went to the right place with that pass?' asked the senioris, his stylus scratching to a halt as he raised his head slightly to peer up at Zefer, one eyebrow raised.

'Yes, senioris, I did exactly as you instructed. When I saw Her Excellency the Princess Gwentria, Matriarchal Heir to the Ancient and Glorious House of Ko'iron' – he decided to give her the full title not just for the sake of form, but mostly to underline the significance of the fact that he had actually met her (he decided not to mention the fact that she was just a little girl) – 'she gave me instructions for a research trip. I assumed that this would have been communicated to you already.' Zefer had puffed out his chest and was trying to look down his nose at the 'Duty Senioris,' whatever his name was. However, the official didn't seem particularly impressed and, slightly disarmed, Zefer felt a sudden pang of doubt that this might not actually be the same senioris as the one he had seen the day before. Looking around at the other seniorises in the area, he realised that he couldn't really differentiate between any of them; none of their desks had name-plates, only their titles, which were all the same.

'No, there is no reason that I would hear anything about your visit at all. Any requisitions for provisions or travel permits would be sent directly to the Historical Provisions Office, of course,' said the senioris impassively, dropping his attention back down to the documents on his desk. He made a little squiggle on one with his stylus, then stamped it and dropped it onto a growing pile of similar documents on the floor next to his desk.

'Of course,' said Zefer, trying to make it sound like he had known that all along. It wasn't very convincing, and he cringed slightly as the words came out. 'I'll be off to the HPO then,' he added, thinking that the acronym might recover some form of nonchalance.

The senioris made no response at all. Zefer hesitated for a moment, then turned and shuffled back down the corridor towards his little booth.

TWO MORE AGENTS passed her as she made her way through the tunnel. She didn't see them and she was sure that they didn't see her, but there had been a whispered acknowledgement as their shadows had merged: the invisible nod of an unspoken confraternity.

The tunnel was longer than Krelyn remembered, and certainly longer than the Wall was wide, but when she reached the end she realised why. The mouth of the tunnel emerged into the commotion of Hive City just above the revolving fan of an air-vent. The tunnel was hidden behind a giant vertical pipe that led up from the fan and through the uneven ceiling. A series of pitons had been hammered into the back of the pipe to provide the suggestion of a ladder for the Red Snake agents to use to gain access to the tunnel. Each piton bore the tiny red snake of the Delaque family crest. Rolling up her sleeve, Krelyn paused for a moment to compare the mark to the tattoo that ran along the inner side of her left forearm.

Krelyn climbed down the hidden side of the pipe and slipped out from behind it, crouching into the narrow trough defined by the downward curve of one of the horizontal ventilation pipes and the roughly riveted wall behind it. She was right next to the fan, which was positioned at the intersection of two giant horizontal pipes and the vertical one that she had just climbed down.

The slow revolutions of the fan blades beat the air and sent pulses rippling through the metal pipes, but the noise was completely drowned out by the raucous tumult going on in the plaza in front of the vent. Krelyn lifted her head and peered over the curving apex of the pipe, smiling broadly at the violent confirmation that she was home again.

As she lifted her head, a tumble of blue-cloaked gangers burst out of the door of a building on the other side of the square followed by a pluming gout of flame. The blue-cloaks dove to the ground, blown off their feet by the concussion, but nobody emerged in pursuit. Instead, a chorus of cheers erupted from Krelyn's right, and she turned her head to see a larger group of similarly blue-coated gangers standing atop the huge horizontal pipe on that side. They started to stamp their feet rhythmically, making the pipe vibrate and rumble.

On the other side of the square, sitting casually on the other horizontal pipe, were a group of ostentatiously clad women. Their silence oozed with condescension and Krelyn could easily see that they were the victorious side in whatever affair was unfolding.

Potentially interesting as the scene might have been, Krelyn had more important things to do than to watch a street brawl – even though she hadn't seen any proper gang warfare for years. Instinctively, her hands traced the shape of the blades strapped in place against her legs and she nodded to herself, delighted that the instinct had returned to her so quickly.

Smiling with contentment, Krelyn slid down the back of the pipe into the shadows underneath it. Landing softly, she pulled her cloak tightly around her to ensure that she would not disturb the fracas in the square, and then she swept along the edge of the plaza and out into the streets of Hive City. She had to make contact with her allies, and quickly.

'WHAT ARE YOU doing here, venator?' Orthios spat the last word as though he were swearing.

'I have come to request your assistance,' replied Krelyn, crouched on the sill of the window through which she'd just climbed, her cloak thrown back over her shoulder so that the people in the street outside would not be able to see her at all.

Orthios laughed, looking around the room at the faces of his comrades in the Snake Charmers gang. 'Excuse me?' he said in amused disbelief. 'You have come to request what?'

'Your assistance, if you please,' said Krelyn, refusing to rise to the bait. In a smooth movement, she vaulted down from the window and landed gently in the centre of the group of gangers. Despite their superior numbers, the men backed away slightly when she landed. If this intruder had somehow managed to penetrate to the heart of Orthios's gang house, the Snake Charmers' Basket, as it was known, then she was probably a dangerous woman.

'Yes, I thought that was what you said,' mused Orthios, taking a step towards Krelyn and propping himself up on his chainsword, as though it were a walking stick. 'I just don't understand why you would be stupid enough to say such a thing.'

Unphased, Krelyn took two confident steps forward, bringing her face to within centimetres of the ganger's. 'Because, Orthios, I bring the seal of House Ko'iron, and you are obliged to assist me, whether I request it or not.' With that, Krelyn flashed open her cloak and revealed the Ko'iron crest hanging as a medallion against her chest.

She had not been looking forward to this moment, and had known that it was a big risk to take, particularly so early on in her mission, but she had nowhere else to go. There was no way that she could have returned to the safe house of the Red Snakes – her own Delaque gang – their response would be even more unpredictable than that of these Snake Charmers of House Orlock. In any case, in theory at least (and in law at best) this Orlock gang was obliged to help her. A number of years earlier, the Orlocks had wrested the lucrative Ko'iron Contract from the Delaque and, in the process, they had bound themselves to the Ko'iron as allies. As a pledged servant of House Ko'iron, Krelyn was entitled to shelter and support from this gang. An unfortunate side-effect of the transference of the Ko'iron Contract, of course, was the escalation of hostilities between Delaque and Orlock gangs in this part of Hive City – and that meant between the Red Snakes and the Snake Charmers. Krelyn, who wore her Delaque lineage like a great black cloak around her body, was just about the last person that Orthios wanted to see in his private meeting chamber.

'This had better not be some kind of Delaque trickery, venator, or you will pay with your life,' muttered Orthios as he grabbed hold of the medallion and studied it closely. The Delaque had a well-deserved reputation for deception and underhandedness, and Orthios had already lost too many men to their treacherous schemes since House Orlock had undercut the Delaque and squeezed them out of their trade agreement with the affluent Noble House of Ko'iron.

Behind him, Orthios's comrades shifted uneasily, adjusting their red bandanas and checking their weapons noisily to indicate their own distrust.

'It is no trick,' replied Krelyn evenly, holding Orthios's eyes with her own but concentrating on the movements of the other gangers in her peripheral vision. Under her cloak, her right hand rested lightly on the stock of her laspistol. 'I want to be here even less than you want me here,' she continued honestly. 'But, since the Delaque are no longer the allies of House Ko'iron, I am left in something of a predicament when it comes to choosing my friends.'

'I did not know that the Noble House retained the services of any of you after the transferral of the contract,' said Orthios, releasing Krelyn's medallion and taking a step back, dragging the teeth of his chainsword along the metal floor.

'Just me, I'm afraid,' conceded Krelyn, her left hand ready at the hilt of a blade in a holster on her lower back. 'My oath was already taken, and Prince Jurod would not release me from it. It seems that he thought I could perform functions that his new Orlock lackeys could not.' The insult was a calculated risk – the Snake Charmers would be even more suspicious if she pretended to be nice.

Orthios hefted his chainsword into the air and it spluttered to life, sending a thin drizzle of blood splattering across the floor towards Krelyn. It was old blood, dark and coagulated, presumably left over from the last time the sword had been used. Then the whirring died and Orthios dropped the blade back against his shoulder. With a broad grin, he stepped forward and slapped Krelyn on arm.

'Well, my venator friend, what brings you down from the airy splendour of the Spire?' As he spoke, he slipped his arm around Krelyn's shoulders and led her off towards the irregularly shaped table at the other side of the room. Even through her inexplicable cloak, Orthios could feel the tension in Krelyn's knotted shoulders. 'Come, come, relax,' he said with a slightly forced laugh. 'You are amongst friends here.'

The other gangers followed their leader at a safe distance, circling around the table to take up positions on the far side as Orthios pulled out a chair for their guest. The table was a torn and jagged sheet of adamantium, presumably it had been ripped out of some other structure and then brought to this gang house as a temporary expedient. Krelyn studied the pockmarked surface as she sat down, wondering whether things had really got so bad for the Snake Charmers that they had to use waste material for their tables. Perhaps they were not doing so well in the war against her Delaque.

Orthios sat opposite and spread his palms flat against the table, as though to demonstrate that there was no weapon in them. For a moment he sat in silence, drumming his fingers against the metal as the rest of his comrades sat down. Krelyn watched him carefully, letting the others move around her peripheral vision, confident that she could deal with anything that the table might hide. She watched Orthios's fingers tapping out a syncopated rhythm and wished that he would stop, but then she noticed something else. Narrowing her eyes, her visor clicked up the magnification and Orthios's fingertips seemed to zoom towards her face. Underneath them, subject to the repeated pummelling of his dirty finger nails, Krelyn saw the red snake of House Delaque etched into the adamantium.

The tension dropped out of her shoulders and she allowed herself to relax for the first time. Orthios smiled at her across the table, realising that she had finally seen what he had wanted her to see. He nodded, returning her insult with firm good humour – Ko'iron's new Orlock allies were easily a match for its former Delaque lackeys.

She returned the nod, grateful that they had reached an understanding without bloodshed.

'If you are all sitting comfortably, gentlemen, I shall begin,' said Krelyn, shuffling the story of Curator Tyranus and his book into an abbreviated form in her mind.

'BUT YOUR PASS says that you are CC9FB2, Curator Tyranus,' said the tubby provisor in the HPO. Zefer couldn't tell whether the man was sitting down or not, since his roughly spherical shape seemed to betray nothing of his posture behind the desk. 'It looks to me as though somebody simply crossed out your number and then wrote in another one. Why should I believe that you are, in fact, CCA04 as you claim?'

Zefer clenched his jaw. 'I don't see why it should matter to you what my number is, provisor,' he said. 'I, for example, care not what my number is, only that I am Zefer Tyranus, curator of the Historical Research Section on a mission for Her Excellency the Princess Gwentria, Matriarchal Heir to the Ancient and Glorious House of Ko'iron. That is what is important. The number is not.' Zefer spoke with a flat hope born of resignation.

The provisor moved towards the edge of his desk, which led Zefer to conclude that he had probably been standing up until this point. His head was bowed and his hands were clasped behind his back. 'I can see your point, Curator Tyranus, but you must also understand mine.' At that, the squat provisor looked up at Zefer as though he were about to relate something far more important than anything that Zefer himself had just said. Yet again, Zefer was slightly taken aback by the complete lack of impact that his mission appeared to have on the officials of House Ko'iron.

'You see, whilst I can understand that your identity as Curator Zefer Tyranus is the most important thing to you personally – since you *are* Curator Tyranus himself – you must try to appreciate that it makes no difference to me in any way at all who you actually *are*, but only who you are *to me*. This, I think, is true of all human relations, and not just those of a professional nature such as we are encountering today. And the fact of the matter remains that *to me* you are CC9FB2, and there are no provisions allocated for you here.' As he spoke, the round little man paced backwards and forwards behind his desk, bouncing his clasped hands off the small of his back.

'I can appreciate your position, provisor…' Zefer trailed off as he realised how much more effective his arguments would be if he knew the names of the people he was talking to. That, he realised suddenly, was probably why the plaques on the desks of senior officials only ever showed their titles. 'If, as you say, it is really of no consequence to you who I am and only who I am to you, could we not proceed from this point as though I had not showed you a paper pass at all and begin our relationship again from the start?'

The provisor stopped pacing for a moment, apparently thinking about Zefer's question. His smooth, sweaty brow wrinkled for a moment, and then he reached a decision. 'Very well,' he said. 'I see no reason why not.'

'Excellent, thank you,' replied Zefer, eager to press on before the little man's brain caught up with events. 'Hello provisor. I am Curator Zefer Tyranus of the Historical Research Section on a mission for the Princess Gwentria herself. She has given me the number CCA04 and instructed me to collect supplies from you. I'm afraid that I have lost my paper pass.'

'I see. Welcome CCA04. Let me just check and see whether there is anything for you,' said the provisor formally, turning sharply from his desk and bobbing off through the door behind it. A few moments later, he returned.

'No, CCA04, I am afraid that there is nothing here for you.'

'What?' cried Zefer, slapping his palm to his forehead in disbelief. 'What? If there wasn't anything here for CCA04 either, why did we have to go through all this?'

'As I believe I explained,' said the provisor, upset by Zefer's manner, 'I am obliged to follow correct procedure here, and I could not check for items for CCA04 until CCA04 turned up to ask for them. Only a moment ago, you were CC9FB2, so you can understand my reluctance to divulge any such information at that time. I'm sure that you would do no less, curator. Besides, I still don't really believe that you are CCA04 at all.'

'If you don't believe me, does that mean that you're not really telling me the truth about whether there are any supplies for me?' asked Zefer, exasperated.

'As far as I am concerned, I can honestly tell you that there are no supplies for you here,' said the provisor carefully. 'You might try the Wall Provisions Office. If your mission is likely to take you through the Wall, that is probably where your supplies would have been sent.'

Zefer just stared at the near-spherical man. Then, without saying a word, he turned and walked out of the HPO, trudging slowly towards the edge of the Ko'iron district, the Wall and the Spiral Gates that led down into Hive City. He was exhausted already, and he hadn't even left home yet. In an attempt to cheer himself up, he told himself that things could only get better.

4: SPIRAL GATES

A CHORUS OF candles flickered around the perimeter of the room, filling the space with dancing shadows and ribbons of warm light. The orange flames bounced off the dull metal walls, as though their lives were diminished with each reflection, leaving the room in virtual darkness despite the hundreds of points of light.

Kneeling in the centre of the floor with his unmasked face raised in rapture at the image of the Undying Emperor that hung from the ceiling before him, glowing as though ablaze, Triar muttered his silent prayers while his blue eyes twinkled in the flickering light. Spread on the floor under his knees were the charred and burnt remains of his cloak, giving off the faint stench of ruin.

There was a hiss from the far corner of the room, as though a snake were tasting the air. Triar inclined his head slightly to the side, but did not look round. Even if he had, he would not have been able to see the cloaked venator standing motionless in the deep shadows beyond the ring of candles, with his light-absorbent cloak wrapped securely around him.

'You're late,' whispered Triar, returning his attention to the icon of the Emperor.

There was a faint shuffling sound, as though the cloaked man had shifted his balance in discomfort or self-consciousness. 'It has been a busy day,' he breathed, not really making an excuse, just stating the facts.

'Indeed it has, Curion. And an interesting one,' said Triar, keeping his eyes fixed on the holy relic. 'Your information about the Escher witch and her Coven was sound, but you failed to warn me of the danger.'

'It is the information that you pay me for. Your security is not my responsibility,' came the sibilant reply. 'I understand that your gangers did not exactly excel themselves,' continued the voice from the shadows, taunting a little.

'What do you want, Venator Curion?' asked Triar, his patience breaking along with his concentration on the idol.

'I thought I was late, sire,' mocked Curion, stepping out of the shadows and into the flickering light of the Redemptionist shrine. 'I should rather ask you what you want.' The candlelight lapped against his cloak, which seemed to absorb it like a sponge soaking up water. Even as he walked towards the kneeling figure of Triar in the centre of the chamber, Curion remained merely the suggestion of a presence in the room.

Triar ignored the Delaque wit. 'Of course you should,' he replied, straightening his knees and rising to his feet. As he turned casually to face in the direction of Curion's voice, he was startled to discover the venator standing directly before him. The red snake tattooed below his dark visor seemed to writhe in the candlelight.

'I have no fear that anything the heretics say contains even the tiniest iota of truth,' began Triar, affecting nonchalance by picking up his blackened, crumbling cloak, brushing it down and folding it into a bundle. 'However, it is easier for the righteous agents of the Emperor to combat the evils of heresy if they are properly informed about their activities.'

'I quite understand,' replied the venator, aware of the importance of sound intelligence. His tone retained an edge of mockery, betraying the fact that he found the Cawdor's devotion to the Cult of Redemption faintly ridiculous. He knew that Triar was aware of his attitude, but he prided himself on the knowledge that his employer needed his services more than he desired his soul.

'If that witch Elria thinks that she has found some evidence that the Undying Emperor was a woman, I need to know what this so-called evidence might be. Of course, I have no fear that it is false, but the power of information only rarely lies in its truth or falsehood,' explained Triar.

Curion watched the Salvationist's leader speak, and nodded, smiling at the redundancy of much of what he said. 'I am sure that you are right,' he said reassuringly.

'You would be more sure, venator, if you embraced the truth of Redemption yourself,' snapped Triar, catching the amusement in Curion's tone. His blue eyes shone brightly in the dark room as he stared into the other's visor.

'Belief is not a condition of true service,' countered Curion. They had had this conversation numerous times before. 'You appear to be confusing belief with payment, sire.'

Fixing a smile onto his face, Triar reached into a pouch on his belt and removed a clutch of tiny gems. 'I am not confused, Curion, but neither am I naïve,' he said as he handed the stones to the venator.

As the man tripped, the tray slipped out of his hands and the glasses went flying. He collapsed heavily to the ground, crashing down onto his face in a pool of red liquid and broken glass. A chorale of laughter erupted around him and he staggered back to his feet, blood trickling down his face from the fresh cuts. An extra bout of hilarity greeted him as he spat out a tooth and then scrambled about on the floor trying to retrieve it.

'Where's my drink?' mocked Jermina, tripping the man back into the pool of alcohol and blood. She planted her boot onto his back as he lay prostrate in the puddle, thrashing his limbs around like a floundering fish.

'S-so-so sorry,' spluttered the man, dribbling spittle and blood as he struggled to breath under Jermina's weight.

'Let him go, Jermina,' called Elria. She was leaning on the metal railing around the balcony, watching the preparations for the gang's expedition in the hall below. From the floor, her gangers looked up at her in surprise.

'I need a drink myself,' she said, vaulting off the balcony and landing into a crouch next to the prone servant. 'If we kill all the men in the house, there will be nobody left to bring us drinks.'

The rest of the women laughed, and Jermina lifted her foot off the hapless servant, who pulled himself up onto his knees and crawled towards Elria's feet. As he reached his hands out to grasp her ankles, Elria stepped back, making him overbalance and fall back onto his face.

'I am not forgiving you, slave, I am simply saving you,' she said without pity as a pulse of chuckles rippled around the hall. 'You may yet live to wish that I had not.' As she spoke, her blue dreadlocks seemed to wave and animate all by themselves, as though thirsting for the blood that oozed from the man's face.

'Now, go and get a fresh set of drinks!' said Jermina, prodding the man in the ribs with the tip of her boot.

Without a word, the man dragged himself to his feet and executed a drab and exhausted bow, streams of blood and drink spilling over his body. Then he turned and limped pathetically out of the hall, prodded and poked by each of The Coven's gangers as he passed them.

'Are we ready to go?' asked Elria, turning her attention back to Jermina and gesturing around the jumbled space of the hall.

'Very nearly, mistress,' bowed Jermina, suddenly serious and formal as she noticed the snaking patterns being defined by the boss's hair. That was never a good sign.

The hall was a mess of half packed crates and kitbags. There were weapons strewn over the top of everything, and some were still stored neatly in their racks against the dirty grey walls. Elria's yellow and red banner was draped colourfully down the wall at the end of the hall, fluttering constantly in the drafts that eased through the cracks in the wall behind it. Hanging off the balcony, which swept around three sides of the hall – the fourth, having collapsed years before, sported the banner – were red bandanas and blue cloaks tinged with blood.

There was a jagged hole in the roof, through which trickled a persistent cascade of green water. It collected into a shallow, mouldy fountain in the hall, in which stood a cracked statue of a man lying in submission before a muscular woman with an axe. Her left arm had been broken off long ago, but it had once held the end of a chain that led to a collar around the man's neck.

Elria's eyes lingered on the statue for a moment. She was proud of her family lineage. Neither The Coven nor even House Escher itself may have the documents, histories and librariums of those effete, naval-gazing Noble Houses up in the Spire, but they had long and glorious histories to match any of them. House Escher even surpassed them, she thought, since only Escher was of pure constitution. She didn't need books and monuments to tell her such obvious things. The knowledge was in her blood.

History only had significance if it gave her power in the present, and the strength of her arm was thus testament to her superior history. Let any man walk into Elria's hall without an army, and she would have him on his face in a pool of his own blood.

It seemed blatantly obvious to her: if an Undying Emperor, or whatever those ridiculous Redemptionists called it, ever really walked the surface of Necromunda, that Emperor must have been a woman. She could feel it in her blood, just as certainly as that servant could feel his inferiority in the blood he left coagulating on the metal deck.

And then her informant had come to her with whisperings of a piece of archeotech, hidden in the depths of the Underhive, an artefact that might prove to the weak willed Redemptionists, to Triar's pathetic Salvationist gang, and to the ridiculous Noble Houses that He was in reality a She. It was pathetic that anyone would require proof, as though Elria's own strength were not proof enough. But proof could open a lot of doors, perhaps even the great Spiral Gates themselves, and Elria was not so entrapped by the power of violence that she did not occasionally dream of the fresh air and natural light enjoyed by the feeble unworthies on the other side of the Wall. If nothing else, material proof would certainly devastate that irritating, pompous Salvationist gang leader, Triar; it would be worth an expedition into the Underhive just to see the expression on his face when she came back with the artefact.

A flutter of motion snapped Elria out of her reverie. Without a moment's hesitation, she slid her favourite blades out of their fixings in her hair as she took three skipping steps backwards. Warned by the alert of their leader, the rest of the gangers snatched up weapons from the floor and racked them purposefully, their aim focussed on the position that Elria had just vacated.

Plummeting down from the rough hole in the ceiling was a solitary, cloaked figure. Its arms were outstretched into the shape of a cross; the corners of the voluminous cape were caught in the figure's hands, and it ballooned up like a parachute, slowing the figure's descent.

With a solid, metallic thud, the dropping figure hit the ground in the middle of the hall, its cloak draped evenly around it, hiding the crouched body completely. The gangers fanned out in a ring around the intruder, unsure of whether it had survived the fall, with their weapons trained on the impossibly black fabric of the cape.

'Mistress Elria,' came a female voice from under the folds of the cloak. 'I bring news from the Spire.' The figure unfolded itself from the ground, standing to face the Coven's leader and executing a curt bow.

With a signal from Elria, the gangers relaxed their weapons.

'We are about to depart, Venator Orphae. Your timing is… dramatic,' said Elria, choosing her words thoughtfully.

'You will want to hear this news before you leave, mistress,' replied the cloaked agent.

Elria looked into Orphae's face and tried to interpret her expression. The dark Delaque visors made it almost

impossible to judge their emotions, and Elria often
wondered whether they actually had any. This was not
the first time that Elria had wished that her spy worked
for something other than profit – Orphae was a powerful and skilled woman. She should be an Escher.

'Will I, indeed?' replied Elria, taking a couple of steps
forward and pressing a cluster of crystals into Orphae's
cupped hand. She knew better than to doubt Orphae's
word. 'Do tell.'

'No, THERE IS definitely nothing here for CCA04,' said
the provisor in the Ko'iron Wall Provisions Office. She
was clearly growing agitated by all of Zefer's questions,
and his insistence that there should be equipment
waiting for him.

'Are you quite sure?' asked Zefer again. 'What about
CC9FB2?'

'Even if there were equipment for that number, I
would not expect it to appear for the next year or two.
The last person to receive provisions from us was… let
me see…' The provisor rummaged through a giant filing cabinet at the back of the little room, trying to be
helpful. She was a huge woman, and the massive cabinet looked decided fragile as she rifled through it. The
scene was comical, reflected Zefer, as he recalled the
tiny little man in the huge HPO and overlaid the
memory atop this giant woman in the tiny little
KWPO.

'Ah, yes, here it is,' bellowed the provisor. 'CC5A1.
That was the last person. A mistress Thelda Grundark.
Oh, it seems that she never turned up to collect her
things,' continued the woman with a scarily broad
smile.

'I think that she probably died before she could get
here,' said Zefer with feeling, thinking back to the old

lady who had collapsed as she left the offices of Princess Gwentria.

'Oh dear, well I wish that somebody had told me. I could have thrown this file away. The Emperor knows that it is hard enough to keep this place tidy without redundant files cluttering the place up.' As she spoke, she tugged the file out of the cabinet and flung it into a gaping waste-shoot in the wall next to her. Turning to make her way back to the little desk, the monstrous woman tripped on the corner of the cabinet and lurched forward. As she fell, she twisted around and grabbed hold of the huge filing cabinet, which upended and crashed down on top of her.

Zefer rushed round the little desk to help the woman out from under the weight, ignoring her protestations that he was not authorised to be on that side of the provisor's desk. He leant his shoulder against the bulk of the filing cabinet and pushed his weight at it, fearing that he might be too weak to shift it. However, almost as soon as he touched it, it slid freely off the woman and smashed onto the floor next to her. All of the drawers opened in a cacophony of clatter, but nothing fell out. It was completely empty.

'No no, you mustn't be over here,' bellowed the woman, clambering back onto her feet and shoving Zefer roughly back to the other side of the desk. Once she was satisfied that he was safely back where he should be, she turned and picked up the filing cabinet all by herself and stood it back in the corner.

'That's empty!' cried Zefer, still trying to process the new information.

'Yes, it is now!' retorted the provisor triumphantly, brushing herself down after her tumble. 'Now that somebody has told me about CC5A1.'

'So, are you saying that nobody has any provisions waiting for them here?'

'Not on this side of the Wall, no,' replied the woman, apparently pleased to be of help.

'Not on this side of the Wall?' queried Zefer, unsure what the provisor might be referring to.

'Yes,' explained the huge woman, leaning forward against the desk and buckling its legs slightly. 'There is another provisions office on the other side of the Wall. The Hive City WPO. It is much bigger and busier than this one, of course. There's not much call for provisions for people *leaving* the Spire, curator. People don't tend to want to do that. But everyone wants to come up here, for some reason.'

'I see. So, are you saying that my paperwork and provisions are likely to be waiting for me on the other side?' asked Zefer tentatively.

'It is certainly possible.'

'Can you check?'

'No. No, I can't check for you, I'm afraid. You see, I am not authorised to pass through the Spiral Gates, and the people who work in the WPO on the other side are certainly not authorised to come up into the Spire. They don't let just anyone through, you know. Or rather,' she added, correcting herself, 'they don't let just anyone into the Spire. Provisors and messengers are not significant enough to be granted access, you see. If I went to check for you, I wouldn't be able to come back again. You'll be fine going down, curator, if you want to go and check the other office for yourself.'

'I see,' said Zefer, trying to understand the logic of what he had just been told. 'You're saying that they'll let me through into Hive City. Will they also let me come back again?'

'When you collect your provisions and paperwork from the WPO, you'll have the correct pass to grant you readmission,' said the provisor simply. 'Besides, didn't you say that your mission was to go down, not up?'

'IT IS NOT only The Coven that is interested in the rumours of this artefact,' reported Curion, tucking the gem stones into a fold in his tunic. 'There is also talk of it amongst the Noble Houses of the Spire. In particular, House Ko'iron has dispatched an agent through the Wall on a mission to retrieve the archeotech.'

'I know better than to ask you how you know this, Curion,' said Triar, gazing into the flickering flame of a candle. 'But it is indeed interesting news. Where is this agent now?'

'I passed her as she made her way through the Wall. When she emerged into the Hive City, she headed for the compound of Orthios and his Snake Charmers.' The venator made the report formally, careful not to betray any emotion at the mention of the gang who had wrenched the Ko'iron Contract from his own Delaque brothers.

At the mention of the Snake Charmers, Triar raised his eyes, wishing not for the first time that he could see Curion's eyes behind his visor. Instead, he could see merely his own reflection, iridescent in the inconstant candlelight.

The feud between the Houses of Delaque and Orlock and their various gangs was no secret, and Triar was not keen to get involved in the wars of other people. He had enough wars of his own to fight. He had never had reason to doubt the information provided by Curion before, but he was always a little cautious when the information had something to do with Curion's gang-masters in the shadowy House of Delaque. The venator may have been in the employ of The Salvationists for the time being, but Triar was not so naïve as to believe that a fist full of jewels would compromise his loyalty to his own house, at the end of the day. Curion was useful, but he was a heretic, after all.

'Do you know the details of her mission?' asked Triar, sidestepping the issue of the Snake Charmers for the time being. 'If you know where she is going, then we will have no need for her, and thus no need to enter into a costly conflict with your Orlock friends.'

'I do not know where she is going,' confessed Curion.

'No, I supposed that you would not,' said Triar with a wry smile.

'However, I also suspect that she does not really know where she is going either,' continued Curion, not rising to the bait. 'She was dispatched after a scholar found reference to the archeotech in an old book in the house librarium. I saw the tome myself, but it was almost impossible to understand. I do not believe that the Ko'iron agent would understand any more of it than myself.'

'So, of what use is she?' asked Triar, raising an eyebrow.

'As I understand it, she is charged with ensuring the success of the mission of another; the scholar himself is to be sent on an acquisitions mission. She may yet prove to be an obstacle to you, if you were interested in acquiring the services of that scholar,' explained Curion.

'I see,' responded Triar, nodding in some amusement at Curion's attempt to keep the information focussed on Orthios's gang. The venator was right, however, that the scholar might be able to help him get to the artefact before the heretic witch, Elria. 'And where is this scholar, of which you speak?'

'His movements have been rather erratic. He appears to be quite skilled in the arts of subterfuge and I have not been able to follow him. I thought it more important to bring you news of the heretic currently being harboured by the Snake Charmers. I am sure that the scholar has not yet passed through the Spiral Gates, but certain that he will do so soon.'

'Then we must prepare a welcome for our honoured guest,' smiled Triar, blowing out the candle and sweeping out of the prayer chamber.

'THERE HAVE BEEN some interesting developments, mistress,' reported Orphae as Elria sank deeply into the cushions on her tarnished throne, below the great banner of her gang. The rest of the gangers had dispersed around the hall, taking up positions within earshot of their leader, reclining across the half-packed kitbags that littered the ground.

The man-servant, or mavant as the Escher were wont to call all men, had returned to the hall with a fresh tray of drinks. His face had been cleaned up, but there were still traces of blood speckled down his sparse clothing. He was walking very carefully, picking his way between the gangers and their kit, trying his best not to be noticed. As he knelt before Elria and extended the tray, his arms trembled so much that the glasses clinked together repeatedly.

'Drink?' asked Elria, directing her question to Orphae but keeping her amused eyes on the tremulous man at her feet.

'No. No, thank you,' replied the venator. Orphae was also watching the subservience of the mavant, but the eyes hidden behind her visor were not filled with amusement. She had never understood the Escher's utter disdain for men but, more than that, she had

never been able to work out what sort of man would
allow himself to be treated in this way. In fairness,
there were hardly any men who would associate themselves with this gang; most held a special place in their
hearts for the hate they felt towards the Escher. But this
man, this *mavant* – how had he come to be a slave of
the Escher?.

The gang leader lent forward off her throne and
snatched two glasses off the tray, throwing the liquid
from one straight to the back of her throat and
smashing the glass onto the floor. She slipped the
stem of the second glass between her fingers and
swirled the red liquid playfully, whispering something that only the mavant could hear.

'What developments?' she asked, reclining back
into the throne and pushing the mavant away with
the sole of her foot. He scurried off, with relief dropping off him like perspiration.

'The curator who discovered the new pages
appears to be in the process of leaving the Spire,'
reported the venator, bowed on one knee to the side
of the throne.

'And where is this woman going?' asked Elria, toy-
ing absently with her drink.

'The curator is a man, mistress,' corrected Orphae,
wincing slightly.

'I see.' Elria downed her drink and threw the glass
across the hall towards the mavant, who was serving
the other gangers on his hands and knees.

'I am not sure where he is going, but I suspect that
he has been sent by the Ko'iron elders to retrieve the
archeotech, of which we have already spoken,' continued Orphae.

'He is aware, I presume, of the significance of the
artefact?' asked Elria, curious to know why a man

would want to discover an artefact that proved that the Emperor was a woman.

'For him, mistress, the archeotech will show that House Ko'iron was here right from the foundations of Hive Primus. Just as it is inconsequential to you that the woman in question may have been a Ko'iron, so it is inconsequential to him that the Ko'iron lineage is matriarchal,' explained Orphae, not relishing the prospect of a debate on gender politics with an Escher gang leader. She realised that Elria had interpreted her account of the content of the lost pages to mean that the artefact would show that the Emperor himself was this Ko'iron woman, which was not quite what she (or the book, she presumed) had meant. 'The significance for us,' she continued, trying to steer the subject back round to the matter at hand, 'is that he is likely to know where to look. As I told you before, the *Paradoxes of the Spire* made little sense to me – he is our best hope.'

Elria shook her head in disappointment. She had heard a great deal about the Noble House of Ko'iron, and she had secretly held out the hope that it was a potential ally of the Escher. It was currently one of the only genuinely matriarchal institutions in the Hive, outside those of the Escher themselves. However, it seemed that she had overestimated their political convictions. But, as Orphae had implied, House Ko'iron's motivations were irrelevant. Weeks before, Orphae had related the book's account of a time in the ancient past, before Hive Primus was the monstrosity that it had since become, when 'a powerful woman walked at the foundations' of Necromunda. Orphae had tried to suggest that this woman was the Ko'iron martriarch, standing at the Emperor's side, but Elria knew in her soul that this woman was the Emperor herself.

'Then we must find this mavant, Orphae.'

'Things are not quite so simple, mistress. I have reason to believe that an agent of House Ko'iron has already descended into the realm of Orthios's Orlock gang, the Snake Charmers. We should assume that she will be seeking the aid of Ko'iron's new allies.' Orphae's voice was low and earnest, but Elria could not help but laugh.

'I see!' she joked. 'So, you would have us attack the Snake Charmers?' Elria was well aware of the Delaque's distaste for House Ko'iron's new allies.

'I am merely a source of information, mistress, not of strategy. You must do with this information whatever you see fit,' demurred the venator, bowed with her face hidden.

'Has this scholar yet come through the Spiral Gates?' asked Elria, beckoning to the mavant for another drink.

'No, mistress. Not yet.'

DESPITE THE FACT that they were the most massive structures that he had ever seen in his life, Zefer stumbled across the Spiral Gates without at first noticing them. He had never been that far from the Ko'iron precinct before, and everything was a wonder to him as he walked through the wide, pristine, statue-lined boulevards.

The streets themselves were paved with marble, and the colonnades stretched magnificently into an only barely visible ceiling. Bright lamps burnt on elegantly twisting poles, filling the wide spaces with brilliant light, which bounced and reflected gloriously off all the marble structures. People thronged through the arcades and pergolas, dressed in luxuriant, plush fabrics, bustling with colour and fragrant with exotic toxins.

Zefer had stumbled through the sights in a blur of amazement, spinning on his heels as each successive beauty passed him by. He was in a spell, enchanted by the sights and sounds of the Spire that he had hardly even noticed whilst cooped up in the dusty seclusion of the Ko'iron librarium, glorious as that was. If anything, these avenues and concourses leading to the Spiral Gates were even more magnificent than Gwentria's Palace, which had been majestic beyond Zefer's wildest dreams.

Before he had even thought about finding his bearings, Zefer was standing in the middle of a vast piazza, gazing back down the grand Helmawr Boulevard, along which he had just drifted. The crowds were thinner in the huge open space, and they got sparser as Zefer backed his way further into it, gazing back along the regal splendour of the boulevard as he went. At the end of the boulevard, at the point where it spilt into the plaza like a great river into the ocean, rose a fifty metre tall statue of Lord Gerontius Helmawr himself, Guardian of Necromunda in the Holy Name of the Undying Emperor.

While he had been strolling in Helmawr Boulevard itself, Zefer had not even noticed the huge statue. But now, walking backwards through the grand piazza and staring back along that street into the Spire, Lord Gerontius seemed to tower over the scene and dominate the vista, his long sword brandished heroically in the air. The shadow of the great man lay across the resplendent scene behind him like a veil over the face of a bride.

Taking another step back as he gazed forward, Zefer's heel crunched into something behind him. He lost his balance immediately, his arms flapping wildly at his sides as he fought against his own momentum, trying to lift his body on wings that he didn't have. But his efforts were futile and he fell, succeeding only in twisting his body around so that he fell straight onto his face.

Still lying on the flagstones, with blood trickling out of his broken nose onto the white rock, Zefer lifted his head and, through the blur of pain-induced tears, he saw the Spiral Gates for the first time. He was barely ten metres away from them.

The arched double-gates rose nearly one hundred metres into the air, supported by vast golden hinges on each side. Their surface gleamed with spiralling pillars of silver and gold, each intertwined with the other into a single, giant plait. Where the threads of precious metal wove together, there were gemstones inset into the structure to fill the gaps. The light that poured out of the Spire crashed against the glorious gates in explosions of colour and blinding brilliance, as though a dazzling star had been harnessed into the structure of the Wall.

Zefer lay prostrate on the ground, with blood gushing out of his nose and tears running down his cheeks, staring at the most incredible sight he had ever seen, almost forgetting to breath.

'Oi! You can't bleed there. You'll stain the marble.' Something was prodding him in the ribs.

'Oi, you! You can't bleed there. Are you deaf? Get up.' The prodding became more insistent and then it was suddenly replaced by hands that gripped his shoulders and dragged him to his feet.

'What's wrong with you?' said the guard. It was not a question.

'I'm… I tripped,' said Zefer, still gazing at the gates. 'Are those the Spiral Gates?' As soon as he said the words he felt stupid.

'Yep, that's them,' said the guard, apparently not noticing the inanity of the question.

'They're… they're breathtaking,' managed Zefer, wiping the blood from his nose with his sleeve, and then wincing in pain as the broken cartilage ground against his nose-bridge.

'Yep, they're pretty nice,' replied the guard, nodding.

'Are you one of the guards?' asked Zefer, finally looking at the man. He was shorter than Zefer, but broader in the shoulders. He wore ceremonial armour that might have been made of gold, on top of a green under-tunic. Around his shoulder he had slung a brown leather satchel. By far his most prominent feature was the good natured smile that creased his face from one ear to the other.

'Yep, I'm the guard,' replied the guard.

'*The* guard?' queried Zefer, looking around for the others.

'That's right. Until Hedred get's here in a couple of hours, that is. I'm the afternoon guard, you see,' he explained earnestly.

'I see,' replied Zefer, not quite sure that he did. 'Listen, I'm not being rude or anything, but I thought that the Spiral Gates were… well, well guarded.'

'Oh yes, I see, sir,' said the guard, not at all insulted. 'Thank you, sir.'

'No, no,' said Zefer, conscious that he was making himself understood. 'I rather thought that there'd be more of you.'

'No need, sir,' said the guard cheerfully. 'Nobody ever wants to go through the gates from this side,' he added, laughing happily. 'Now, if you were on the other side, sir, that would be a different matter entirely. There's *lots* of guards on that side. *Lots*.'

'I see,' replied Zefer, looking around. The guard appeared to be right. The piazza was virtually empty on this side, with nobody at all near the gates themselves. 'So, if I wanted to go through the gates, would I have to talk to you about it?'

'I'd say you should talk to a doctor about it!' laughed the guard good naturedly. Then he stopped laughing. 'You serious, sir?'

'Yes.'

'Well then, sir, you'd better come with me,' said the guard, a smart formality snapping into his manner as he turned and marched off towards the side of the gates.

CUT INTO THE adamantium of the Wall itself, hidden behind one of the huge pillars that supported the great golden hinges of the Spiral Gates themselves, was a tiny, buckled and patched cast-metal door.

'You'd better go through there, sir,' said the guard, indicating the little door. 'We never open the big ones.'

'I see,' said Zefer, adjusting his nose and peering at the incongruously shabby metal. 'And when I come back, do I come back through here too?'

'No, sir. People coming up into the Spire go through the Spiral Gates themselves, sir,' said the guard, puffing out his chest proudly.

'But, didn't you just say that you never open those gates?'

'That's right, sir,' nodded the guard affirmatively.

'I see.'

The guard pulled an oversized key from his satchel and stooped down to slot it into the keyhole in the little door. 'You're sure, sir?'

Zefer just nodded wordlessly, clenching his jaw and exhaling through his nose in an attempt to muster his courage. The key clicked round in the lock with a resounding clunk making him start abruptly, his nerves suddenly shot.

A wave of sound crashed against the little door, literally blowing it open and sending the guard staggering back under the force. He stood there braced against the door as the torrent of sound funnelled through the tiny hole in the Wall. The sounds of heavy machinery pounded through the gap, punctuated by yells and screams of hundreds of voices. Zefer swayed weakly in the onslaught, feeling slightly nauseous.

'Well? Are you going or not?' yelled the guard, struggling to make himself heard over the din.

Zefer stared through the doorway, tasting the squalid stench of stale air that blew out of the darkness of the tunnel beyond. The noise was deafening – louder than anything he had ever heard in the Spire. He turned his head to look back into the unspeakable beauty of the piazza, with the towering statue of Lord Gerontius glaring down at him. And he shook his head in disbelief at what he was about to do.

'Yes,' he said resolutely, ducking down into the doorway. 'I'm going.' And he went.

THE TUNNEL THROUGH the Wall grew noisier, smellier, narrower and lower as it progressed, until it finally terminated in a metal grille, no more than a metre square. Zefer dragged himself towards it on his elbows, pulling his body along behind him like a dead weight. He pressed his face up against the grille and peered out.

All he could see in front of the exit was a row of unmoving, dirty black boots but the most unholy cacophony that Zefer had ever heard was emanating from the other side. He coughed politely, waiting for somebody to notice him. Then he called out. Then he shouted, trying to make himself heard above the din. Finally, gripping hold of the grille with his fingers and lifting his face as high as he could, he screamed.

One pair of boots twisted round and came towards the grille. After a few moments, a face came down from above them and peered into the tunnel.

'By the Emperor!' said the grimy, scarred face of the guardsman. 'What in the world are you doing there?'

'I'd like to get out, if you please,' said Zefer, wide-eyed with excitement and fear.

'I'll bet you would… sir.' The guard added the last word as though he had dredged it up from the furthest recesses of his memory. 'Hold on a sec. I'm not sure that I have the key. Oh, no, here it is,' he said as he slipped it into the rusty lock. 'I've just never had the call to use it before, see… sir.'

The guardsman played with the lock for a little while, trying to get the old mechanism to work. In the end he just smashed it off with the butt of his gun and swung the grille open.

'Come on out, then,' he said in a friendly tone.

Zefer climbed out of the little hole in the Wall and clambered to his feet, finding himself behind a line of armed guardsmen that stretched as far as his eyes could see in both directions. The guard who had let him through had already slammed the grille shut and jammed a huge padlock into place.

Looking over to his right, Zefer could see the back of the Spiral Gates, dirty and pockmarked, but with tiny flecks of shiny metal glinting here and there. Before them a full scale riot was in progress, with hundreds of people pressing into the little open space that served as a plaza. The momentum of the crowd pushed towards the gates, but the guardsmen in front of them had their weapons drawn, and they were laying down a constant stream of fire into the crowd, felling row after row of screaming rioters. The line of guards was three men deep, so that they could rotate as the front line began to run low on ammunition. The plaza was in chaos, with guardsmen and rioters hacking at each other with machetes and bludgeoning with pipes, leaving growing numbers of dead bodies to mount into piles before the gates.

'What's going on?' shouted Zefer to the guard next to him, horrified.

'What? What do you mean?' yelled the guard, leaning his mouth right up to Zefer's ear to make sure that he would hear.

'This… this riot,' said Zefer, not really sure what to call it as he waved his arm vaguely at the mass of violence in front of the gates.

'Oh, that,' replied the guard, nodding casually. 'Yeah, it's quiet today. Welcome to Hive City… sir.'

5: THE HC

THE DOOR HISSED shut behind him, dulling the cacophony of the riot outside, but not silencing it completely. As he stood in the doorway, stooped in concentration, brushing the soot and dirt from his robes, Zefer muttered to himself in disbelief. He mumbled and shook his head from side to side, his eyes bulging hysterically as he obsessively patted down the torn, stained fabric of his curator's robes. Fixating on one spot where the threads had worn through and a dull red stain had bled out into the cloth, Zefer scrubbed and scrubbed with his fingers, spitting over and over again. But it hurt when he scrubbed and the red stain seemed to grow rather than shrink. Peering even more closely, almost bending double to bring his face within centimetres of his knee, he saw that the stain was actually his bloodied kneecap, and that there was simply a large hole in the material of his robe, with its edges stuck into the coagulated blood around the wound.

Zefer just stared at his skinless knee, and tears started to well up in his eyes. It was all just too much for him. First there had been the excitement of his discoveries in *The Paradoxes of the Spire*, and then there had been all the furore about getting somebody to acknowledge his discoveries. He had been all the way up to the throne room of Princess Gwentria's palace, and then had even come down through the Wall into Hive City. And what a place this was. Over the last few weeks, he had hardly slept at all and, now that he was here, with a riot blazing in the corpse-strewn plaza outside, events were finally catching up with him. Only three weeks ago, the most exciting moment of his life had been spending seven extra minutes reading a book in the librarium.

What am I doing here? he thought, as he collapsed into a crumpled heap on the floor, with tears cutting trails of cleanliness down his grime-encrusted face.

'What are you doing here?'

It took Zefer several seconds to realise that the voice was not in his head.

Slowly, he lifted his face from the floor and looked up towards the source of the voice, still slumped on his hands and knees. For the first time, he realised that he was in a long, narrow waiting room. There were seats running the lengths of both sides, each one occupied by progressively less sanitary-looking people. At the far end, perhaps eighty metres away, was a single counter that ran across the width of the room. Leaning on it from behind was a firmly muscled figure of indeterminate gender. Its skin was a shocking blue, as though densely tattooed from head to toe in solid colour, and its hair was a dirty yellow mop. A sprinkling of metal fragments encrusted its right arm, which was pointed directly at Zefer. Above its shoulders hung two security drones, bristling with camera lenses and gun barrels, which were also pointed directly at Zefer.

Shaking his head and laughing hysterically, Zefer's mind spiralled with answers to the deceptively simple question.

'I'm… I'm CC9FB2,' he began, but then changed his mind. 'I'm CCA04, here to collect my papers and provisions.' As he spoke he grinned and pulled himself up to his feet. 'I'm from the Spire, on a mission for Her Excellency the Princess Gwentria, Matriarchal Heir to the Ancient and Glorious House Ko'iron.' If titles hadn't made any difference to the officials in the Spire, Zefer was sure that they would have some intimidating effect on the grubby and unscrupulous creatures before him now. After all, they had to mean something to someone other than him.

'What?' bellowed the figure at the desk. 'You need up speak up, man, or down counter come and me talk.' The voice echoed faintly through the corridor-like room, but some of the sound was absorbed by the bodies of the other people who were waiting. From the way that the official's neck strained, Zefer could tell that it was yelling, but he could hardly make out what was being said. For a brief moment, the memory of little Princess Gwentria asking him to make echoes flickered in his mind.

The man behind the desk (Zefer had decided to consider the muscular and intimidating figure a man) was not the only one to notice Zefer's surprising appearance. As he shuffled through the waiting room, Zefer was intensely aware of all the eyes watching him. The entire room was in silence, and Zefer could clearly hear his own nervous, heavy breathing against the muffled, background booming of the riot outside. He hoped that nobody else could hear his anxiety, but he was sure that they could.

He was equally sure that he must have cut a bizarre looking figure as he shuffled along in between the parallel lines of seated locals. This may have been the first time that some of the people had seen a curator from the Spire, and even his long, grey, curator's robes must have seemed odd to them. Zefer scanned his eyes over the faces that stared at him; they were attached to rough, scarred, dirty people with wild eyes, elaborate tattoos and ostentatious piercings. There were bright red bandanas and grubby, colourful cloaks under which glinted the half-hidden menace of bladed weapons. Never before in his life had Zefer come across such people, not even in the salubrious atmosphere of the Quake Tavern. With all the grime and the bloodstains on his clothes, Zefer wouldn't exactly have felt at home in the Quake at the moment.

'I'm CCA04,' said Zefer quietly, leaning onto the desk, suddenly realising that it may be better if the other people in the waiting room didn't overhear him. 'I'm from the Spire. There may be some documents and provisions for me.'

'What name?' barked the blue man, his black pupils set within startling white irises flicking up and down to take in Zefer's broken form.

'What?'

'You-name. What?' said the man simply, in an abrupt dialect that Zefer had never heard before.

'I'm...' Zefer looked back over his shoulder at the people in the waiting room. Hundreds of eyes flicked self-consciously to the floor, to the occasional pictures on the wall, or suddenly took deep interest in the pattern of light fixtures on the ceiling.

Zefer leaned even further across the desk. 'Zefer Tyranus,' he whispered, wincing slightly at how loud his voice seemed in the cavernous room. 'Don't you need my number?'

'No. Here, no number. Just you-name,' said the blue man firmly. 'Number is Spire thing. Hive City have you-names.'

SLOUCHED INTO HIS chair in the Hive City WPO, Koorl was nodding on the edge of sleep. It may have been a boring assignment, but at least it was warm and dry in there, and it saved him from his place in the riot rota.

It was the first time that he had been in an authentic Hive City office of any kind; there were precious few of them where he was from, and Koorl had never really seen the point of them. The further away from the Wall you went, the fewer official premises you would find. But you couldn't get any closer to the Wall than the WPO, which was actually built into the substance of the Wall itself, tucked up against its sheer side, just along from the Plaza of the Spiral Gates. It was always busy, stuffed to bursting with people trying to scam passes into the Spire. The riots in the plaza outside were testament to the invariable failure of virtually all such attempts.

Koorl had burst into the waiting room, expecting to find the kind of raucous rabble that he was used to in the rest of Hive City. He had literally kicked open the door, swearing loudly at an Orlock who had been trying to shoulder his way around him. The silence of the waiting room had hit him like a wave, and he had dropped his head and shuffled over to one of the seats, biting back his shock and anger at having to share the space with Orlocks, Escher and even Goliaths. He noted with interest that there didn't seem to be any Delaque representatives in the room. The official line was that such communal spaces would help to ease the frictions between the great gang houses, but the riots out front provided plentiful evidence that it wasn't working.

The whole place seemed unbelievably artificial, and Koorl had sat uncomfortably sandwiched between a huge ganger, with rows of metal spikes grafted into his arms, and a robust Orlock, with a grubby bandana and daggers stitched into his vest like fashion accessories.

After nearly an hour of alert agitation and staring people down, he realised that nobody was going to cause any problems in the WPO itself, and he settled in to catch up on some sleep. It was then that the door squeaked open and the wretched man in effeminate grey robes staggered in, crying like a girl and talking to himself.

Koorl listened to the bizarre looking stranger yell across the waiting room, shouting some kind of code number. And he watched the man shuffle slowly through the room, wondering all the time whether he was the man that Triar had sent him to find. He was certainly different from all the other people in the WPO, and he seemed to speak with an odd, pompous lilt that made him seem both incomprehensible and instantly loathsome.

Shifting his attention from the shuffling stranger to the faces of the other people in the waiting room, Koorl noticed that everybody was watching him. Rather than fixing their eyes deliberately on the scuff-marks that criss-crossed the metal floor, trying hard not to meet the gaze of anyone else in case they took offence and poked their eyes out with their thumbs, every head in the room traced the pathetic gait of the bedraggled, grey stranger. Silence gripped the atmosphere of the room as though it were trying to strangle it.

The stranger appeared conscious that everyone was watching him, and he leant over the reception desk to talk with the provisor in conspiratorially low tones. But the gangers in the waiting room were accustomed to filtering out huge amounts of background noise as they spoke – nowhere in HC was as quiet as this room – so even the faintest whispers seemed to boom like shouts in this strangled atmosphere. Besides, the man's voice carried clearly through the hushed, echoing waiting room, and Koorl was not the only one to leap to his feet and dash out of the door into the street outside when he heard the man speak his name.

'No. TYRANUS, NOTHING,' said the androgynous blue figure without moving.

Zefer turned back to look at the provisor, his attention having been momentarily distracted by the flood of people who had suddenly sprung to their feet and fled the WPO. They had all done it at the same time, as though released by some invisible signal.

'What? But you haven't even looked,' complained Zefer, feeling his heart sink into the pit of his stomach.

'No need look,' replied the provisor, throwing his left arm out to the side to indicate a small, empty shelving unit. 'Nothing there,' he added, as though an explanation were needed.

'But what about that side,' asked Zefer, pointing to the stacks and stacks of documents, folders and packages on the provisor's right.

'HC to Spire. Not you.' The blue provisor shrugged, and Zefer wondered whether there was meant to be any sympathy in the gesture.

The empty shelves stared back at him ominously, taunting him with the blatant reality of their condition.

'But there must be something,' said Zefer, slumping forward against the counter with his tear-streaked head in his hands. 'There must be something.'

'No. Nothing,' replied the provisor flatly, and Zefer realised that there had not been any sympathy in his shrug.

'But I have to be able to go back. You'll let me back through, right?' said Zefer, lifting his hysterical eyes to meet the shocking white irises of the blue provisor.

'No pass. No passage.' For the first time in weeks, perhaps in his whole life, Zefer heard a simple, sensible and logical explanation tumbled from the mouth of a Hive official. The man's expression was blank and unmoved, but Zefer thought that he could sense a hint of vitriolic satisfaction under the blue surface. It occurred to him, at last, that the people of HC might not be pleased to have him descend from heaven into their midst. They might resent him. They might just think that he was stupid. Perhaps he was.

'Can I wait?' asked Zefer hopefully. 'It must take time for documents to come down through the Wall, right? The provisor in the Spire explained that it was sometimes hard to get messengers through the gates. My papers could still be on their way, right?' Since the man behind the desk did not appear willing to offer Zefer any solace, he decided to offer it to himself.

'Sure. Wait.' A finely muscled blue arm waved casually in the direction of the chairs in the waiting room, and Zefer turned to see that the packed waiting room was now completely empty. Suddenly, Zefer noticed that he could hear the whirring of he camera lenses in the security drones that hung above the provisor's desk and, at the same moment, he realised why. The background din of the riot outside had stopped. An incredible silence descended on the WPO, and even the almost inhumanly calm provisor looked uneasy.

Nodding quietly, Zefer virtually tip-toed over to the nearest chair, wanting to stay as close to the desk as he possibly could. Just as he was about to sit down, the provisor's voice shattered the silence and made Zefer spin nervously.

'Tyranus?'

'Yes. Yes, that's me,' replied Zefer, suppressing his excitement in case it was a false alarm. As he turned back to face the blue figure at the desk, he saw that it was holding out a small, white envelope.

'Was waiting. Top shelf. Not see it. Apologies,' explained the provisor without any outward signs of contrition. Instead, the man was looking nervously around the waiting room, checking back over his shoulder from time to time as though expecting to see a platoon of Helmawr guardsmen come storming out of the storeroom.

Zefer almost skipped back to the desk, feeling the weight of panic and disappointment dropping off him, as though he had suddenly been freed from the restrictions of gravity itself. He snatched the envelope out of the provisor's hand and read the neat calligraphy on its face: *Zefer Tyranus, Ko'iron Curator – First Class.* A broad smile broke out across his face as he realised that, somewhere along the line, he had been promoted from his designation as a second class curator. When he got back to the librarium, he would have access to the very highest levels – perhaps even to levels above the permanent cloud line.

He turned the pristine envelope over and over in his hands, looking for the blue Ko'iron seal, but it was nowhere to be seen. Instead, there was a tiny red icon stamped across the seal, which looked like a representation of a little, coiled snake. Zefer presumed that this was the mark of the Wall authorities themselves, and he slipped the envelope up into his sleeve, tucking it into the document pouch that all curators kept in the sleeve of their undergarments.

'Thank you,' he said, bowing formally to the increasingly shifty, provisor behind the desk. Then, with a newly confident swirl, he spun on his heels and strode off towards the exit, ready for the start of his little jaunt into Hive City.

A HUGE CRUMPLE of paper and dust tumbled across the empty street in front of him as Zefer stepped out of the WPO. Nothing else was moving, but the side-streets on the far side were congested with people, all of them standing in silence. As Zefer looked up and down the narrow street that ran along the side of the Wall, he saw that crowds of people were blocking the way at the end of the road in both directions.

Not knowing what else to do, Zefer simply stopped moving. He stood, motionless in front of the door to the WPO, fearful that he had walked right into the middle of something. He wondered whether he should quietly take a couple of steps back into the waiting room. He could certainly wait in there, until whatever was going on out here had finished. That's what it was for, after all.

Slowly, without wanting to make any sudden movements, Zefer moved his foot back towards the door behind him. At the same time, a murmur arose from the crowds, as though there had been a collective intake of breath. Zefer froze again, bringing his rear foot back in line with the other one. There was silence again.

He tried once more, moving his foot towards the door and then bringing it back again, listening to the tension rise and fall in the crowds around him. The realisation was slow and terrifying; he had not stepped into the middle of something, something had collected around him.

Just as the significance of the murmuring crowds began to sink in, there was a stir within the crowd that blocked the street towards the Spiral Gates. The people were jostling against each other, trying to create a passageway between their densely packed forms. As they shuffled, shoved and tripped, Zefer could see the flamboyant flashes of their blue cloaks. It was as though they were wearing a uniform of some kind. He peered into the seething mass with gathering trepidation. For a moment he thought that he caught a glimpse of one of the men from the waiting room.

A great commotion made him snap his head back round to the other end of the street, where a motley assortment of huge, barbarous looking giants were pushing and prodding at each other in a similar way. They appeared to be riddled with piercings and etched from head to toe with tattoos. Zefer could see no sign of the neat uniformity of the blue-cloaks on the other side, but he supposed that it was possible that this was a uniform in itself. He had seen people of a similar appearance before, although he could not quite place the memory in his exhausted brain.

'May I bid you welcome!' yelled one of the blue-cloaks, now standing out in front of the crowd near the gates. Zefer wondered why his welcome needed to be shouted from so far away, but he was relieved to know that this was a welcoming party of some kind. It made sense, he supposed, that the people of the Hive City would want to welcome an official from the gleaming Spire. He had just been so caught up in his own, petty, bureaucratic concerns that he had forgotten how much of an event his arrival would probably be for the locals.

'You may not!' boomed a crude, metallic voice from the giants, almost giving Zefer whiplash as he spun to meet the noise. The speaker was the largest human being that Zefer had ever seen. He must have been more than two metres tall – a clear head taller than the others in his gang, who were in turn head and shoulders taller than anyone else. As far as Zefer could see, the man's jaw was made of some kind of metal, bolted into the side of his head, and his hairless scalp glinted like a sheet of adamantium. Fat chains the thickness of his arms were wrapped around his neck, punctuated with spikes and what looked like fragments of bone. The man's arms were tense with the weight of a huge gun, almost as big as him, which he made no attempt to hide from the authorities... wherever they were. The mass of huge heavies behind him was swaying with motion, pounding clubs and pipes into their palms and tossing blades menacingly from one hand to the other; impatient chuckles rolled out of them.

'Curator of Ko'iron,' called the man in the blue-cloak, using a mode of address with which Zefer was not familiar. Zefer turned back to face him. 'I place myself, my men – The Salvationists – and the patronage of House Cawdor at your service,' continued the man, sweeping his cloak into a deep bow. Slightly concerned by the unorthodox greeting, Zefer nodded a return greeting, relieved that the man's intentions were good.

'Triar Cawdor!' yelled the metal-jawed man, making Zefer spin back to face the jostling giants. He didn't look even nearly as friendly as the man with the cloak, but the massive ganger was not looking at Zefer. His eyes were set on the opposing orator and animosity lanced out of them. Zefer was relieved that the man's hatred was focussed elsewhere, but it gradually dawned on him that he was, indeed, trapped in the middle.

'Triar Cawdor! You will not take this man. He's mine!' The voice resonated through the street, bouncing off the Wall and making it vibrate like an amplifier. As he spoke, he took a couple of steps forward, racking the mechanism of his autocannon.

'Uglar Goliath, how charming to see you so high in the hive,' countered Triar, his voice slipping smoothly along the street, like oil over metal. 'I didn't realise that you and your Subversives ever made it out of your pit. How delightful that you find the time for a trip into town from time to time.'

Even from where he stood, Zefer could see the twinkle in the eyes of Triar. There was a confidence in that gaze that Zefer could not understand in the face of the threatening forms of the Goliath gangers opposing him – the Subversives towered over the Salvationists in physical stature.

'Perhaps we should ask this gentleman whether he would rather join us,' continued Triar, gesturing openly with his empty arms, 'or whether he would like to go down into the cesspits with you?'

Zefer's eyes bulged and he felt his heart pumping faster and faster. There was absolutely no way that he wanted to make a decision about this. He didn't want to have anything to do with it at all. If he thought that he could get away with it, he would have simply turned and gone back into the WPO waiting room. The thought of having to go anywhere at all with the giant Uglar filled him with horror, but there was something about the glint in Triar's eyes that scared him even more.

'No. No choices!' thundered Uglar, his forward momentum pushing him into a run. With an excited cheer, the rest of his gang erupted into motion, yelling and braying like huge lumbering animals as they started to close the gap between them and Zefer.

STRUGGLING FOR BREATH, Zefer snapped his head from one side to the other, watching the two gangs storming towards him along the street. The Subversives had a head start, but they were heavier and slower than the lithe blue-cloaked men of Triar's gang. The Salvationist gangers were streaming towards him with their capes billowing out behind them like wings. From under their cloaks they had produced a dizzying array of weapons, which they flourished with well practiced skill as they ran.

Under his feet, Zefer could feel the metal road vibrating under the thunderous charges. Instinctively, he backed up towards the Wall until he felt the adamantium pressing against his shoulders. He watched the opposing gangs charging towards him with terror bursting out of his eyes, twitching his head from side to side and hyperventilating. His jaunt into Hive City had not started quite as he had planned.

A fraction of a second later and Uglar pounded up to him, flipping his huge autocannon onto his shoulder and firing out a tree-trunk arm towards Zefer, his hand open and reaching towards Zefer's neck. The curator screamed, closing his eyes and waiting for the end.

There was a loud crunch, and a spray of liquid splashed against his face. Zefer opened one eye experimentally and then screamed again. Uglar was staggering back away from him with a huge gash sliced across his chest; blood was spurting out of it and showering all over Zefer. A smaller man would be dead already.

Triar's blade flashed again, sparking against the heavy chains around Uglar's neck and severing the straps around the massive autocannon, which clattered down to the ground before the Subversive could catch it.

The Salvationist gang-leader was a blur of motion, spinning with long-bladed daggers in both hands, slicing the air all around the staggering figure of Uglar. For an instant, Triar froze, letting his long cloak whip round behind him as he balanced his blades for the final strike. But, at exactly that moment, the wave of gangers from the Subversives caught up with their leader and burst past him, bearing down on Triar. Simultaneously, the blue Salvationist tide crashed past Triar and smashed into the Subversives in a frenzy of metal. Triar and Uglar were engulfed in the tumult and dragged away from each other in the backwash, leaving Zefer standing in the middle like an island.

Zefer had seen blades before, and he had seen flames on the candles in the librarium and in the antique fireplace in the front bar of the Quake Tavern, but he had never seen blades being jabbed into human stomachs or flames jetting out of weapons and dousing the screaming forms of people writhing on the ground. He pressed his shoulders back against the Wall, praying to the Undying Emperor to make him ethereal so that he might fall through it back into the Spire.

The two gangs ploughed into each other and the street was immediately transformed into a battleground, making the riot at the gates earlier look like a child's birthday party. Shotguns coughed and autoguns barked, riddling the air with lethal fragments, cut through by the sizzling hiss of laspistols. Despite the close range, the gangers brought all of their weapons to bear at once, hacking with blades, pounding with bludgeons, and snapping off projectiles in all directions at once. The smoky discharge from the firearms hazed into the air, progressively clouding everyone's vision. In between his terror and his panic, Zefer found himself wondering how the gangers avoided damaging others in their own gang.

A sudden blast of concussion threw Zefer's head back against the Wall and he felt his knees give way. As he slumped down the Wall, collapsing onto the ground as his legs failed beneath him, a strong arm caught him. The arm was muscled but hairless, with intricate tattoos snaking all over it. Dazed and confused, with his strength deserting him, Zefer looked up along the arm and into a pair of burning red eyes, around which seemed to hiss and writhe a brood of bright blue snakes. Then he passed out.

'THERE IS NOTHING that we can do,' said Orthios, shaking his head and sitting back onto the flat metal roof.

'What do you mean, nothing?' spat Krelyn, convinced that the leader of the Snake Charmers was being deliberately lax. 'We *must* recover that man, don't you understand?'

Krelyn took a step forward, right up to the edge of the roof, and looked down into the street. The blue cloaks of the Salvationist gangers were pouring along the road into the immovable might of the Subversives. Their leaders were already locked in combat, directly in front of a petrified Tyranus. In a few seconds there would be the rare sight of an all out gang war in the street next to the Wall.

'We will not die on your whim, Red Snake. Enough of us have already died at your hands,' said Orthios, clasping his hands behind his head and lying back on the roof. If he had remembered to bring his tox-sticks, he would have smoked one.

'This has nothing to do with the Red Snakes, Orthios. This is about House Ko'iron, of whom we are both servants.' Even after she had explained about her mission, and the possible importance of Curator Tyranus's discoveries, Krelyn had suspected that Orthios had remained suspicious of her. It hadn't helped that she had been unable to explain the content of the newly

discovered pages of *The Paradoxes of the Spire*. Her igno-
rance had seemed shifty and obfuscatory, and her
insistence that she was not well enough educated to
understand the significance of the lines had looked like
false-modesty to a gang of illiterate thugs; the Delaque
were well known for their wit and intelligence.

'As I said, there is nothing that we can do here,'
repeated Orthios, staring up at the dancing shadows
and the reflections of flames that flickered on the
underside of the next level of the hive above the
rooftop. He was bathing in the echoes of the fight
below.

'Will none of you fulfil your oaths?' asked Krelyn,
turning and facing the other gangers of the Snake
Charmers on the roof. But they were all already imitat-
ing their leader and lounging casually. Some of them
had broken out their tox-sticks and were smoking happily, dangling their legs over the side of the roof and
watching the gang war raging below them. One or two
were taking bets on the outcome.

Shaking her head in despair, Krelyn turned back to
the scene in the street just in time to see the women of
The Coven charge out of the side streets into the fray.
Despite her frustrations, Krelyn could not help but be
impressed: they were much more organised than either
of the other gangs, who simply hacked into each other
with varying degrees of individual skill and strength.
The Coven's gangers seemed to have a strategy: pouring
out of three separate sidestreets and fighting their way
into a single united incision, piercing the battle like a
dagger into its soft underbelly. In less than a minute,
the tip of the dagger was approaching Zefer and then,
out of nowhere, a huge fireball erupted from the road
directly in front of him. Salvationist and Subversive
gangers scattered out of the flames while one of The

Coven's women leapt forward into them, her shocking blue dreadlocks thrashing in the smoke behind her.

In a matter of seconds, the Escher warrior had grasped hold of Zefer and carried him back through the flames into the heart of The Coven's incision. Then, almost as though the scene were thrown into reverse, the women fought a controlled withdrawal. To Krelyn, from the vantage of the rooftop, it looked like a death-dealing dagger was being slowly extracted from the corpse of the battle, as the forces of The Coven pulled out of the fight and bled back into the side streets from whence they had come.

The gang war in the street raged on, as though none of the gangers had yet noticed that the purpose of their fight was already lost. Zefer had gone, stolen by the women's raid. Krelyn watched for another few seconds, intrigued to see the relish with which the gangers threw themselves into combat – she wondered whether they simply didn't care that the curator was no longer there. The Snake Charmers sitting on the edge of the roof, whooping and whistling at the action, certainly suggested that battle had an energy of its own in these parts.

Turning her attention away from the streetfight with a sudden and decisive twist of her body, which sent her cloak fluttering out into a whirl around her, Krelyn started to track the passage of the Escher kidnappers. She ran along the rim of the roof, her visor clicking and whirring as it zoomed down to street level, working to pick out the figure of Zefer in the seething side streets.

Reaching the edge of the building, Krelyn sprang into the air, spreading her cloak out behind her like a sail, and flew across to the next rooftop, trying to keep her targets in view. But the streets were high and narrow, and they were increasing busy with people. The women from The Coven kept running through the blind spot in Krelyn's goggles, making her swear and twitch her line of sight. Every time she did it, one or two of the women would vanish, as though into thin air, presumably slipping into even narrower side streets.

Jumping building after building, Krelyn tracked the kidnappers through the increasingly narrow, labyrinthine streets of the Wall Quadrant of Hive City. After a few minutes, there were only a couple of Coven gangers left, one of them carrying the unconscious curator like a baby. Gradually, the ceiling above the rooftops started to drop, squeezing the gap between it and the roofs on which Krelyn was running. She could clearly see that the ceiling of the city quadrant was uneven and fractured, as though hive-quakes had shattered the structure over and over again.

She vaulted from the apex of a tiled roof, bicycling her legs and spinning her arms to give her extra momentum, keeping her eyes fixed on the slumped figure of Zefer below her. As she flew, her hand smacked against the adamantium ceiling, scraping the skin off her fingers and upsetting her balance. She tugged her hand back, wincing in pain, and her momentum faltered; she started to fall. Tumbling and reaching, Krelyn caught hold of one of the structural trusses that crisscrossed the streets, catching her weight and swinging herself around on top of it. Immediately she scanned the darkness of the alleyway below her, but there was no sign of the curator or his captors. Not only had the Snake Charmers failed to fight, but she had lost her man.

6: MAVANT

CONSCIOUSNESS RETURNED SLOWLY and reluctantly to Zefer, as he pulled the covers up around him, languishing in their warmth and security. For a while he simply lay there, his eyes firmly closed, not wanting to know what he would see when he opened them. In the darkness he could imagine that the bedding was that of the Quake Tavern, and that the commotion he could hear in the background was merely a lively night down in the bar.

Drifting on the edge of sleep, he found himself wondering whether he had left his stylus out on his desk on level seventy-three of the librarium. Despite his current situation, he was anxious about it, and he rolled fitfully because of the failure of his memory. Then, almost involuntarily, his eyes flicked open as he realised how ridiculous his concern was. A guttural convulsion gripped him and he coughed, trying to suppress it and feeling his diaphragm wrench painfully. He realised that he was trying to laugh, and that horrified him. Another convulsion pulsed through his abdomen, and he snorted painfully, feeling a thread of blood trickle out of his nose.

Trying not to draw any attention to himself, he was laughing and coughing up blood. His eyes were wide now, as his mind raced to find reasons – any reason at all – for his mirth. In a dark corner of his brain, he realised that it was probably hysteria, but an internal voice mocked him about the banality of his concerns about the stylus. It was as though his mind was being split in two by the events around him.

Squeezing his eyes shut, he tried to remember the librarium. He forced images of book stacks, candles and misty daylight into his fractured mind. He dragged the memory of the luxurious carpet in the Quake's bedchambers before his eyes and saw the beautiful figure of the lady in the strategically ill-fitting red shirt in the bar. But, as he concentrated, screwing up his eyes with the effort, Prince Jurod roared through the scenes on the immense engine that Zefer had seen on the fresco in Gwentria's palace. The spiked ram pierced the beautiful woman through her stomach, dyeing her red shirt a deeper shade of blood. The giant tires ripped up the deep pile carpet and crushed the spindly desks of the libarium, knocking the candles flying into blazing fires in the bookstacks. Finally, Jurod dismounted and strode towards Zefer's desk. He picked up the errant stylus and, turning to face directly into Zefer's mind, he snapped it in two.

'No!' screamed Zefer, wrenching himself out of sleep and sitting bolt upright. The sudden movement made him wince with pain as his broken ribs ground and splintered. Tears cascaded freely down his face, but he wasn't sure why: it could have been the pain; it could have been the sense of loss and of being lost; but a dark part of Zefer stirred in the depths of his psyche, and it could have been fear of that.

'Looks like he's awake.' The voice was nearby, but Zefer couldn't see its source and didn't recognise the tone.

'Yep, we'd better get him out of those clothes before Elria gets back,' said another, a bit louder than the first, as though moving closer.

Zefer twitched his head nervously from side to side, trying to take in his surroundings. He appeared to be lying in between a couple of huge kitbags, which seemed to be stuffed with hard, metallic objects. They chinked and clunked as he shifted his weight against them. To his right was a dirty metal wall, cast in deep shadow by what looked like a balcony overhead. Turning painfully to his left, he saw that he was at the edge of a huge hall, speckled with kitbags and weapons, with a balcony running around three sides of it. Sitting casually on some of the bags were implausibly well-muscled women with shockingly coloured hair and rich tattoos scribbled all over their shamelessly exposed flesh. Zefer gawped.

A hand gripped his shoulder and Zefer's neck spun round instinctively. He cried out in pain as the sudden motion sent javelins of agony down his spine, and he slumped back onto the ground, whimpering.

'Easy,' said the man as he climbed over the kitbags, pressing gently down on Zefer's shoulder. 'You're in a bad state as it is. There's no need to be hurting yourself even more.'

Zefer peered up into the bloody face of the man. He had a couple of teeth missing and a series of scars cut into his face. There were some small circular burns on his skin that looked like they had been caused by tox-sticks. But his eyes seemed to smile compassionately, as though he understood everything.

'We need to get you out of those clothes, before the mistress returns. You will not want to displease her. At least, not while you are still so weak, eh?' The man winked and nudged Zefer with his elbow.

'What?' asked Zefer, confused and vague. Out of all the thoughts spiralling around inside his head, he was most acutely conscious of the fact that he had said 'what' more often over the last day than in the whole of the rest of his life put together. 'My clothes?' he asked, uncertainly peering down along his own body and seeing the ripped, threadbare cloth, tinged with blood. 'The mistress?' Finally his brain had locked onto the most pressing question.

'Never mind about that now,' said the man, scooping his arm around Zefer's shoulders and helping him to his feet. In the background, Zefer could hear a half-hearted cheer raised from the women in the rest of the hall.

'Just ignore them,' reassured the toothless grin. 'We'll make you presentable in no time at all. Can you walk?'

'Yes. Yes, I think so,' said Zefer hesitantly, leaning most of his weight against his new friend. As the two of them faltered, another arm swooped in from the other side, catching Zefer before his stumble became a fall.

'Easy there, friend,' said the second man, stooped and bleeding freshly from a broken nose. Like the first, this man was smiling broadly, clearly happy to see Zefer, and sincerely keen to help him. 'Let's get you changed.'

UNCONCERNED ABOUT THE stealth of her entry, Krelyn vaulted through the window, turning a slowly revolving somersault before landing into a crouch in the middle of the adamantium fragment that served as the Snake Charmers' conference table. The gangers seated around the perimeter leapt to their feet, staggering back away from the intruder. Only Orthios remained seated, apparently unsurprised by the arrival of their newest ally.

'Venator Krelyn, how nice of you to join us, *again*,' smiled the gang leader, rocking back casually in his chair.

'Orthios,' nodded Krelyn, determined to maintain at least the appearance of composure, despite her desperation. 'I realise that it pleases you to have me here asking you for help–'

'Begging,' interrupted Orthios, flicking a tox-stick into his mouth. One of the gangers at his side hefted a two-handed heavy flamer and lit the little narcotic tube with its pilot-light.

'*Asking* for your help,' continued Krelyn with firm resolution. 'But, the fact of this matter is that by obstructing me, you are also obstructing Prince Jurod of House Ko'iron, whom, I might remind you, you are pledged to obey under the terms of the Ko'iron contract.' She was standing now, and staring down at the smoker as he rocked in his chair. 'If you breach the contract you will lose it.' She let the menace hang in the air, as though it infused itself with the smoke.

'My dear venator,' oozed Orthios, drawing heavily on his tox-stick, 'you are neglecting a number of very important factors in our relationship, which, I might add, is not something that I have come to expect from your kind.'

'I have told you, Orthios, I am no longer of the Red Snakes, nor even of House Delaque itself, and I thought myself in trustworthy company. Am I mistaken?' Krelyn bowed slightly, in mock deference.

'It is true that you do not behave as I would expect of the Delaque, Krelyn, but you have been away a long time. You may be rusty. Or you may be clever. I know not which, and it bothers me even less than I know.

'My point here is simple. I could see no reason why my gangers should shed their blood at the command of a Del… a Ko'iron agent' – he smiled, correcting himself – 'when there was no obvious threat to the Ko'iron. Your curator means nothing to me, venator. Nothing at all. Elria can have him and I'm sure that he will enjoy himself for a while. Until he dies.'

'Your failure at the Wall will not have gone unnoticed,' replied Krelyn, stepping towards Orthios and dropping onto one knee, flicking a blade from her fatigues up under the chin of the gang leader. The toxstick trembled momentarily in his lips, but then he breathed a long, slow plume of smoke out into her face. The room echoed with the sound of guns being braced and blades being drawn.

'I am sure that I could persuade the Ko'iron to overlook your unsavoury conduct if you were to help me now,' said Krelyn, keeping her gaze fixed in the soft browns of Orthios's eyes, whilst mentally tracking the motion of the other gangers in the room. 'All I need is some help to recover Curator Tyranus from the enclave of The Coven. That is all.'

With his chin resting delicately on the tip of Krelyn's dagger, Orthios smiled. 'Ah, so that is all. Your point is well made,' he said, chuckling at his own joke. Krelyn smiled back sarcastically. 'But, I think you will find that my first point still stands: I can see no reason why we should shed our blood against the Escher of The Coven when we have to save ourselves to kill your brothers in the Red Snakes… for the good of your precious House Ko'iron, of course. It is hard to imagine what Prince Jurod could offer us as an incentive to serve a Del… a Ko'iron agent such as yourself. We already have the Ko'iron Contract! And, what's more, Ko'iron *needs* us to fulfil it for them.'

'You are too confident, Orthios. There are many other gang-houses who would be more than willing to take on the responsibilities of the contract, and Jurod would have no qualms about terminating his relationship with the Orlocks, if he learned that you were uncooperative. I am sure, for example, that the gangs of House Delaque themselves – including the Red Snakes – would be delighted to return to their duties.' It was a calculated jibe, and Krelyn winced inwardly as she made it and risked linking herself back to her old masters in Orthios's mind.

'No, no, sweet Krelyn, it is you who are too confident.' He was clearly enjoying the poisonous banter, like a chess-player who thinks that he has already won. 'You see, Prince Jurod – may the Undying Emperor preserve his soul – would only be able to make such a misjudged decision if he were ever informed of our occasional, and entirely justified, reticence.'

Krelyn realised where Orthios was heading with this and she let her eyes glance rapidly around the room while he continued. 'So, you see, there really is no need for us to spill any more of our own blood for the effete snobs of the Spire, since their only source of knowledge about our conduct is already under our control. Without their Delaque spies, Ko'iron is without eyes in Hive City. After you are dead, Venator Krelyn, I will send word that we fought to defend you but that you died without imparting any information about your mission. Or perhaps,' he added, a malicious glint sparkling in his eyes, as though something brilliant had just occurred to him, 'I will explain that you were a double agent, and that you were threatening to sabotage the mutually beneficial terms of the Orlock-Ko'iron Contract, in the hope that the Delaque might once again curry favour.'

Krelyn nodded. She was genuinely impressed. 'It is a good plan, Orthios, worthy of the Delaque themselves.

Knowledge is power, as they say.' As she spoke, her blade drew a trickle of blood from Orthios's throat, but her eyes had already left his face. She was scanning the movements of the other gangers in the room, and noting the distribution of weapons.

ZEFER WAS NOT wholly convinced that his new clothes were any better than his old ones. They seemed tatty and worn – not at all the kind of things that he could wear in the splendid streets of Gwentria's Fringe. Although he had to admit that he wouldn't want to wear his old clothes there in their present state. In any case, he was not in Gwentria's Fringe, and he was not oblivious to the fact that his old clothes did not exactly help him to blend into the streets of Hive City. Part of him wondered whether all the fuss at the Wall had been caused by his inappropriate dress; he had heard stories of people having their heads cut off for wearing the wrong things in the company of Lord Gerontius Helmawr, Guardian of Necromunda in the Holy Name of the Undying Emperor. He hadn't been prepared for the people of Hive City to be so sensitive to fashion errors.

He rolled his shoulders experimentally and regretted it at once, as stabbing pains fired through his ribcage. But, the soft leather jacket flexed comfortably over the fabric of his undergarments: after some protestations, the men had permitted him to retain his curator's undergarments when he explained that they contained pockets and pouches of considerable value; the men had nodded appreciatively, apparently thinking that such storage systems were very sensible.

From the front, the jacket looked like it had been cropped around the waist, but the back dropped into a long tail, like a cape. Various implements had been jammed under his belt, and their hilts were readily accessible because of the short cut of the jacket-front. Zefer wasn't sure what all the hilts were attached to, but he nodded in sudden appreciation at the design of the jacket. It made sense, and that realisation touched something half asleep in his mind.

His boots were also of leather, and they were covered in a lattice of buckles and ties, into which had been fixed short daggers, the like of which Zefer had never seen before.

Finally, after he had finished admiring his new look, Zefer noticed the smell. His new clothes stunk. There was the stench of dead animal about them – something that he had only read about in books. And there was also the smell of dried blood. Searching the coat, Zefer found three slits above his kidneys, each about the width of a broad-bladed dagger. The cuts were rimmed with spongy, coagulated blood.

'Good coat, that one,' said one of the men, as he cast Zefer's old, shapeless, grey smock into the burner. 'Belonged to Seraphia. She was quite something, that one.'

'What happened to her?' asked Zefer, not really wanting to know the answer.

'She died in the brawl at the Wall. Mistress Elria's burning her now,' explained the man with the broken nose eagerly. 'She'll be back soon, don't worry.'

'Mistress Elria?' asked Zefer, picking at the coagulated blood to try and dislodge it.

The two men stopped dead, as though they had just heard the worst possible heresy.

'Mistress Elria is the leader of The Coven, *friend*.' The last word had become a question, as though Zefer had somehow stepped outside its usual parameters. 'She is a great warrior... and a *wyrd*.'

This was all getting a bit too much for Zefer. 'A weird?'

'No, no, a *wyrd*. You'll see. It's fantastic. She's amazing.' Both of the men were nodding with such enthusiasm that the various wounds on their faces started to bleed again. 'She can make fire.'

'Enough!' came a powerful, even voice from the hall behind them. 'Bring the curator. We should be going.'

'It's her! She's back.' Zefer couldn't tell which of the men was speaking. Perhaps it was both of them. Their features were suddenly animated, as though the sun had finally risen after a barren night. 'Come, come.'

The men stooped into hunched postures and shuffled along next to Zefer, guiding him back into the hall, where he had awoken only an hour earlier. They limped and larked around his feet, suddenly like deformed jesters. And, as the three of them entered the hall, a chorus of jeers erupted from the gang of woman that, literally, lay in wait. A few thrown scraps of food splashed against the man-servants, to the great delight of the women and, apparently, the men themselves. Zefer noticed that none of the projectiles struck him, and he wondered whether this was the product of luck or skill. He stood upright between the faux hunchbacks, and absorbed the scene before him.

At the far side of the hall, under the fluttering reds and yellows of a great banner, one of the women leapt forward off a huge, rusty chair, which might have been a throne of some kind. Her hair seemed alive with blue snakes, and her eyes burned red as she strode across the hall towards him. When Zefer met her eyes, he found himself utterly unable to look anywhere else. The other women might all have spontaneously disappeared, for all he knew.

The scene seemed to shift into slow motion, and Zefer watched the incredible woman stride towards him as though that was the only thing happening in the whole of Necromunda. With an abruptness of motion that shattered his amazed reverie, the woman kicked out with one leg and then spun to kick with the other. Zefer heard two loud crunches and yelps of pain, followed by dull thuds as the two man servants on either side of him flew back under the abuse and smashed against the wall.

Just as Zefer braced himself for the inevitable assault, he heard the spluttered, mumbled thanks of the men together with the malicious jeers of the other gangers. Without a word, the blue haired, red eyed woman in front of him stared into his face, as though searching for something in his soul.

'I am Zefer Tyranus, Curator of House Ko'iron, First Class,' said Zefer unevenly, attempting to inject some pride into the first public announcement of his recent promotion. His voice trembled, but not as much as he expected.

'We know who you are, *mister* Tyranus,' replied Elria in curious, dulcet tones, edged with acid. 'And we know why you are here.' She was walking in a slow circle around Zefer, and he was not enjoying it.

'I am confused, however,' continued the gang leader. 'Why would the Noble House Ko'iron dispatch its agent so woefully unprepared for his journey into the Underhive?'

Zefer started slightly and gulped. 'The Underhive?' Collecting himself, he added: 'I too found it odd that my supplies were not waiting for me at the WPO.'

Elria nodded slowly, as though assessing the response. 'No matter,' she said. 'You are better equipped now.' She looked him up and down one more time. 'You will do.'

'Thank you,' replied Zefer, unsure of what else he could say.

'I should apologise for our sparse hospitality, but we are unused to *male* company of your kind and, in any event, we are in a hurry, as you will appreciate.' Zefer couldn't quite look at Elria. It was as though she were coiled, ready to pounce into his mind at the slightest opening. Her eyes patrolled around his face, looking for gaps, and Zefer kept his gaze fractionally averted all the time. It was obvious that she didn't trust him, which was understandable, although he suspected that it was for reasons that he would never fathom.

'We should get going,' she said, without making any sign of moving.

'Where are we going, Mistress Elria?' asked Zefer, repeating the title that he had heard from the men earlier.

'Why don't you tell me? You're the expert,' said Elria, her tongue hissing with acid.

'What?' Zefer cursed in his head, disappointed that he had said that word again. 'I'm not sure what you mean, Mistress Elria. How am *I* supposed to know where *you* are heading?' He was genuinely confused.

'It is simple: we are going to follow you,' explained Elria, as though to a child.

'But I have no idea where I'm going. I don't even know where I am,' countered Zefer. He realised that everything he was saying was true, and panic started to well in his stomach again.

The gang leader laughed, looking back around to the other women, who laughed with her. 'Do you really expect me to believe that the mighty House Ko'iron would be so stupid as to send a curator who didn't know their way?' She laughed again. 'Do you take me for a fool?'

'He knows the way,' hissed another voice from the shadows under the balcony, and Zefer turned to see another women apparently step into existence as she came into the light. She was wrapped in an impossibly black cloak that seemed to defy his gaze, and her eyes were hidden behind a dark blue visor. 'He even took notes of the directions in the notebook which he keeps in his undergarments.'

'Ah, my sweet Orphae, your timing is immaculate, as always,' said Elria, without taking her eyes off Zefer, but raising an amused eyebrow at the new information.

THE BLADE SLID slowly forward and Orthios's eyes bulged. The muscles of his jaw bunched momentarily, as though he wanted to scream, but then they fell slack as the dagger severed them. There was no great fountain of blood – Krelyn knew infinitely more subtle methods of death – but a wide stream oozed out from around the blade and coursed down Orthios's neck onto his chest.

She stared intimately into his fading eyes, with her own hidden behind the dark reflectivity of her visor, and she smiled. 'For House Ko'iron,' she whispered, with her breath caressing his features, watching the shock and incomprehension bleed out of his face.

The intimate scene exploded abruptly, as the other gangers saw the growing pool of blood gathering around the feet of Orthios's chair. In an instant, the chamber was a confusion of red bandanas and flashing weapons, as some of the gangers pounced forward with blades drawn and others held back, bracing their heavy weapons against the walls.

Krelyn held her nerve, crouching on the adamantium table with her blade still pushed into the neck of the gang leader. In her peripheral vision, she could see the gangers fanning out to surround her, and the yells of death filled the air with their outrage. In her chest, her heart was racing, and a thrill tingled her spine like an electric charge. She had been looking forward to this for years.

The air to her right rippled, as though being shunted towards her. A bludgeon arced horizontally across the table as one of the gangers tried to knock her away from their leader. But Krelyn was ready. In one swift movement, she swept her dagger out of Orthios's neck, sending a rain of blood spraying across towards her attacker. In the same motion, she flipped into the air, rolling horizontally and kicking out with her left leg. Her foot smashed against the side of Orthios's skull, wrenching his head from his shoulders and sending it flying.

The ganger with the bludgeon recoiled and dropped his weapon as his boss's decapitated head smashed into his face, breaking his nose with a bloody crunch. As he fell to the ground, his comrade instinctively reached out and caught the head, dropping his whirring chainsword in the process.

In the commotion, Krelyn leapt forward, pulling longer bladed swords into each hand from their leg holsters. Her movements were rapid and fluid, spinning the blades into an almost impenetrable sphere around her. She cleared the space between the table and the disarmed ganger in less than a second, piercing him through the stomach with one blade whilst flicking the head out of his hands with the other. Using the impaling sword as a pivot, she turned a curving kick and sent the head arcing across the room towards the stubguners on the other side.

In confusion, the gunners opened up, spraying the flying head with shot. From the side of the room, a great plume of fire jetted out from a heavy flamer and incinerated Orthios's head before it could reach the gangers with the stub guns. The sheet of flame cut the room in half, obscuring everyone's sight of Krelyn. When the flames finally died down, she was gone.

Orthios's riddled and smouldering head crumpled into ash as it thudded to the ground in the middle of the room and, over by the table, his body finally lost its balance and fell off its chair.

Krelyn glanced back into the chamber from the high windowsill and smiled at the chaos that she had unleashed. How she had missed this part of her job while she'd been in the Spire! With a flutter of her cloak, she vaulted out of the window and off into Hive City.

'IT WOULD BE such a shame to mess up those new clothes,' said Elria, eyeing Zefer with an expression that he had never seen before. He suspected that she was lying about the clothes.

'I assure you–'

A metallic clink made everyone spin, turning to the middle of the room next to the huge statue of the chained man. A tiny metal sphere was spinning to a halt on the floor, with a little red light pulsing rhythmically. The next second passed in slow motion. A wave of recognition washed over the faces of the Coven's gangers, and, as one, they dove to the ground.

Zefer watched the sudden urgency of everyone around him. He stood looking at the prostrate forms of the women, moving his head from side to side in bewilderment. The red light on the little spinning orb blinked once more, then it shifted to green.

The next thing he knew, there was an impossibly bright flash and Zefer was flying backwards. He smashed into the wall at the edge of the hall and slumped down into a heap at its base, his consciousness flickering like a candle. He could hear cries and yells, the bangs and rattles of gunfire, and could see the occasional flare of flames misted behind the clouds of smoke.

As the stinking smoke began to settle, Zefer looked up over the clouds and saw teams of giant warriors abseiling down a fat chain that had been dropped through a jagged hole in the ceiling. They looked vaguely familiar, and Zefer realised that they were the Goliaths from the battle at the Wall.

Fire strafed up from the ground, flashing past the descending figures and blowing chips out of the fabric of the ceiling. One abseiler caught a slug in his arm and was left hanging by the other one until it was shattered by a shotgun burst. But for every Goliath Subversive that fell, two or three more made it down into the smoke cover and Zefer had no idea how many were already in the fog-filled hall.

Silhouettes were moving in the smoke, and Zefer was watching the shadow-puppets hack at each other with axes and swords. He felt utterly disconnected from the cacophony as his eyes stung and streamed in the wisps of smoke. But then, bursting out of the cloud line, Elria came storming towards him with her hair writhing in her wake. Close on her heels was the huge Subversive from the Wall, with bloody bandages tied crudely across his chest, covering the wounds inflicted by the Salvationist ganger earlier on. His massive adamantium jaw was wide open and a hideous, bellowing scream was being forced out as he ran, pumping his two-handed autocannon from side to side.

A staccato of fire rattled behind the two charging figures, and another of The Coven's gangers emerged slowly from the cloud-line. A chunky ammunition belt was wrapped around her waist and over her shoulder, and the tip of her heavy stubber was smoking.

Uglar stumbled as the shots impacted on his back. He was close enough for Zefer to see his bright green eyes widen in anger as he tripped and fell forward onto the ground, skidding to a halt as his momentum failed, and the metal plate on his scalp glinted into Zefer's face.

From his crumpled heap against the wall, Zefer watched the scene in horror, as blood started to ooze out of the gaping wounds in the giant warrior's back. But before he could formulate any coherent thoughts of his own, Elria was at his side, slipping her arm around him and trying to drag him to his feet.

'We have to get out of here, curator.'

Zefer simply nodded, wondering why she had bothered to say such a blatantly obvious thing. The battle in the smoke cloud was reaching fever pitch, and he could hardly even hear her voice, despite the fact she was yelling directly into his ear.

'Jermina, take his other arm!' shouted Elria as the ganger with the stubber came rushing over to help her mistress. She slung the huge weapon around onto her back and gripped Zefer under his arm, making him cry out as his ribs stretched apart.

'How did they know about the roof entrance?' yelled Jermina over the din and over Zefer's hanging head.

'There must be a traitor in our midst,' replied Elria, as she ducked her head under Zefer's other arm, making him scream and pass out. 'But this is not the time to worry about that.'

'You're right, Mistress Elria,' came a deep, resonant voice that didn't belong to either of them. They had been so preoccupied with getting Zefer onto his feet that they had not noticed that Uglar had climbed up off the floor.

'He's mine, Uglar,' said Elria with immaculate calm, fixing the huge Subversive with her burning red eyes.

'I don't think so,' boomed Uglar, as a squad of barbaric warriors came storming out of the smokescreen and lined up behind their boss. 'Put him down, and we'll let you live.'

Elria didn't move a muscle – knowing that if she showed any signs of fear, they would take her instantly. But she let her eyes scan backwards and forwards along the line of muscled men before her. Each brandished at least two weapons. Most had blood drenched battleaxes or spiked clubs in one hand and heavy stubbers or autocannons in the other. It took Jermina all of her strength to heft just one of those guns.

Behind the wall of muscle, Elria could hear her gangers fighting desperately against the superior weight of the Goliath gang. Once the brutes had got inside the enclave, the chances of a victory for The Coven had plummeted. She sighed and shook her head, imagining the ridicule that would be heaped on her by the other Escher bosses if they even found out that she had been taken by surprise by the Subversives. Of all the gangs by whom to be ambushed, the huge, hulking, clumsy and loud Goliaths had to be the most embarrassing for an Escher. It was hard to think of anyone that represented the *male* more than Uglar.

A high pitched scream cut through the gunfire and explosions, bringing the battle to a momentary standstill, and Elria realised that her girls were dying. She took one more look at the line of testosterone in front of her, with flames flickering in her irises, and then she stooped back away from Zefer, letting him collapse back onto the ground as Jermina followed her lead. Already unconscious, he dropped like a dead weight.

'Take him and go,' she said, keeping her voice velvety and smooth. 'But this is not the end, Uglar of the Goliath.'

Uglar made a motion with his head; one of his goons stepped forward and took hold of Zefer's legs, swinging him over his shoulder with one arm. 'Thank you,' grated Uglar's metal jaw. The muscles on his face twitched grotesquely, and Elria realised that he was trying to smile.

SHE WAS FAR from certain that she was doing the right thing. It had been a long time since she had been properly embroiled in the politics of the HC, and things had certainly changed a lot. The last time that she was down here, the Ko'iron Contract had been held by House Delaque, and the other gangs struggled around the edges picking up the scraps. But now the Orlocks had the contract, even though they didn't appear to know what it meant, and everyone seemed suspicious of the various Delaque gangs. Actually, people had always been suspicious of the Delaque, so that hadn't changed. What had changed was that the Delaque gangs never used to care that nobody trusted them, because they had the power and the money already. That had changed, it seemed. Now, nobody trusted them, and they probably needed a bit of good will. The Undying Emperor alone knows how much the people of HC needed a bit of good will.

Killing Orthios had seemed like the natural thing to do. He was failing in his duty to the Ko'irons and, furthermore, he was threatening to kill her. Krelyn reassured herself that his death had nothing to do with the little red snake etched into the adamantium sheet that he was using as his table. She killed him as a Ko'-iron agent, not as a Delaque venator or a Red Snake ganger, no matter what her name was, and no matter what her clothing suggested.

Besides, she added in her internal monologue, she needed the practice.

There were a cluster of potential problems, however. Most pressingly, she had failed to recruit any assistance in her quest to appropriate the curator. The Snake Charmers had simply refused. Whilst their refusal had led to certain *complications*, it did leave Krelyn with the problem of whom she could turn to now. She briefly entertained the idea that she might go back to the Delaque masters or to the bosses of the Red Snakes and throw herself on their mercy, but then she realised that they had none. In any case, the Delaque would be the last people who would want to help House Ko'iron at the moment.

Sitting on the roof of the *Breath of Fresh Air*, letting the breeze from the giant ventilation fan on the other side of the plaza wash over her, Krelyn tapped her fist against her head, trying to bang some political sense back into her brain. It had been too long since she last had to think in this way. Life in the Spire had been easy and soft. Too easy.

She stared across at the huge ventilation pipes that dominated the square, and watched the slow revolutions of the four-bladed fan. Should she go back through the tunnel in the Wall, behind the vertical shaft, and tell Prince Jurod that she had lost her mark? No, she couldn't do that. The surviving gangers of the Snake Charmers had to be dealt with, otherwise they might report to House Ko'iron that she had killed Orthios – with a little wit they could easily make it look as though she had defected back to the Red

Snakes as soon as she had re-entered the HC, and used her erstwhile connection with Ko'iron to ingratiate herself into the company of Orthios. Despite those red bandanas cutting off all the oxygen to their brains, Krelyn was sure that even they would be able to think of that. They might even believe it, despite what she said to them. Either way, going back to Jurod now would be a mistake.

As she sat there, the waft of roasting food seeped up out of the door below, along with a constant column of tox-smoke. She breathed it in deeply, remembering the richer, cleaner smells of the Quake Tavern. She hadn't been in the *Fresh Air* for years, but the putrid fragrance brought the good-times flooding back. Although it had never been in Red Snake territory, she had frequented it more often than most other places. It had a peculiarly relaxing atmosphere, and there was always a good fight on tap when you needed one. And drink. Drink like you could never find in the Spire. She remembered that the little barman – Squatz was his name, she thought – he used to say that it was because of his house special brew that his growth had been stunted. And, for some reason that she could no longer fathom, that had made her want to drink a lot of it.

Wondering whether, perhaps, she needed a quick shot of Squatz's special brew to help her settle her thoughts, Kreyn swung her legs off the rooftop and dropped to the ground next to the front door. She pushed it open a crack and breathed in the ghastly, toxic fumes that billowed out into her face. With a smile, she kicked it open and strode into the bar.

THE GANGERS IN the corner were hunched over their drinks and muttering amongst themselves, their faces hidden in the shadows of pale blue, hooded cloaks.

Krelyn recognised them at once as the Salvationist gangers from the Wall, and she noted the blood stains, tears and burns that speckled their capes. They didn't appear to notice her entrance or, if they did, they weren't concerned about her.

Krelyn walked up to the counter and leant her elbow onto it, peering down behind the other side to see whether Squatz was still around. Behind the metal bar were a series of heavy barrels and a single row of bottles, all of which appeared to contain the same, brown, foaming liquid. At fairly regular intervals, Krelyn could see the butts of guns protruding from under the counter itself, and she smiled as she realised that Squatz himself was permitted to break the house rules regarding firearms. She patted her own laspistol instinctively, and realised that she had still not had it repaired, so she wasn't really breaking the code.

'He's out back,' called one of the gangers, without looking up. 'Getting some more brew.'

Krelyn nodded, but said nothing. She pushed her visor up onto her forehead and rubbed her eyes. She needed a drink. Reaching over behind the bar, she grabbed one of the bottles of brown froth and bit the cork out of its neck. The acrid smell that wafted out of the bottle almost made her vomit, and she smiled faintly at how soft she had become. To spite herself, she placed the bottle to her lips and threw her head back, tipping the liquid straight down her throat. It was vile.

'How is it?' asked Squatz, appearing at the end of the bar and wandering along the counter towards Krelyn.

'Like the nectar of gods,' she replied, grimacing and trying not to gag.

Squatz stopped walking and tilted his head to one side. 'I know you.'

As he spoke, the gangers in the corner fell into silence and their heads twisted round to watch.

'Possibly,' conceded Krelyn. 'I haven't been in here for a while, but I used to be something of a regular.'

'You're with that other venator, right? The one with the little tattoo under his eye.'

As Squatz described the man, an image flashed through Krelyn's mind. She was waiting at the Red Snake tunnel through the Wall, and a venator had sprung out of the darkness with a red snake writhing under his eyes. He had knocked her over and then vanished.

'The red snake,' confirmed Krelyn, slightly hesitantly. 'Like this?' she asked, pushing up her sleeve to reveal her own tattoo.

'Yes,' said a charming voice next to her. 'Just like that.' Before she even knew that he was there, the Salvationist ganger had taken hold of her arm and was tracing the lines of the snake with his fingertip.

Krelyn yanked her arm away, bringing the blade that she had slipped into her other hand straight up to the man's throat, slipping it under the chin of his silver face mask.

'Forgive me,' he said smoothly. 'I am Triar Cawdor, friend of Venator Curion, our mutual acquaintance.'

Krelyn considered his startling blue eyes for a moment, and then flicked her dagger, severing the ties that held the man's mask to his face. Behind the silver, he was a young and handsome ganger, but his eyes contained his real power, and Krelyn was not about to succumb. She withdrew the blade and nodded a silent greeting, not yet willing to disillusion the young gang leader.

'Are you here at Curion's bidding? Do you know what happened to the curator?' asked Triar, relaxing his shoulders a little.

Krelyn dropped her visor back down over her eyes and smiled. 'Yes. Yes, I am, and I do.' She could feel her political cunning running back into her veins like Squatz's special brew. 'The Snake Charmers took him while you were fighting. They were tipped off about the curator by one of their agents from the Spire, and they went to fulfil their obligations under the Ko'iron Contract. They have him in their enclave – I can show you the way.'

Triar looked at her sceptically, but then nodded with resolution. He had been searching for the Snake Charmers' base for years. 'Good. We will go now.'

THE DARKNESS WAS almost complete, and the darker than black robes that shrouded both figures rendered them virtually invisible.

'How are things developing, Curion?' The voice hissed from everywhere at once, and Curion did not know which way to look.

'Exactly according to plan, master,' he replied, bowing his head deferentially to the ground instead of trying to face towards the source of the voice. 'Exactly as you planned.'

7: BADZONE

THE FLOOR WAS strewn with bodies and puddled with blood. Smoke hazed through the room, rich with the discharge of flamers and shotguns. The walls were pockmarked and lacerated, and the metal furniture had melted into unrecognisable shapes. Crouched in the corner, with the silver glint of a blade in her hand, Krelyn peered down into the face of the last of Orthios's gangers. He was mumbling, inchoate with fear and the certainty of death.

'You should have listened to me,' she hissed in a whisper that only he could hear. Then she slit his throat.

'What did he say?' called Triar from the centre of the room. He was bracing a two-handed flamer, sweeping its barrel slowly across the room in case they'd missed someone. A clutch of Salvationist gangers stalked through the mist, their cloaks stirring eddies into the smoke and their masks glinting as they caught moments of light. They prodded at the bodies with daggers to make sure; vengeance was a code of law, and they could not risk survivors escaping to inform the other Orlock gangs.

'The Coven,' said Krelyn, turning her head to face Triar, but letting her body shield his view of the ganger at her knees. Even through the haze, Krelyn could see the startling blue of Triar's eyes flashing behind his silver mask. If anything, they seemed to burn brighter after the battle.

'Elria?' mused Triar. 'Of course, I should have known.' The gang leader turned away and strode off towards the door, his cloak stirring the smoke into a whirl. 'Finish him,' he called back over his shoulder. 'These heretics will meet judgement in the gaze of the Undying Emperor. There are others still awaiting cleansing at the hands of his righteous servants.'

'As you wish,' smiled Krelyn, turning back to the bubbling slash across the Snake Charmer's neck. 'You should have listened to me.'

A RINGING PAIN pulsed in Zefer's ears, as though he had been smashed in the head by something heavy. The muscles in his neck were knotted and they seared with fire at even the thought of movement. He could feel a delicate, cold and wet impact drumming on his temple, as though an icy liquid were dripping from a great height. But he couldn't move.

Experimentally, he opened his eyes, one then the other, convincing himself that deliberate slowness would somehow make the scene more palatable. It didn't work.

He awoke to find himself slumped into the corner of a small, dark cell. The walls were rough and uneven, as though they had been dug out of rock, not at all like the smooth metal structures that he was used to. And they seemed to glisten with moisture.

Without moving his head or neck, Zefer cast his eyes around, trying to work out where the light was coming from. It was faint and tinged with green, but there was enough to make the water on the walls glint and sparkle.

As far as he could see, the cell was completely sealed. There was no way for light to get in. He couldn't even see a door, although common sense and a faint draft across the floor told him that there must be one. The eerie, greenish light seemed to be emanating from the droplets of liquid on the walls. Tiny, dull stars trickled down into glowing pools on the rocky floor.

Tentatively, he brought his hand up in front of his face, as though seeking reassurance that he was really there, wherever there was. His hand pulsed gently in the green light, itself speckled with droplets, and a trickle of the strange liquid was running down his arm from his shoulder. The cold dripping on his temple told him the source.

Straining the muscles in his neck, he sniffed at the liquid on his finger tips, remembering in a flash of melancholy how he used to sniff at the pages of the books in the librarium. The green water was sticky and viscous, and it smelt sweet, like a rich perfume that had been condensed into treacle.

He had no idea what it was, and he dropped his arm back to the ground, letting his head fall back against the wall with a dull thud. Without any sense of where he was or how he had got there, and without the strength even to push himself off the wall, he closed his eyes and passed out again, lapsing into a sleep of violent visions and unspeakable shadows.

A PUNGENT FIRE roared in the centre of the camp, sending curdling spirals of thick black smoke billowing around the cavern. The walls and floor were cracked and uneven, as though the cave had once been in several other places that had all been crunched together in a gigantic hive-quake. Thick, ichorous fluids rolled and pulsed down through the cracks, collecting into pools on the floor. Crude runnels had been cut into the ground, through which the pools evacuated themselves into a great pit in the centre of the cavern which bubbled and frothed with the congealing liquids. The immense fire danced over the surface of the pit-lake, with flames flickering through the colour spectrum as the chemicals in the liquids flared and burned. Puffs of gas and belches of putrid stink erupted as parts of the pool boiled while some of the liquids vaporised instantly.

Sitting comfortably on the burnt out wreckage of an overturned battle-wagon, Uglar gazed into the dancing pattern of flames, as though staring into the cryptic prefigurings of a dark and dangerous future. The light bounced off the adamantium of his jaw and scalp-plate, rendering him into a starburst of noxious colours. He had ripped the bandages from his chest, and the huge gashes through his pectoral muscles bubbled and hissed as the toxic fumes invaded the wounds. He showed no sign of noticing the agony of infection and kept his expression fixed on the fire.

The other Subversives gangers were dispersed around the camp. A bunch of them had pinned the dead body of a Coven ganger against the wall and were firing volleys from their shotguns into it, laughing and drinking. Others were prodding at their weapons and cussing, obviously displeased with equipment that had failed on their raid. Some simply smashed the butts of their guns against the ground and then cast the ruins into the pit-fire, whooping and cheering as the ammunition detonated and sprayed the cavern with shot. But most were slumped into the wreckages of vehicles with bottles in their hands, enjoying the heat of the flames and the toxic liquor.

'He is a puny man. We may have broken him already,' mumbled Uglar, apparently to himself. His gaze was fixed on the fire, and its reflection danced in the depths of his brown eyes.

'He will not die yet,' hissed a disembodied, low, female voice from the shadows. 'He is tougher than you think – why else would he have been chosen?'

'It doesn't matter. If he dies, nobody will get there. If he lives, I will get there. Either way, I am the strongest,' reasoned Uglar, nodding slightly as the warmth of the fire singed his face.

'Indeed,' agreed the voice.

'Don't patronise me, venator,' growled the Subversives' boss, turning suddenly and staring into the shadows behind him. He couldn't see anything at all, but he knew that she was lurking there, enwrapped in that cursed shroud of hers, oozing with her condescending tone. 'I know the value of artefacts. It is not only the snobs of the Spire or the weaklings of the upper levels of Hive City that know of objects of power. Hive Primus rests on the shoulders of the Goliath gangs in these pits, we in the Subversives know of power, venator. And we do not fear the shadows.'

In fact, Uglar had not been quite sure what 'subversive' had meant when he had named his gang. He had a vague sense that it had something to do with being 'under' everything else, and it had a pleasantly dynamic sound to it. He liked to think that the uphivers shivered when they heard the name, since it should make them aware that the ground under their feet was held aloft through the power of his gang.

'I meant no offence, Uglar, and I do not doubt your strength.' Orphae was smiling sickly. 'But you realise that the other gangs will not give up on this? Triar and Elria both will want revenge for your attacks on them.'

'Let them come!' boomed Uglar, rising to his feet and smashing the butt of his autocannon against the wreck beneath him. 'They could not beat us on their turf. Let's see them try to bring battle to the pits of Uglar.'

'Perhaps we should attempt to retrieve the artefact *before* they come?' prompted Orphae, leading Uglar's anger.

'It must indeed be an object of great power, if the pathetic houses of Hive City are willing to fight about it. They don't know the value of battle – let them come, and the Subversives will teach them!' Uglar was roaring now, and the other gangers raised a drunken cheer in support of their boss's bravado.

'As you wish,' hissed Orphae, realising that she had done all that she could.

KOORL SPRINTED FOR the door, spinning to press flat against the wall next to the doorframe as he reached it. In his wake three more gangers took up positions on either side of the door. Further back in the street, Triar crouched in a deep trench that had cracked into the ground, torn out between two of the huge metal slabs that made up the surface of the road. Poised in the trench, another ten gangers were in support. Krelyn had vanished, leaping up onto a nearby roof and disappearing from sight.

As Triar looked up at the ramshackle structure of Elria's enclave, he thought he saw a flash of shadow dancing over its roof. Although the light was dim up there, dimmer even than in the narrow streets below, he also thought that he saw some wisps of smoke.

Despite himself, he hoped that Krelyn was okay. She may be a Red Snake Delaque, but for some reason he trusted her more than Curion. Curion had been trying to convince him to attack the Snake Charmers for years, never wasting an opportunity to slight them or to implicate them. He had never actually come out with it and directly asked Triar to attack them, but it was something that seemed to underlie everything he said. Krelyn was different. She had turned up without ceremony and told Triar that Orthios had taken the curator. There were no games and no cunning convolutions. She had just said it: They have him in their enclave – I can show you the way.

Of course, Triar had been sceptical, and he remained slightly suspicious because Krelyn had not asked for payment. Curion would have held out on such information and waited for a substantial reward, knowing how important the curator was to the Redemptionist cause and to the Salvationists themselves. Then, as the battle in the Snake Charmers' Basket raged and he saw Krelyn fight, he thought that he understood why she had not demanded gems or jewels for her tip-off: killing the Snake Charmers gangers was enough reward in itself. She had thrown herself into the task with the kind of righteous fury that Triar would have admired in a Redemptionist. By the time his blue-cloaks had ploughed into the fray, she had already dispatched most of the red-heads, or at least slashed them across their throats in a frenzy of cuts. It had taken a while to find a survivor still able to talk.

And it made sense that Elria would have kidnapped the curator from them. After all, this whole affair had begun with Curion's tip-off about Elria's quest into the Underhive to find her sacrilegious archeotech. If anyone had wanted the grey-smocked fop from the Spire more than the Ko'iron's own allies, it would be that heretical Escher witch. Well, now they had him and it fell to Triar to deprive them of his guidance and appropriate his knowledge for the glory of the

Undying Emperor. In any event, he had been waiting a
long time to take the battle to Elria's front door.

At the signal from Triar, Koorl planted his melta-
bomb onto the plasteel of the door and then turned
back into cover, vaulting over a pile of the debris that
was strewn throughout the area. From his position, he
could see the plasma-gunner in Triar's trench take aim
with his heavy, shoulder mounted weapon. There was
an almost indiscernible nod from Triar and the gunner
squeezed off a shell of bright glowing plasma. It seared
across the street and punched directly into the melta-
bomb, detonating the thermal charge in its own
super-heated explosion.

The door melted and blew in all at once, spraying
molten plasteel into the building. The entire wall
rocked and rippled under the impact, raining fragments and debris down into the street, dusting the
Salvationist gangers as they leapt out of cover and
charged towards the door.

HE FLOATED IN and out of consciousness, feverish and
increasingly soaked by the pungent liquids that dripped
from the walls. After a while, his posture slumped even
more, and he ended up laying on the floor, bent at
ninety degrees with his back against the wall and his legs
sticking out into the middle of the cell. The shift
brought his mouth directly under the dribbling effluent,
and gradually its sickly sweet taste began to fill his
senses.

Spluttering and spitting, Zefer's eyes pried themselves
open, as though his unconscious was rebelling against
the assault on his senses. For a moment, he actually
thought that he was drowning, and he rolled over onto
his belly, coughing and gagging in an attempt to evacu-
ate his lungs. Nothing came out, but the sour taste of

vomit seeped into his mouth, making him scrape his tongue against his teeth in revulsion.

Sitting back onto his ankles, spitting the residue from his mouth, Zefer looked around the cell once again. He could see more of his surroundings now, as though the glowing liquid on the walls was brighter. But it wasn't brighter in there, reflected Zefer, it was simply that he could see better than he could before. He could see each of the glistening walls in the little cell, and even the low ceiling. The entire space was probably only eight cubic metres. There was still no door visible, and no windows of any kind. The only light, faint and tinged with green, came from the sweet tasting moisture on the walls.

Tentatively, Zefer stood up. If he reached his hand into the air, he could touch the slimy ceiling. He took a step forward and pressed both of his hands against the rough rock of the wall before him. Leaning his weight forward, he sniffed, drawing in the sickly scent of the moist rock in front of his face. Somewhere on the other side of the wall, he could hear the muffled sound of gunshots and shouting.

'Who are you?'

Zefer spun on the spot and backed up against the wall, banging his head abruptly on the uneven surface. The voice had come from somewhere inside the cell. It had not even been a whisper and, for some reason, the shock of conversational volume was almost as great as the shock of hearing a voice at all.

'What?' said Zefer, instinctively. 'Who said that?'

He strained his eyes in the faint green light, snatching his head from side to side. The cell certainly wasn't big enough for anyone to hide in, and it was small enough that even the dim light was enough for him to be able to see the whole thing. But he couldn't see anything at all.

'Where are you?' he asked, when he got no answer to his first question.

'I am with you,' came the reply, even and measured, as though perfectly crafted in a foreign language. The voice seemed slightly surprised that Zefer needed to ask.

'Show yourself.' Zefer was in no mood for this.

'I am not hiding.'

'Then why can I not see you?'

'Perhaps you are not looking in the right place?'

'So, *where* are you?' cried Zefer, his exasperation over-coming his fear. Anybody willing to have this conversation was probably not going to kill him.

Something tugged at one of the tails of his coat, and Zefer instantly snapped his head down towards the movement. At first he couldn't see anything at all, but gradually a shape began to form in the darkness. The problem was not with his eyes but with his brain – there was enough light in the cell for him to see the creature in the corner, but he had not known how to look for it. Eventually, his brain started to process the negative images that the cell provided, showing him silhouettes against the pale green sludge as three dimensional shapes. But it took a little time.

'W-what are you?' asked Zefer, staring shamelessly at the creature now.

'I am Ruskin,' came the reply, as the creature shuffled silently in the corner, rocking backwards and forwards as though curled into a ball.

The voice in the corner seemed to belong to a normal sized human. But the man was stooped and folded, curled into a ball on the floor, as though chronically self-conscious. His voice was incongruously clear and his speech articulate, despite the fact that there was the suggestion that he wasn't quite sure what he was saying. Whatever he was wearing, it had a pale sheen to its surface that closely matched the dim glow of the glistening walls, making it incredibly hard to see his profile clearly. The oddest thing about him, however, was the shape of his head. As far as Zefer could make out, the man's head was elongated like that on an animal, with a long jawbone and jagged teeth. He seemed to be able to speak without moving his jaw at all.

As he stared down at Ruskin, a realisation hit Zefer like a sudden dose of spur. All of his pain had gone. The muscles on his neck were loose and supple, his head had stopped hurting, and even his broken ribs seemed comfortably set. He shuffled back along the wall away from the man-animal in the corner, trying to remember when he had arrived in the cell, and how long he had been there.

As HE RAN, Triar lobbed a couple of smoke grenades through the wrecked hole where the door used to be. They blew just moments before his blue-cloaks ducked into the building, keeping low to make the most of the cover provided by the smoke. The gangers fanned out into formation, interspersing heavy gunners through their line. Triar pulled his sword free and clasped it heroically as he pushed forward of the rest looking for the first kill. But there was no hostile fire. He charged onward, yelling out for Elria.

'Show yourself, witch!' But there was no response.

Unsure about how to proceed in the absence of a battle, the blue-coats waited for word from Triar, fidgeting anxiously with their weapons and snapping them incautiously from side to side.

The smoke thinned as Triar swept on through the hallway, and then it vanished completely when he kicked open the double doors into the great hall.

Behind his mask, his mouth dropped. The hall was in chaos: the balconies were shattered and broken; the banners were torn and burnt and there were bodies lying all over the floor. Half-packed kitbags had been abandoned haphazardly. Elria's throne had been over-turned and her family statue decimated.

Standing in the middle of hall, surveying the car-nage, was Krelyn. Two bloodied and bruised men were fussing around her, bowing and kneeling, but she was ignoring them. With one hand, she held a thick chain that ran up into a jagged hole in the roof. Triar pre-sumed that this was how she had got in before him.

'What happened here?' he asked, picking his way through the corpses in genuine shock.

'Looks like the Subversives got here first. It seems that we are not the only ones interested in this curator,' replied Krelyn, pushing the bumbling mavants out of her way as she stooped to check the pulse of one of the women.

'Dead,' she said. 'They're all dead.'

'No, mistress. No no,' intoned the mavants, almost in chorus. 'Not all dead, mistress. No no.'

'There were survivors?' asked Krelyn, surprised.

'Y-yes… oh, yes.'

'Where are they?' demanded Triar as he joined them in the middle of the hall, turning his sparkling blue eyes on them.

The mavants recoiled at his gaze, grabbing hold of each other and quivering like frightened animals. 'T-they've g-gone to f-f-find you, mister,' they managed.

A commotion by the main doors to the hall made Triar turn. His gangers were edging their way into the huge chamber from the corridor outside with their weapons still primed and ready. They were deploying into a wide line to make a sweep through the hall.

Triar held up a hand. 'Hold there.' And the gangers stopped. Each of them scanned the scene in silence.

Regardless of the masks that hid their faces, Triar knew that his men would be shocked by the scene that greeted them. They may hate Elria and her Coven of witches, and they may even have been looking forward to the chance to fight them today, but he was sure that they would be shocked to see what had been done to them in their own enclave. Triar and Elria had been at each others throats for years and, if they were perfectly honest, they had learnt to accept a roughly equal balance of power between their gangs in the sector. They fought every now and again, and even killed a few on each side, just to keep everyone on their toes. But the situation was actually pretty stable. Triar harboured a genuine desire to save their souls and, in the meantime, the conflict gave him an opportunity to exercise his righteousness. The Subversives were brutal people, and they had no place this high up in the hive.

'I suspect that we will find them in the Breath of Fresh Air,' announced Triar, after some thought. 'That's certainly where I always go when I want to irritate them.'

THE SUBVERSIVES WERE hard at work, smashing at the floor of their cavern with huge mallets and pickaxes, gouging out channels around the perimeter of the cave and digging miniature pits into the mouths of each of the access tunnels. They were stumbling and drunk, but this made little difference to their progress, as Uglar patrolled the gangers, punching and kicking at any who slacked off.

In the absence of any electric light, the Subversives worked by the roaring light of the fire, sweating in the darkness as they laboured in the stifling heat. The glittering phosphorescence of the walls sparkled and twinkled in delicate incongruousness, shining in stark contrast with the crude bulk of the gangers themselves.

One or two grew rapidly bored of digging and shouldered their heavy bolters, shattering the rock with stuttering barrages of explosive shells. Stone shrapnel and errant shells ricocheted around the cavern, sizzling into the burning liquids or burying themselves into the flesh of other gangers, who roared with pain but threw their rage into their work rather than turning on their brothers.

Uglar watched the crude ingenuity of his men and nodded. He knew that the upper hivers looked down on all the Goliath gangs. He knew that they were horrified by their brutal existence in the lower levels of the hive, where electricity was scarce and water was richer in toxins than oxygen. Even the air was thick with sludge and the unwanted gases of the Hive City. There were no great paintings or beautiful statues of women down there in the deepest and harshest areas of the hive. But there were no weak saplings either. That genteel fop, Triar of Cawdor, would not last a day down in the furnace halls or the slag pits. He would not even have the stomach for the water, let alone for the epic barbarism of the great Feast of the Fallen. Let him come, and Uglar would throw him into one of the ancient fighting pits, and then those pathetic Cawdor Salvationists would see the meaning of strength and of despair.

There was not a single member of his gang who had not triumphed in the ceremonial pit fights after the Feast of the Fallen. Goliath gangs would not admit just anybody, contrary to the assertions of the softer hivers. It was not enough to be strong or robust. It was not enough to have survived into adulthood in the harshest environment that the hive had to offer and to have become inured to the toxins and deprivations of life on the cusp of the Underhive. Every Goliath ganger had to make a kill in the pit following the great feast. Every Goliath currently breaking their massively muscled backs against the rock in the floor of this cavern had killed one of their own in the oldest ceremony known to Hive Primus.

Whenever he thought about it, Uglar's huge heart welled with pride. The Goliaths were the very foundations of the hive, holding it up with the immense strength of their arms and their industry. The slack upper hivers may mock at their supposed lack of sophistication, but it was down in the fires of this hell that Hive Primus was built, and the Subversives stood as testament to that glorious heritage. They were there at the start, and they were still there now, holding the place together from the foundations. Without the various gangs of House Goliath, Hive Primus would be nothing but a gibbering crowd of slack, foppish uphivers, weak and pathetic to the point of suicide.

If this curator that Orphae and the other uphivers thought was so important really knew the whereabouts of an ancient and powerful archeotech, it was probably in the Subversives' domain anyway. And nobody was going to come down here and steal artefacts of power from Uglar of Goliath.

Taking a clutch of melta-bombs, Uglar made his way around the central pit of the cavern, fixing a bomb between it and the end of each channel that his gangers had carved into the stone floor. Making a second pass with a roll of shielded fuse-wire, Uglar rigged the place for the welcoming party. The uphivers always tried to keep their enclaves so pretty, he laughed in his head. Down here, nothing stays pretty for long.

THE SQUARE IN front of the Fresh Air was deserted, filled only by the breeze from the great four-bladed fan. Garbage and dust skidded around in little demons, swirling in the air currents.

Triar and Krelyn stood side by side at the edge of the plaza, watching the scene for signs that the quiet was unnatural. It certainly seemed unnatural, because the Fresh Air was usually the busiest joint in the sector. However, times had changed. Orthios's Snake Charmers gang had been completely wiped out and Elria's Coven had been decimated. Of the three gangs whose territories criss-crossed around the Fresh Air, only the Salvationists were at anything like full strength. It was only natural that the plaza would be deserted today, but it seemed like the most suspicious scene in Necromunda. It wouldn't take long, certainly, for gangs from neighbouring districts to attempt to fill the power vacuum. Triar and Krelyn both knew that this could mean House Delaque and the Red Snakes.

'Looks clean,' said Triar, but Krelyn knew that it was a question.

'Yes,' she replied, striding confidently across the square towards the Fresh Air.

The door was ajar when they arrived. There would usually be a blast of noise and the fumes of toxins wafting out, but there was nothing. Peering in through the crack, Triar could see the women of The Coven seated around their usual table in the corner. Elria herself was perched on the back of her chair with her feet on the seat and her back to the wall. She was talking quietly to her gangers and nodding her head to emphasise certain points, letting her dirty blue dreads cascade freely. Suddenly she stopped talking.

'Who is that with you, Triar of Cawdor?' she asked, without looking over.

Triar shared a glance with Krelyn and turned to beckon a group of his gangers from the other side of the square. Then he pushed open the door and stepped into the Fresh Air.

None of the Escher women turned to face the new patrons, and Elria did not lift her gaze to them. Squatz, on the other hand, was more jovial than usual, sliding down off the bar and running over to greet them.

'It is good to see you again, sir,' blurted the little man with a little too much urgency. 'And you, madam.' He bowed.

Triar smiled behind his burnished mask and nodded a greeting. 'Ah, Squatz, I see that you're still not very discriminating about your clientele.' He turned his face towards the women in the corner.

'Times are hard, and we cannot all uphold principles as stringently as you, sir,' replied Squatz with uncharacteristic deference.

Triar reflected that the little man was probably telling the truth. The cunning business strategy that he had developed to keep the Breath of Fresh Air running for so long had collapsed overnight. It was no longer the case that his tavern occupied contested, but stable, ground at the intersection of three rival, roughly equal gangs. Now it was merely an unclaimed tavern in front of the most valuable source of fresh air in the sector. Triar was his best and only possible source of security. Even on this day, Triar could see the perfect opportunity for a conversion to the cult of Redemption.

'I understand,' said Triar, his generosity taking Squatz by surprise.

Krelyn brushed past the men and reached over the bar to grab a bottle of the house special. She pushed her visor up onto her forehead, popped the cork and took a long swig from the bottle.

'That stuff will stunt your growth.'

One of the Coven's women had come to the bar and was propping it up on Krelyn's right. The venator turned to her left, looking back towards the door; Triar and Squatz were still talking in the middle of the room. She shrugged and turned back to her bottle.

'I don't think I've seen you in here before,' continued the ganger.

Taking another swig from her bottle, Krelyn didn't reply, but she was smiling inside. It had been a long time since anyone had flirted with her. In the Spire, people tended to scattered like shrapnel whenever she approached a bar. Nobody would try and pick up a venator in the Quake Tavern.

Unperturbed, or even reassured by Krelyn's silence, the ganger reached behind the bar and grabbed a bottle for herself, smashing the neck off against the metal counter and tipping half the liquid straight down her throat.

'I am Elria,' she said. 'I am acquainted with a colleague of yours. Venator Orphae?'

Krelyn thought about the name for a little while and then shook her head. 'I am not familiar with Orphae. But it has been a long time since I was last in Hive City. Much has changed.'

'It has indeed,' replied Elria, casting her eyes back over towards the table in the corner, where eight of The Coven's gangers were drowning their sorrows. 'Will you join us... for a drink?' she asked, leaving her pause deliberately ambiguous.

'We are drinking now, Elria,' said Krelyn, turning to face the blue-haired woman for the first time. She started slightly at the red burning in the ganger's eyes, leaning back involuntarily to get a little distance.

'I should be honest with you, Elria,' continued Krelyn, realising that the flames in her eyes were a mixture of anger and grief. 'I am not a venator of House Delaque, but am an agent for the Noble House of Ko'-iron. Our purposes coincide today.'

'The curator?' asked Elria, piecing things together for herself.

'Exactly. It is in neither of our interests that he should be in the hands of those Subversive creatures.'

Elria's eyes flashed. 'What makes you think that the Subversives have him?'

'We have just come from your enclave, Elria,' said Triar smoothly as he propped up the bar on the other side of Krelyn. Despite his religious beliefs, he too reached behind the bar and snatched a bottle of the house special. 'What?' he said defensively. 'It's been a hard day.'

'You were going to attack us in our own compound?' asked Elria, evidently impressed. 'I didn't think that you had that kind of courage, Cawdor.'

'In the end, there was no need.' It was true.

'Why are you with these deluded freaks?' asked Elria, leaning in toward Krelyn and dropping her voice. 'Don't the Orlocks hold the Ko'iron Contract these days?'

'Othios is dead, and the Snake Charmers are finished,' said Krelyn flatly.

'As you know,' added Triar concentrating on his drink.

A look of shock flashed over Elria's face, but she said nothing as she processed the news. Then, realising the

necessary conclusion, she spoke. 'We must do something about these Subversives. They may be brutish
and stupid – even for men – but they are powerful. We
should move together.'

Standing between the two gang leaders, Krelyn
picked up her bottle again and drained it into her
mouth. In her head, she was smiling.

'The enemy of my enemy...' said Triar, still not looking across at Elria, leaving the end of his sentence
hanging in the air.

'We are not and will never be friends, Triar of Cawdor,' said Elria. 'But it is within both our interests that
Uglar does not gain anymore power. It was enough
that he felt able to come into the upper levels of Hive
City today – I have never seen him this high before.'

'It seems that he is already powerful enough to deal
with The Coven on its home ground,' said Triar, finally
turning to face Elria, his eyes glinting and blue behind
his mask. He realised that his words were insulting, but
they were also tinged with fear – he knew that Uglar
could take on his Salvationists just as easily, if he was
confident enough to come so high in the city.

'What do we know about this archeotech? What do
we *really* know?' he asked, changing the subject slightly.
'Why would Uglar want it?'

'It is an artefact from the ancient history of the hive,'
replied Elria. 'My information suggests that it locates a
woman at the foundations–'

'A Ko'iron woman,' interrupted Krelyn.

'Even leaving aside the obvious and terrible blas-
phemy of what you are saying,' said Triar, only half
joking, 'would such an item really grant Uglar any
more power?'

'It certainly seems that he thinks so,' said Krelyn, and
the others nodded. 'After all, our information is

incomplete. Only the curator really knows what's down there – he's the only one who could really understand that stupid book. Can we take the risk?'

Triar and Elria stared at each other along the bar, watching each other's eyes burning in vivid colours. They couldn't believe what they were about to do.

'THE ROCK MOVED, and then you appeared,' explained the man-animal called Ruskin.

Zefer gazed blankly, trying to work out whether the creature was deranged, or whether he simply found himself in a deranged place. Instinctively, his hand worked its way up his other sleeve, feeling for the envelope that he had tucked into his undergarments. He needed to know that there was a way home, if he ever made it out of this little cell.

'The rock moved?' asked Zefer, deciding to play along.

'Yes. And from the bright light beyond, you came. You are Kuhnon?' said the crawling figure hopefully, reaching out for Zefer's feet with its hands.

Zefer recoiled, but there was nowhere to go. 'What?' he kicked himself mentally for saying that again. 'Kuhnon? Who is Kuhnon?'

'You. You are Kuhnon. You come from the light and you bring the light with you. You will lead the Ratskins into the lost Garden of the Slump.' The creature had a hold of Zefer's ankles and was just lying there on the floor clutching them.

'Um,' said Zefer. Despite his disorientation, he was reasonably certain that we wasn't called Kuhnon, and that he didn't know where anything called the Garden of the Slump might be. The last few days had been such a blur, however, and it wouldn't surprise him that much to learn that he was wrong about this. Reality was something that seemed to be slipping through his fingers at the moment.

'Where is this garden?' asked Zefer, deciding to fix his attention on a practical problem.

'Ruskin can show Kuhnon,' said the ratskin, rolling himself back onto his heels and looking up at Zefer with huge reflective eyes.

Staring down at the man-animal, an image flashed through Zefer's mind. He could see figures just like it cowering on the ground as one of their brethren was run through by the spiked ram on the front of Prince Jurod's battle-bike. In the caverns of his memory, he could hear the echoing giggles of Princess Gwentria: 'That's my brother! Doesn't he look wonderful! He killed them all you know...'

The squalid little cell wasn't quite as glamorous as the shimmering corridor in Gwentria's palace, and Ruskin didn't seem as dangerous or evil as the man-beasts in the epic fresco. Zefer struggled to remember his response to the picture when he had first seen it – he recalled a vague sense of awe, but now it just seemed farcical.

Slouching back against the wall, Zefer realised that something was changing in him. His world had been turned upside down, and his mind was spinning into spirals with it. He clutched his head into his hands, trying to stabilise his thoughts with sheer pressure. But he froze and then pulled his hands away from his face; his left arm was pulsing with a radiant green. He could actually see the blood vessels throbbing through the leather of his coat. Frantically, he scratched and clawed at the sleeve, hoping without hope that the lines of light were simply streams of the bizarre effluent, dripped down from the ceiling. The sleeve was smooth and dry, and the radiance was undimmed.

'Kuhnon,' nodded Ruskin. 'The bringer of light.'

Zefer craned his miraculously healed neck back, and peered up into the darkness of the ceiling. A steady drizzle of the liquid was seeping through a crack in the corner. There was a shallow pool on the ground where he had been lying, and he could still feel the residue on the side of his face where it had dripped into his mouth.

'Did I come from up there?' asked Zefer.

There was no response. Taking his eyes off the little, glowing crack, Zefer turned to face Ruskin, but the ratskin had gone. 'Ruskin?' he called, taking a couple of steps forward, holding out his arms in front of him like a blind man. The glow from his left arm shed just enough light for him to see that he was quite alone.

A sudden and dull boom sounded, and the cell shook. Debris rained down from the low ceiling and a light spray of the glistening liquid sprinkled across his face. Another series of far-off booms rattled the cell, and the delicate spray from the ceiling became a shower. The crack in the corner had expanded and the liquid was gushing through like a waterfall, cascading down the uneven rock of the wall and rapidly collecting into a expanding pool on the floor. Zefer backed away to the other side of the cell, trying to keep his feet out of the liquid. After a few moments, the entire floor was a glowing pool of pale green, and the water level was rising steadily.

PRESSED UP AGAINST the wall of the narrow tunnel, Krelyn could see out of its mouth and into the huge cavern. The Subversives were simply standing their ground around the great pit in the centre, spraying the other tunnels with flame, bullets and bolter shells from their heavy weapons. They stood and absorbed impacts from the hail of slugs that flashed across at them from the tunnels. A few of them were bleeding from bullet wounds on their limbs and abdomens, but none had yet fallen.

On the other side of the cave, Krelyn could just about make out the glint of Triar's silver mask in the shadows. He and his men had followed one of the winding tunnels around to the back of the cavern, twisting and snaking through the rocky substructure of the hive like animals in warrens. With the magnification of her visor thumbed up to maximum, she could see Triar's men preparing a string of grenades, but the cursed blindspot on her goggles prevented her from seeing exactly what sort of grenades they were.

Elria's Coven had split into two groups and they had worked their way around to opposite sides of the cavern in an attempt to catch the Subversives in the crossfire. They had a clutch of autocannons, braced by two women each, that were sending out constant streams of screaming shells, but most of The Coven's gangers carried lighter weapons, and Krelyn could see Elria itching to close the range.

Krelyn herself was not keen to get involved in the fire-fight. She was here for Curator Tyranus and, frankly, didn't really care about the outcome of the battle as long as she could recover her mark. The cavern was too vast and too dark for her to see all of it from the tunnel mouth, and she resigned herself to having to infiltrate the camp itself if she was going to find her man. Pulling her cloak around her as camouflage, she slipped out of the tunnel and dropped down into what looked like a narrow, manmade trench that seemed to have been cut into the floor of the cave. It gave her perfect cover as she crouched with her cloak swept around her.

As she crept through the trench towards the heart of the camp, a series of explosions shook the cavern, and Krelyn knew that Triar had deployed his grenades. She risked a peek over the lip of the trench, and saw the Subversives unmoved in their positions around the pit in the centre. Four or five of them had fallen now, with limbs blown clear of their bodies, but at least two of those were still firing their weapons with whatever limbs and whatever strength they had left. Krelyn had to admit that these were seriously tough gangers, and she wondered why Ko'iron had never thought to offer their precious contract to them. As Uglar stooped down and ripped the firing arm off one of his fallen brothers, casting the arm into the immense fire behind him and spitting off a hail of autocannon fire from the pilfered gun, she realised the answer to her own question. The Subversive on the floor at Uglar's feet roared with pain, and Krelyn realised that he was still alive.

Bizarrely, the body-shock seemed to spur the fallen, dismembered ganger into action, and he jumped to his feet, screaming a guttural call out into the cavern like an injured animal. In a second he was lumbering and running towards Triar's tunnel. But his intention was never to reach the Salvationists. Instead, he stopped suddenly and threw himself onto the ground. As he did so, another explosion shook the ground and the superheated, vaporised remains of the ganger were sprayed back into the faces of his brethren. By throwing himself onto the grenade, he had certainly saved a number of the Subversives. Krelyn was impressed that he had not allowed himself to bleed uselessly to death at the feet of his boss.

As the explosion died down, Triar stood forward of the tunnel with a gleaming silver orb and hurled it forward towards the centre of the cave. Krelyn instantly knew what it was, and she threw herself flat into the trench, pulling her cloak up over her head as a thermal shield.

Uglar watched the plasma grenade spin through the air towards him and swore. He yelled an order to his men to scatter and, at the same time, punched the detonator for the charges that he had planted around the great pit.

The Subversives sprinted from their positions and launched themselves into the relative cover of the ruined vehicles that decorated their lair. Seeing their opportunity as the massive gangers scattered, Triar and Elria jumped forward of their tunnels into the cover of the pits that had been hacked into the stone in front of them.

The plasma grenade and the melta-bombs detonated at the same time. If anyone had been watching they would have been blinded instantly by the starburst of plasma that erupted into an orb above the flaming pit, and then they would have been cooked and flattened by the thermal concussion that rippled out from the blast through the cavern. At the same time, they would have seen the melta-bombs detonate in a staccato sequence around the perimeter of the pit, blowing shards of rock into lethal shrapnel and rupturing the little dams that held the flaming liquid out of the channels in the floor. As the plasma ball radiated death into the air from above the flaming pit, tendrils of burning, toxic liquid gushed into torrents through the trenches towards the little pits in the tunnels' mouths.

8: CONVERGENCE

IT WAS UTTERLY dark and the air was thick with dust. In his ears, Triar could hear only the ringing echoes of perforated drums. Suddenly associating the darkness with the piercing pain in his ears, he wondered whether he had been blinded by the plasma explosion. Deaf and blind were not the ideal characteristics of a warrior, especially not of a warrior buried deep in the Subversives' sector of Goliath territory on the cusp of the Underhive.

He rolled over onto his back and searched his pockets for anything that might serve as a temporary light source. His clothes felt unpleasantly damp, and Triar lifted his head to look down over his body. There was a dim, greenish tinge to his cloak and, with his head craned towards it, he could just make out the sweet smell of toxins wafting through the air. The cloak was not giving off enough light for him to see by, but he was sure that other people would be able to see it, if there were any other people still alive in the cavern. Awkwardly, he rolled and shuffled on the ground, slipping his cloak off and laying it out on the ground next to him. He didn't relish the idea of that toxic sludge pressed up against him, but he also didn't relish the idea of Uglar popping a slug into the glowing green target.

Finally, he found a bunch of metallic tubes tucked into his belt and he tugged one free. Unscrewing the cap and clicking the primer, he lobbed the photon flare into a high arc, making sure that it would not detonate close enough to him to give away his position. After a couple of seconds, it exploded with a burst of intense, white light, showering the cavern with brightness as it incinerated its own shell and sizzled slowly back down to the ground.

Squinting and shading his eyes, Triar struggled to make out any shapes in the sudden light, but at least it meant that he wasn't blind. Half closing his eyes this time, he threw another flare along the same path as the last one. When it burst into life in the centre of the cavern, he was looking away from it, around the perimeter of the cave. The tight point of bright light cast heavy, deep shadows throughout the space, stretching the burnt-out wrecks of battle-wagons and bikes into grotesque misshapes. In the few seconds of light, Triar saw the prone forms of Subversives gangers laid out on the cavern floor, and a number of others flopped unceremoniously over the edges of the ruined vehicles. He couldn't tell whether they were dead, but they were certainly not moving. Closer to him, he could see the shapes of a number of cloaked Salvationist gangers, prostrate and broken against the rocks. As the light died, he saw that their cloaks retained some of it as a pale green glow.

'Doesn't look good does it,' came a voice at his shoulder, making him start.

'Krelyn?'

'The same,' she said. She had been sitting behind him and watching his antics with the flares. Clicked to infra-red, she could see pretty well through her visor in the almost complete darkness of the cavern. She could also see that large numbers of the gangers on all sides had been killed by the blasts and the torrents of toxic fluids – their body heat was already ebbing away. Hardly anyone from the upper hive could swim, and about half of Triar's men had drowned as their pit flooded. Of the lucky ones who had managed to vault out of the pit before the waves gushed in, another three or four were fried by the thermal blast from Triar's plasma grenade. Triar himself and a couple of his clos- est aides had made it into the shadow of an upturned battle-wagon, which was now an amorphous lump of melted plasteel, after it had absorbed most of the heat wave directed towards the Salvationist gang leader.

'How many left?' asked Triar, reclining gently against the warm and still slightly soft metal blob at his back. 'How many were saved by the grace of the Undying Emperor?'

Even in the dark Krelyn could see Triar's eyes flash when he mentioned the hallowed name. 'I am not sure about that,' she answered, rising invisibly to her feet, 'but there are about four of you and perhaps the same of Elria's people – they're on the other side of the cave in a similar condition to you. As for the Subversives – maybe fifteen. They're tough slag-shovellers, those guys.'

'What about Uglar?' asked Triar, his voice quivering very slightly at the thought of all the death that had already surrounded him today. When Uglar had unex- pectedly turned up at the Wall and challenged him for the curator from the Spire, Triar had been surprised, but he had actually been pretty pleased at the chance to dance a little with the Subversives. It was not an opportunity that the uphiver gangs got very often, and new opponents were the best way to sharpen one's wits. Had he known that the battle at the Wall would have led to the almost complete eradication of three uphiver gangs and to an apparently suicidal attack in the best-forgotten and hellish depths of the hive, he may have acted differently, for the glory of the Undying Emperor, of course.

'Uglar is fine,' said Uglar.

FLAMING TORCHES FLICKERED around the walls of the cavern and fires burned in the wrecks on the cave floor, filling the space with shadows and an inconstant, warming light. Uglar directed the surviving Subversives to collect up the weapons from the remnants of the Salvationists and The Coven gangs, who had been herded down into the great pit in the centre of the cavern. The liquid that until so recently had filled the huge pit, had all run out of the cave or been evaporated by the tremendous heat of the plasma explosion. The air remained dense with pungent humidity and sulphurous smoke.

Krelyn stood apart from the uphivers, and Uglar appeared to be ignoring her, as though he had either not noticed her presence or simply didn't consider her worth worrying about. This had not escaped the attention of Triar and Elria, who were muttering to each other and throwing glances over towards the venator.

Despite the heavy losses suffered by Uglar, the uphivers were now outnumbered and outgunned by the Subversives. The explosive pit-defences had taken them by surprise, and the plasma grenade that they had hoped would have dealt with the bulk of the Subversives force had actually fried as many of their own gangers. Fighting down in the substructure of the hive turned out to be a completely different enterprise from the often clandestine gang wars that they had fought with each other in Hive City.

From its edge, Uglar watched the uphivers being corralled into the pit. He had dragged the chassis of an old battle-bike over to the lip, and he sat on it now as though it were a throne.

'What–' began Elria, shrugging off the hands of a Subversives ganger and firing her defiant eyes up at Uglar. Her words died in her mouth and the flames dancing in her irises winked out as the ganger punched her squarely in the stomach. She doubled over and collapsed, her dirty blue hair brushing into the dust. Instinctively, Triar stepped forward to catch her, but the Subversive brought his foot round is an arc and smashed it into the side of Triar's head.

'No questions,' said the ganger simply. From his throne, Uglar looked down and laughed.

'What will you do with them?' asked Krelyn, approaching Uglar quietly from the side. Although she had no idea why she was receiving special treatment, she realised that she still didn't know where the curator was and that she couldn't leave without him. Besides, it seemed very unlikely that Uglar was unaware that she was there. In which case, he obviously had some sort of reason for treating her differently from the others, and she wanted to know what that was.

'You see, venator,' said Uglar, still laughing at his captives in the pit below, 'I told you that Uglar could pound these weak uphivers without your precious artefact! Didn't I tell you?' He turned to face Krelyn and slapped her heartily across her shoulders, as though emphasising his point.

'Erm, yes. Yes, you told me,' said Krelyn uncertainly, searching her memory for any recollections that might corroborate what the giant man was saying.

Uglar paused and stared at Krelyn for a moment, tilting his head slightly to one side as though deep in thought. 'You look different today, venator,' he said.

'Indeed?' replied Krelyn, pulling her impossibly dark cloak more tightly around her to hide her figure. 'Perhaps it is the thrill of the battle?'

For a couple of seconds, Uglar said nothing. He just stared at her. Then, abruptly, he laughed and slapped her again. 'Perhaps, Venator Orphae, perhaps. Battle invigorates us all – you may even have made a Goliath,' he mused, 'if you had been born as a huge man in the bowels of the world!'

Orphae? Krelyn had heard that name before, and her mind raced trying to locate it in her memory. The images and sounds of the last few hours and days cycled back through her brain at a lightning pace. Triar had mentioned the name of another venator, but she was sure that it had been a man's name: Curion. That was it. It was after that, she thought, and her memories fast-forwarded like a movie, clicking into normal speed as she remembered leaning up against the bar in the Fresh Air talking with Elria for the first time: *I am acquainted with a colleague of yours. Venator Orphae?*

'You're too kind,' said Krelyn, unsure of what else she could say in response to that.

Clearly, Orphae's most important characteristics in Uglar's mind were the facts that she was a venator and that she was a woman. Both of these things must be pretty unusual to a Goliath; the Delaque are not well known for their rugged enjoyment of the brutalities of the substructure. For them, delight is found in the more subtle and sinister arts of death and deception. If there was a gang-house that could truly bridge the social divide of the Wall, it would be the politicking Delaque.

Besides, realised Krelyn suddenly, it is really dark down in Uglar's territory, and venators must be almost impossible to see, hidden under their light-absorbing cloaks, with half their face obscured by their visors. No wonder the Goliaths were so brash and bold with their hair, tattoos and piercings – otherwise they wouldn't be able to tell each other apart except, perhaps, by smell.

Of course, Elria seemed to have assumed that Krelyn would know Orphae, just because they were both women. And Triar had assumed that she would know Curion, just because they were both venators. They had all been wrong, just like Uglar. At least he had the excuse of not getting out much, and of the dark. It seemed that everyone had their blinkers when it came to House Delaque, which was the finest possible testament to their ability to maintain an aura of sinister mysteriousness.

'You too have been kind, venator. I should thank you for your counsel. Without it, things may have turned out differently.' He was still distracted by the events in the pit, since Triar and Elria had now launched themselves at the Subversives ganger who had struck them, and the three of them were rolling about the pit-floor in a brawl. The other Subversives down there had formed a cordon between the rest of the uphivers and the fight, which they were watching enthusiastically.

'Just doing my job,' replied Krelyn, remembering the official line that she used to give whilst she was still part of the Red Snakes of House Delaque. As she said the words, a realisation stuck her like a branding iron. Orphae must have been a double agent – working as an informant for both Elria and Uglar. If this were true, it could only mean that the venator masters in the Red Snakes and in House Delaque itself were manoeuvring somewhere in the shadows. She wondered whether they knew that she was back in town.

'So, what are you going to do with the curator now?' asked Krelyn, realising at last that the whole affair with the Salvationists and The Coven was actually a sideshow.

'Ah, I'm sure that he'll be dead soon. He is a weak, sappy Spireling, venator, and hardly suited to a life in our cells.' In the pit, Elria had set the Subversive's hair on fire and Triar had a choking grip around his massive neck. Uglar was laughing boisterously now.

'Why not give him to me, if he is of so little importance to you?' asked Krelyn, trying to make the most of the gang leader's good humour.

A weak cheer rose out of the pit, making Krelyn look down. Triar and Elria lay panting on the ground, exhausted but alive. The Subversive was motionless, face down in the dirt, with charred and melted skin dropping off his head. The cheer, such as it was, had been raised by the remaining uphivers, although they instantly regretted it as the cordon of Subversives turned back to face them.

'These uphivers are too weak to make good sport,' complained Uglar. 'It took both of those to kill Burgla, and he is the weakest of us. And those are their leaders, aren't they? It's pathetic.'

As he spoke, he stood out of his throne and vaulted down into the pit, thudding heavily as he landed. 'I will fight you all at once!' he yelled. 'Blades only. This is an ancient Goliath fighting pit – it is an arena for warriors. To the victor go the spoils!'

Triar and Elria struggled to climb back onto their feet, leaning against each other for support. Meanwhile, their gangers struggled with each other to get to the back of the group, as the huge figure of Uglar strode heavily across the pit towards them.

'I will fight you, Uglar of Goliath!'

The shout made everybody freeze. Uglar stopped walking and turned slowly. All eyes tracked up the far side of the pit to the source of the voice. And there, standing on top of Uglar's makeshift bike-throne, was Krelyn, flickering in and out of visibility as her cloak fluttered around her in the drafty cave.

'Venator Orphae?' boomed Uglar. 'Why should I fight you?'

Elria strained her eyes in the darkness, struggling to see whether it was really the treacherous Orphae. It suddenly made sense: she was the one who betrayed the location of the roof-entrance to The Coven enclave. But it didn't really look like her.

'I am Krelyn Delaque of the Noble House of Ko'iron, and I will fight you. To the winner the spoils.' announced Krelyn with calm confidence.

Uglar laughed. 'What? You're who of what? What do you offer if you lose?'

'I can offer your Subversives the Ko'iron Contract – something that both of your prisoners down there would kill each other for.'

'Never heard of it!' countered Uglar. 'Never heard of the Ko'iron. They must be a distant and weak people. But I'll fight you just for the novelty. Then, when I win, I'll get these two to try and kill each other for it, like you say.'

HER CLOAK BALLOONED out behind her as she sprung down into the pit, slowing her fall so that she looked as though she were floating. As her feet touched the ground, she jumped again, letting the grav-shooter in her cape reduce her effective weight. She seemed to bounce, flipping up into the air to a height similar to that of the pit's edge, turning a slow somersault and landing again on the far side of the pit, a short distance from the group of uphivers.

Uglar watched her display with a grin. He didn't really care who this person was – whether it was Orphae, Krelyn or Gerontius Helmawr himself. The way she flipped and leaped around the arena actually made his mouth water in anticipation. 'Are you going to fight or dance?' he bellowed playfully.

In response, Krelyn kicked back up into the air and angled herself towards the giant Goliath in the centre of the pit. As she headed back down to ground, she saw Uglar hold out his hand to the side. One of his gangers tossed him a long, broad and heavy looking sword and, as he caught it, he stepped back so that he could bring it to bear when Krelyn landed before him.

He timed his swing well, starting his horizontal arc before she landed so that the huge blade would cleave her through the stomach as her feet hit the ground. But she twisted in the air, flicking her cloak like a rudder and redirecting her flight slightly to throw off the giant's timing. As she hit the ground, she ducked into a roll, and Uglar's blade whipped through the air above her head, taking some folds out of her cloak but leaving her otherwise unscathed.

Before he could bring his hack under control, Krelyn was back up on her feet behind him. She spun and flicked out with a short dagger, plunging it into Uglar's lower back where his kidneys should be. He roared and spun, bringing his great blade round in a driven crescent. But Krelyn was already a metre out of range and the sweep served only to turn Uglar himself; Krelyn was standing casually, as though waiting for him to do something.

Hefting his sword into one hand, Uglar reached the other one around behind his back, feeling for the wound. As he drew it back, he lifted his bloody fingers to his face and wiped them against the adamantium of his jaw.

'Not bad, venator,' he barked, realising that he may have a serious contender on his hands.

With a roar, he lunged forward with his blade, trying to close the gap on the woman. Krelyn sprung backwards, maintaining a zone of safety between her and the tip of the blade. As she jumped, she tucked her hand into her fatigues and slipped one of the little, strapped knives between her fingers.

Uglar lunged again, breaking into a roaring charge towards the venator, trying to prevent her from maintaining her safe distance. But again Krelyn skipped backwards, much lighter on her feet than the giant who lumbered towards her. As she stepped back, she whipped her hand forward and released the little knife. It flipped end over end until it slit into Uglar's chest, burying itself completely through the half-healed gash that Triar had left there at the Wall.

The Subversives' boss roared in frustration and batted blindly at his chest, trying to dislodge the blade that had already sunk into one of his lungs. As he roared, he coughed, and a mouthful of blood vomited out onto the pit-floor.

He knew that he needed to close the range – he couldn't let the nimble venator use her speed and these sneaky projectiles. He needed to get in close and overpower her. He lowered his chest and bent forward to hide the gaping wound there, and prowled from side to side, advancing slowly and pushing Krelyn towards the sheer wall of the pit.

After only a few steps, Krelyn had nowhere to go and she knew it. She didn't have enough space for a big jump – the giant would hack her down before she left the ground. As her retreating foot crunched up against the wall, she knew that she had to do something. Without much hope, she whipped out a couple more throwing knives and darted them at Uglar. One stuck into his exposed shoulder, just inside his collarbone, but he swatted the other one away with a grumpy flick of his sword.

Her hands were empty now, and Uglar saw his chance. He pushed his sword out over his right shoulder and stepped forward, bringing the immense blade slicing down and across his body as he closed the gap to nothing.

Uglar had committed himself now, and Krelyn saw her chance. Ducking down to her left, she rolled forward towards the huge ganger, tugging long-bladed daggers from her boots with each hand as she went. She streaked under the descending arc of the broad sword and emerged at Uglar's right shoulder, dragging her two blades through his ribs as she rushed past and out in the middle of the pit once again.

The gang leader bucked like a wounded beast, throwing his head back and screaming into the darkness of the great cavern. The tip of his heavy sword scraped a diagonal grove through the rock-face where Krelyn should have been and then buried itself in the ground.

With blood gushing out between his ribs and dribbling down his chest, Uglar yanked the blade free and turned to face Krelyn again. He was dragging the tip of the heavy sword along the ground now, as though the strength to lift the mighty weapon had deserted him. His posture was broken and slumped, as he tried to hold his body in a position that didn't rely on any of the lacerated muscles. As he staggered forward, he stumbled slightly and coughed, and blood started to spill over the edge of his metal jaw.

Krelyn stood in the centre of the pit, holding her two curving daggers in an elegant combat pose, with one horizontally before her and the other pointing forwards over her head. She stared at Uglar and met his smouldering brown eyes. He growled, almost half-heartedly, trying to maintain his momentum, but Krelyn simply shook her head.

'It's over, Uglar,' she said simply and without venom. It was just an observation.

'Ss not 'ver,' managed Uglar in response, pulling himself upright despite the agony.

As the Subversives gang leader broke into his final charge, Krelyn seemed to see the whole thing in slow motion. He came lumbering towards her, his head thrown back with blood and a tremendous roar spilling out of his mouth. His huge sword was chambered over his right shoulder, ready for a last great hack, and his eyes were fixed on the impenetrable darkness of Krelyn's visor.

Krelyn flourished her blades and reholstered them, breaking into a charge herself. As she ran towards the lumbering beast, she flicked out a cluster of throwing knives, exhausting the supply strapped to her thighs. Then she dropped into another roll, reclaiming her curved daggers from her boots, and plunged them forward as her spin brought her up onto her knees.

Looking up from her crouch, she could see the bulging eyes of Uglar staring straight down at her, as he leant his weight forward against her hands, with her daggers buried up to their hilts in his stomach. His chest was peppered with throwing knives and there was one sticking out of his forehead.

Slowly and without strength, the great sword fell from his right shoulder, clattering to the ground behind Krelyn. The last of Uglar's strength bled out of him and his massive weight fell forward, forcing Krelyn to duck out from underneath him or be crushed by his bulk. He crashed down onto the pit-floor, his weight driving the knives straight through him, so that their tips protruded out of his back.

A constant stream of blood coursed out of his metal mouth, but his eyes still twitched with the last residue of life. Krelyn touched her knee to the ground next to the giant's head.

'When you look up, there is nothing but the sky,' she whispered.

'Ss 'ver now,' replied Ulgar. Then he died.

THERE WAS ALMOST complete silence in the cavern, and Krelyn could actually hear the hiss and crackle of the fires that provided the flickering light. Not quite knowing what kind of reaction to expect from the gangers, she decided to take her time. She rolled Uglar over onto his back and dug her knives out of his body, wiping them one at a time on her ragged cloak and repositioning them under the various straps on her legs.

When she stood up from the corpse and turned to face the others, she could see that they were just as uncertain about how to proceed as she was. The Subversives had dropped down onto their knees and were staring fixedly into the dirt, although it wasn't clear whether this was out of respect for their dead boss or out of reverence for her. The Coven and the Salvationist gangers just looked stunned, staring at her wide eyed as though she had just performed a miracle.

Krelyn decided to take the initiative.

'To the victor go the spoils,' she said, trying to sound assertive. 'This is the way of the fighting pit. You!' she called, hoping that one of the Subversives would look up.

A couple of heads lifted to look at her, and she pointed directly at one of them. 'You are now my second,' she said, hoping that she had picked a good one. The gargantuan man looked from side to side and then back at Krelyn. He pointed at his own chest like he was asking a question. 'Yes, you. Now, tell me where the prisoner is.'

The hesitant ganger clambered to his feet and bowed uncertainly. Then he rushed towards the side of the pit, where he paused and turned back to face Krelyn again. She realised that she would have to follow him, but she was not entirely confident that could leave Triar and Elria unsupervised. Both of them must have been a little surprised by recent revelations, and she didn't want them to transform their surprise into violence.

'The rest of you,' she called, calmly but firmly, 'stay here and watch them.'

With that, the other Subversives gangers were on their feet and reforming their cordon around the uphivers as though nothing had changed. Evidently, they were relieved to have something to do, no matter who told them to do it. It seemed that the victor really did get the spoils, in a refreshingly honest and uncomplicated way.

Krelyn walked off with her new second. As they wandered towards the edge of the great cavern, she tried to strike up a conversation with the man, but he would not be drawn on any subjects. He would not even reveal his name, and Krelyn began to wonder whether the man actually had any capacity for speech at all. She supposed that eloquence was not the most highly prized trait amongst the Goliaths, although Uglar had actually been quite charming, in his own distinct way.

The man suddenly stopped moving and pointed down at the ground.

'There?' asked Krelyn, looking down at the rough but featureless rock on the floor at the very edge of the cave. 'The prisoner is down there?'

The dumb man just stood there and nodded.

'Very well,' continued Krelyn, trying to encourage him, 'Can I see him?'

Again, the man nodded, but this time he also bent down and picked up a long metal bar from the ground. He proceeded to jam this bar into an almost imperceptible crack in the rock. Standing behind the bar, the man gripped hold of it and threw himself backwards towards the ground, dragging the rod down with him. As he did so, a huge slab of rock dislodged from the floor, defining itself as it lifted out of the ground. The man paused, drove the rod even deeper into the crack, and then threw himself down once again. After a few such exertions, the slab had been prised out of the ground, and the man rocked his shoulder against it to move it aside.

'Help! Please, somebody, anybody, help!' The voice sprang out from under the slab with a burst of green light as the slab was gradually moved out of the way.

Down below, in a small pool of stinking green effluent, Krelyn finally caught sight of Zefer, squinting at the relatively bright light that suddenly flooded his cell. He was splashing about in the glowing liquid and spitting mouthfuls of it. From the look of the water level, there couldn't have been much room down there for him to breathe whilst the huge ceiling slab had been in place.

'Curator Tyranus of House Ko'iron librarium?' asked Krelyn politely, reaching down her hand to help him out of the pool.

'What?' said Zefer, absolutely stunned to be greeted so formally. 'Y-yes,' he said, spitting slime and treading

water. 'That's me, yes. Have you come to help me? I did
wonder when my help might arrive. I rather thought
that I would have met you at the Wall–'

'Shut up,' said Krelyn sharply, grabbing hold of his
outstretched arm and dragging him out of the cell. She
had already forgotten how hideously officious and
pathetic people from the Spire could be. 'It is enough
that we have met now,' she said as he flopped down
onto the dry ground. She didn't have the heart to tell
him that she was really an insurance policy rather than
an assistant. Frankly, if she had never told Prince Jurod
that she had been his baby-sitter whilst he went round
pretending to be an Underhive hunter, she felt no com-
pulsion to disillusion this bedraggled bureaucrat.

'Let's get you dried out, and then we should get moving. This is no place for the likes of you, curator,' said
Krelyn, helping Zefer back to his feet and leading him
over to the fires next to the pit in the centre of the cavern.

'I HAVE TO confess,' said Zefer, huddled up next to the
fire, 'that I'm not entirely sure where we are… not, not
exactly.'

The green liquid was gradually evaporating from
Zefer's clothes, and it gave off an awful stink as it did
so. Krelyn was sitting on the other side of the fire, in an
attempt to keep the stench at tolerable levels. She was
watching him mumble to himself as he dried, and she
thought he looked slightly different from the Curator
Tyranus that she had been watching for years back in
the Spire. It could have been that her perceptions had
shifted after being back in the HC for a while, but it
was equally possible that being out of the Spire for the
first time in his life had done something to the curator
himself.

'We are in the domain of the Subversives, a Goliath gang, just on the cusp of the Underhive itself,' explained Krelyn through the flames.

'The Goliaths?' asked Zefer, not sure what she was talking about.

'These giant, barbarian warriors,' replied Krelyn, shaking her head. She had been through so much to keep track of this man, and he didn't even know who the main gangs were in the hive. Still, she supposed, that was not his skill – that was not why he was important. He was significant in this affair because he was a curator and a scholar, not because he was a great explorer or a warrior. Each has their place, she reminded herself.

'And it is better to be well defined at the top than lost in the paradoxes of foundations,' added Zefer, as though in response to her thoughts. 'Unless it isn't.'

'What?' snapped Krelyn, disarmed. 'What did you say?'

'It's from *The Paradoxes of the Spire*, a book I have been studying. Have you heard of it?' replied Zefer innocently.

'Yes, yes. I've heard of it. But *why* did you say that just then?' persisted Krelyn.

'Because you said that each has their place, and I was reminded of those lines from the book. I remember that they were very confusing for me when I was in the librarium, but their meaning has become much clearer since I set off on this little adventure,' he explained.

'But, curator, I didn't *say* that each has their place.' Krelyn was on her feet now and moving round to Zefer's side of the fire.

'What?' Zefer kicked himself again mentally for saying that. 'What do you mean? Of course you said it. Who else could have said it?' he wondered, looking around.

'I didn't say it, and neither did anybody else.' She was genuinely unnerved now, and not entirely sure that this was Zefer at all. She had heard legends about strange creatures in the Underhive who could take on the form of anything or anyone they consumed. Such creatures were said to be telepathic, luring their victims to their doom with reassuring platitudes injected directly into their minds.

'What happened to your arm?' she asked, pointing. Most of the greenish fluid had dried now, but his left arm was still aglow, as though the veins from his shoulder to his finger tips pulsed with light.

Zefer shrugged and reached the arm out towards her. 'I don't know,' he answered honestly, as Krelyn stepped back cautiously. 'It happened when they put me in that cell. I thought that it might have had something to do with the water.'

'Has anything else changed?' asked Krelyn, fingering the hilt of a dagger under her fatigues. This didn't look good at all.

'No, I don't think so. But my neck feels much better now, and I think that my ribs have healed.' Zefer seemed genuinely cheerful about it.

'Curator, do you know what wyrds are?' she asked carefully.

A cry from the fighting-pit made them both turn. Triar was standing forward of the gangers and pointing up towards the fire around which the two servants of Ko'iron sat. His tarnished silver mask danced with firelight and his eyes burnt with a searing intensity.

'Mutant and witch!' he was pointing at Zefer, who looked all around in fear, as though trying to see who the Redemptionist might be talking about.

The other Salvationist gangers were on their feet, and the Subversives were peering up to the edge of the pit with anxiety on their faces. Triar may have been a fire-brand of righteousness in the uphives, bringing the judgement of the Undying Emperor to those wyrds who showed even the slightest signs of their powers – people like Elria, who was a genuine pyromaniac. But down here in the depths of the hive, the Subversives had to deal with creatures far more terrifying than telepaths and weakling pyros. All of the wyrds from the upper levels who were too mutated or too powerful to pass as ordinary citizens would eventually find their way down here, where the short arm of the authorities would not bother to look for them. When a Goliath ganger yelled 'mutant,' he really meant it.

'We have to get out of here, now,' said Krelyn, gripping Zefer by his glowing arm and almost dragging him off towards the edge of the cavern. Down in the pit, she could hear the arguments erupting between the remnants of the three gangs but, worse than that, she could hear the bracing of weapons. Even if they didn't all come after them, at the least she could expect a hunting party of Subversives on their tail.

You'd better be worth all this fuss, she thought as she half dragged and half carried Zefer in an attempt to get him to move faster.

'Yes, I hope so too,' said Zefer. He meant it.

Krelyn stopped abruptly. 'I didn't say anything!'

She let go of his arm and dropped her hands onto her hips. She stared at him, watching him shift uneasily from one foot to the other, seeing his obvious discomfort in his surroundings and his complete obliviousness about the danger he was in. The thing that worries you most, she thought, is probably that you're wrong about your interpretation of that bloody book.

'Yes, that does worry me,' he said, nodding anxiously. 'But I'm sure that I'm right,' he rallied, puffing out his chest in pathetically false bravado.

It certainly seemed like him. It would be a weird wyrd creature that would not only take on the form of this curator but also his neuroses.

She shook her head in resignation, and the sound of at least twenty pairs of boots pounding up the edge of the fighting pit made her reach out to grab Zefer once again. 'We have to go,' she said, with calm determination.

'What's that?' asked Zefer, pointing into the shadows where the floor met the wall of the cavern.

'Curator, come. We don't have time for…' She trailed off. 'That,' she said, 'is hope.'

'But he is a mutant!' cried Triar, addressing all the gangers in the pit. 'We cannot suffer him to live. It is the will of the Undying Emperor that heretics must be exterminated.'

'Boss lady said to keep you here,' said the most vocal of the Subversives' guards. 'We keep you here.'

'But she's not really your boss. Don't you understand about vengeance?' asked Triar rhetorically. 'Vengeance is what makes us human. It is what places us above the level of animals. It is what makes us the chosen of the Undying Emperor himself.'

Triar was never one to miss the chance to preach, and this sermon might also have the advantage of saving his life.

'The venator killed Uglar! She killed him.'

'That is the way of the fighting pit, as it has been since ancient times,' said the ganger simply, as though he was repeating something that he had heard many times before. 'To the victor go the spoils. We are the spoils, see.'

'But she was deceitful in the pit. She fought with hidden blades and throwing knives, not with the honour of a Goliath warrior.' Triar had no idea whether the Subversives had a sense of honour in this way, but it was worth a shot. He fixed the ganger with his sparkling blue eyes and explained: 'This wasn't the fighting pit of old, it was a Delaque trick to free the mutant.'

The Subversives didn't cheer or speak, and their expressions hardly seemed to change at all. Then, one of them nodded, and the others started to hand the confiscated weapons back to the uphivers.

'You're right. Uglar was a good boss. We will kill the cheating venator and her mutant lackey.' With that, the Subversives turned and ran out of the pit, collecting an array of autocannons, bolt guns and chainswords from the pit-wrack as they went.

As Triar checked his weapon, Elria strode up to him and pulled his mask clear of his face. 'I do not share your feelings about the mutant, Triar, but the venator woman has deceived The Coven. We will hunt with you until she is dead. Then you are on your own. The artefact is now fair game.'

'I do not seek your help in this, witch–' began Triar.

'I can see into your eyes,' interrupted Elria, gazing deeply and closely. 'Do not cross me about wyrds.'

KRELYN HEFTED THE weapons onto her back and stuffed the grenades into a munitions bag that she slung over her shoulder. Zefer stood around, kicking his feet together and looking back towards the growing chorus of shouts and yells that were emerging from the pit.

'Don't worry, I'll carry them,' said Krelyn dryly.

Zefer nodded.

With the weapons loaded up, Krelyn ducked down into the nearest exit tunnel and disappeared into the darkness. A couple of seconds later, her face reappeared in the tunnel mouth.

'Come on,' she said to Zefer, who had still not moved.

An abrupt shout from further back in the cavern was followed by the rattle of gunshots and a dusting of rock from the wall around the tunnel mouth. Zefer turned and looked back.

'Are they shooting at us?' he asked.

'Yes, they're shooting at us,' yelled Krelyn as she grabbed hold of Zefer's sleeve and pulled him into the tunnel. Without letting go of his sleeve, Krelyn dragged Zefer around and pushed him out in front of her so that she could drive him along through the tunnel.

'Move!' But Zefer wasn't moving.

'Move!'But Zefer still didn't move. Instead he seemed to be talking to someone further along in the tunnel, but Krelyn couldn't hear what was being said. It was as though only half the noise of their voices was actually vocalised. It was little more than a sequence of rasping breaths.

'What are you doing?' asked Krelyn, pushing Zefer aside to see who he was talking to.

She flicked her visor to infra-red and saw a figure crouched in the darkness. It looked only vaguely human, with a strangely elongated head, as though an animal's jaw-bone had been grafted on. The man-animal was sitting on its ankles and staring up at Zefer with unnaturally big eyes, leaning its weight forward on a staff. It was huffing and mumbling incoherently, and showing no signs of having noticed Krelyn at all.

'What's that?' she asked, shoving Zefer in the arm to get his attention.

'What?' said Zefer, cringing again at his choice of word. 'It's Ruskin. He says that he knows a good place for us to hide, and that we should follow him.'

'When did he say that?' asked Krelyn, confused and suspicious.

'Just now. You must have heard him too. He really is terribly articulate, isn't he, considering he appears to be an animal of some kind?'

'We don't have time for this now,' said Krelyn, checking back over her shoulder and hearing the rush of footsteps approaching. 'We have to get out of here.'

Ruskin nodded and turned. He beckoned to Zefer, took a few steps forward, and then seemed to vanish into the wall of the tunnel. Pushing from behind, simply eager to keep moving, Krelyn bundled Zefer along to the vanishing point. The darkness was severe, so she scanned the walls urgently with her thermal sensors, but she found nothing.

'Where did he go?' she asked, her voice tinged with exasperation. As she spoke an arm seemed to reach out of the wall itself and drag them both through it.

9: METASTASIS

THE NARROW TUNNEL twisted and snaked through the rocky substructure of the downhive, growing lower and more constricted as it went. To get through, Krelyn had swung her weapons around in front of her and stooped forward, ducking under the jagged rocks that jabbed down from the uneven ceiling. She praised the Emperor for her infra-red visor, without which she would surely have brained herself against the roof. The odd, man-animal guide could clearly see in the pitch-blackness, and he kept disappearing ahead of them, only to be found sitting patiently in the meandering tunnel, waiting for them. And, somehow, Zefer managed to wander on through the darkness, avoiding all of the dangers without any apparent effort, muttering and grunting in response to noises from Ruskin.

They had lost their hunters almost instantly. A few bursts from a shotgun had smashed into the wall next to them as Ruskin had pulled them through into the concealed side-tunnel, and Krelyn had been able to hear the crashes and punches of frustration as the hunting party had been unable to work out where they'd gone. Rattles of gunfire had ricocheted down after them once or twice, but she was confident that these shots were just flukes – the angry discharge of hunters who had lost their prey.

After what seemed like an hour of walking, Krelyn turned a sharp corner in the passageway and came to an abrupt halt. As far as she could see, she had hit a dead-end. She pressed her hands up against it, not willing to trust her eyes after the incident in the tunnel off the Subversives' cavern, but it was solid and cold. It looked as though the passageway ran through a fault line, and there had been a vertical slip at some point that had severed the passage in two.

Looking around, there was no sign of Zefer or Ruskin, and she sighed loudly, slouching back against the side of the tunnel, needing the rest in any case. Typical, she thought, shaking her head.

'Are you coming?' It was Zefer's voice.

Krelyn pushed herself off the wall and looked around again. 'Where are you?'

'Down here,' came the reply.

Peering down through the darkness, Krelyn saw a narrow slit at the base of the stone wall that blocked the tunnel. Faintly, perhaps ten metres below, she could see the pale green glow of Zefer's mutant arm – it was waving happily. The crevice was only just wide enough for a human body to slip through, and it was almost invisible, unless you knew exactly where to look. Even then, had Zefer's radiant arm not been showing her the way, Krelyn doubted that she would have found it without falling in and breaking her neck.

Remembering Zefer's clumsy and near fatal attempts to climb down from the Ko'iron librarium's exit tunnel, Krelyn could not help but laugh as she dropped the weapons down to him. How in Necromunda did he ever make it down through there?

'I'm not sure,' replied Zefer, as though responding to her thoughts. 'It just seemed like the best thing to do.'

With all of the weapons safely down, Krelyn took a final look behind her in the tunnel and then jumped, pulling her arms and legs flat so that she would drop like a dart through the narrow fissure.

The tunnel below was just like the one above, as though it had indeed once been part of the same passageway. By the time Krelyn held her hands out for the weapons, still looking around her for some sign of Ruskin, Zefer had already slung a couple of the heavy guns onto his own back, and he was slipping a string of grenades into the custom pouches around his belt. Without a word, he handed the remaining equipment over and then started off into the darkness.

'How can you see where you're going,' asked Krelyn, struggling to keep up with the curator in the perfect black.

'I look,' replied Zefer curtly, as though the question made no sense at all. His manner had changed significantly, and Krelyn noticed that the guns on his back had been strapped combat-fashion, for quick access.

'But it's so dark,' she insisted, ducking under a sudden and vicious drop in the roof level, which Zefer had navigated without comment or visible hardship.

'Is it? It's not too bad,' said Zefer. 'We must catch up with Ruskin. It would not do to lose him now.' With that, Zefer seemed to click up a gear, and he started to pull away from Krelyn, who was moving as fast as she could in the restrictive environment.

After a few minutes, Krelyn was on her own, struggling forward under the weight of the weapons, banging them against the narrow walls, and concentrating hard on keeping her head on her shoulders whilst not falling down any of the apparently bottomless potholes in the floor. Zefer had vanished into the darkness up ahead. Clearly he was not suffering the same problems as her. Only a few hours ago, the curator had been utterly oblivious about what a gun even looked like, and a few days ago he had been a gibbering wreck of a bureaucrat in the Spire, but now he seemed fitter and more confident than a Delaque venator.

Rounding another bend, Krelyn saw Zefer and Ruskin sitting on opposite sides of the tunnel, Zefer leaning on the barrel of a shotgun with his green arm, and Ruskin propping himself against his staff. Behind them was the faint glow of a fire, which must have been in a cavern further along the passageway. The pale light presented the conversationalists as silhouettes, and seemed to carry their grunting and hissing discussion through the tunnel towards Krelyn.

'Ah, Krelyn!' exclaimed Zefer climbing to his feet at the sight of her. 'Let me help you with those.' He strode confidently towards her and reached out to relieve her of the weapons on her back.

'I'm fine, thanks,' she said, suspicious of his latest mood change, shrugging his hands off and trudging forward towards the light. She was reasonably sure that she had not told him her name.

BURNING LIKE SAPPHIRES in the darkness of the tunnel, Triar's eyes scanned the walls. He could see the impacts left in the ceiling from the shotgun blasts that had chased their prey, but there were no such marks on the side wall.

Behind him, the Subversives were raging, stamping their feet and smashing their fists against the other walls, firing their weapons in frustration. Great clouds of debris crashed down from the low ceiling, dislodged by their fury, making the already confined space seem even more claustrophobic.

Elria came running back along the main tunnel – she and her Coven had run on ahead in case the escapees had gone that way.

'Nothing,' she said simply, with bright red light spilling out of her eyes into the dust riddled air.

In the strips of red light, Triar saw the dust and debris swirl. The air in the tunnel was being disrupted by a side-draft, not simply being sucked along in a line. He turned back to the wall that had no shotgun marks in it, and he reached out a hand to push it, wondering whether there was perhaps a concealed doorway.

He leant forward and met no resistance at all, stumbling through into a side-tunnel. From behind him he could hear the shocked cries from the gangers, wondering where he'd gone. Mumbling under their noise, Elria's voice muttered something about hypocrites and wyrds.

A second later, and Elria herself stepped through alongside Triar, pushing her arm through tentatively at first.

'Very clever,' she said. 'I have seen many concealed doors before, but this is the first time that I have seen a concealed opening.'

'Obviously a trick of the light,' commented Triar, not convinced.

'Or of the shadows.'

THE TUNNEL OPENED out into a hab-dome, of the kind that Krelyn had thought only existed in the uphive. It was rather smaller than those found higher up, but its huge vaulted structure was similar in design. Unlike the epic domes of the Spire or even the upper HC, the roof was clearly visible, perhaps no more than fifty metres from the ground at its apex. Giant cracks ripped through the structure, and rains of dust and liquid

effluent sprinkled down into the cavern. The rain and
the cracks themselves were lit with an uneven green
light of the kind that radiated from Zefer's arm, casting
the whole scene into a pale and noxious aura.

Ruskin seemed to spit and gargle as he pointed his
staff out over the vista, and Zefer nodded appreciatively, burbling some kind of guttural noise in
response.

At least half the dome was made up of a lake. The
water was smooth and calm for the most part,
although it shimmered with the drizzle of impacts
from the effluvial rain. In a couple of places on the far
side, where the waters lapped up against the edges of
the dome, huge outflow pipes spilt vast quantities of
liquid into the mix, like waterfalls. Around the out-
flows, the lake swirled and eddied as the rusty, red
waste splashed into the pale green water, stirring up silt
and residue from the lakebed below. A group of boats
circled the waterfalls, and their crews cast nets into the
tumult, dredging the swirling mess for anything that
may have fallen into the waste pipes higher up in the
hive or been dislodged from the bottom of the lake.

Piled into huge mountains around the coastline were
heaps of garbage. Fleets of tugs and barges, belching
smoke from their filthy chimney stacks, constantly
called into these ports and dumped their loads before
setting off back into the lake for more fishing. As they
unloaded, hundreds of figures swarmed over the
mounds of refuse, scrambling and fighting to be the
first to reach the fresh pickings.

Further away from the coast, there was a fair-sized
settlement of, perhaps, fifty or sixty lowrise buildings.
None of them were more than two stories high, and
they were of an uneven, random architecture that
spoke of no design whatsoever. The structures

appeared to have been fashioned out of the garbage found in the lake, thrown together with varying degrees of ingenuity. It was clear, even from the mouth of the little tunnel where Krelyn stood, that many of the buildings had collapsed in the past, but they had just been left as they were, perhaps with some of their most useful parts pilfered and incorporated into other structures.

Something that struck Krelyn straight away was the fact that there appeared to be electricity in the settlement. There were a series of dull, bluish lights punctuating the spaces between the buildings and, at the back of the dome, behind the little settlement, there was a huge chimney that vomited thick columns of smoke into the already thick air. A chain of barges queued up at its base, and huge flares of fire leapt out of a colossal grill that overlooked the water. It was probably a furnace of some kind, generating tiny amounts power and vast quantities of pollution using a steam turbine.

While Krelyn soaked in the view, catching her breath at the end of the tortuous journey through the maze of tunnels, Ruskin and Zefer had fallen to their knees on a little plateau that overlooked the ratskin settlement. Ruskin had planted his staff into the ground before them, like a totem, and the two of them were muttering incomprehensible sounds with their heads bowed.

Not knowing quite what to do, Krelyn just watched them, wondering whether the curator had any idea what he was doing and, if so, how he knew. She had been down into the Underhive a number of times before, mostly to oversee the mock heroics of Prince Jurod during his youthful spyrering adventures. She had even seen ratskin settlements before – although mostly through the red-dot laser sight of a needle rifle. And she had no idea what Ruskin was doing.

After a few moments, Ruskin nodded and climbed back to his feet, leaning heavily against his staff for support. As he turned back to face her, Krelyn saw his features for the first time in the relative light of the dome. He was much, much older than she had thought. Indeed, he looked like an old man, with scars and wrinkles etched into his grimy face. The odd shape of his head turned out to be some sort of headwear – a giant rat skull had been sliced in two and fashioned into a kind of helmet, with the elongated jaw sticking out over the man's face and sheltering his huge black eyes from even the tiniest trace of light.

She could see that he was stooped and supporting his weight on the staff, which had been carefully carved into elaborate, snaking patterns, and decorated with a series of miniature animal skulls. The craftsmanship made her gasp as she realised that the staff would probably be worth a small fortune in the curiosities markets of Helmawr Boulevard, in front of the great Spiral Gates. Seeing it clutched in the hands of this decrepit old ratskin, surrounded by the rubbish and waste of the hive, hardly seemed believable. And yet, it seemed perfectly appropriate.

Ruskin was dressed in a series of furs, tied around his body in patches with an intricate system of cords and twine, and a short cloak dropped down out of the base of the rat-skull on his head. If he were to crouch on the ground, that cloak would cover most of his scrawny body and the skull would distort his head; he would look like one of the giant rats that scavenged around in the badzones.

'We must talk with the elders,' said Zefer, back on his feet. 'They may be able to help.'

With that, Zefer and Ruskin set off down the slope towards the ratskin settlement, leaving Krelyn to collect her thoughts, her breath and her weapons, and to hurry down after them. Things were not developing quite as she had anticipated.

As THE THREE strode through the outskirts of the ratskin settlement, Krelyn started to notice faces appearing in the cracks in walls, between habitation structures, and in doorways. Highly reflective black eyes shone out of the deep shadows, burning red in her infra-red goggles. Ruskin and Zefer seemed to be oblivious to the attention that they were attracting, but it put Krelyn on edge and her arms were tensed, ready to pull round one of the guns from her back at a moment's notice.

The street was criss-crossed with little runnels, in which flowed fine streams of the glowing green liquid. It seemed smoother and less viscous than the liquids that they had encountered up until now, and Krelyn wondered whether the ratskins had some form of filtration system that made the vile substance less noxious, so that they could use it as a form of street lighting. It was possible, she conceded, that this was simply a completely different type of liquid from the others – less volatile and much less pungent. After all, if even she could tell that it was different from the nauseous stuff in the Subversives' cave, then she was sure that there were any number of variations that she couldn't identify. The ratskins, who lived with this stuff everyday of their lives, would probably ridicule her stupidity if she suggested that all of the noxious green slime looked the same to her. In a similar vein, she recalled being staggered when she learnt that it was only the Delaque who had twenty-seven different words for shadows, depending on their density and utility. Looking around her, it wouldn't surprise her at all if the ratskins had even more.

Eventually, the ambling little street opened out into what passed for a town square. It was a relatively open space, devoid of built structures and paved with what appeared to be door-panels salvaged from vehicles. The strange green liquid flooded out underneath the entire space, lighting it eerily from below through all the myriad cracks and joins between the panels. In each of the four corners of the square were vertical pillars, atop which shone pale blue electric lights. The light that they gave off was negligible next to the general glow from the floor, but they added a sense of ceremonial importance to the place.

The most striking feature, however, was a huge column in the very centre of the square. It must have been a couple of metres in diameter and at least ten metres high. Roughly cylindrical, it could have once been the barrel of one of the great cannons that bristled around the very summit of Hive Primus, protecting House Helmawr from air-raids and attacks from outside the hive. But that would have been long, long ago, and the cylinder oozed such an aura of permanence that it seemed to have been rooted down here in the foundations of Necromunda since ancient times. Perhaps it had never seen the heady heights of the Spire. Perhaps it dated from before there was a Spire to protect, when the battles for land in the wastes of Necromunda raged horizontally across its surface rather than vertically into the skies. Krelyn knew that the ratskins sometimes constructed their settlements around sites of ancient archeotech, and built cults around them.

Whatever its origins, the column was now carved into a gradually rotating spiral, as though it had been wrapped diagonally in thick metal rope. Etched into each strand of the spiral were little icons and friezes, depicting battles and what looked like angels. Right in the middle was a panel in the shape of a family crest, but its details were partly eroded and mostly obscured by grime; a hint of a blue K peeked through the dirt. There were images of animals at regular intervals, and the skulls of giant rats had been installed into dedicated alcoves cut into the material of the column itself. In each skull burnt a single, fat candle, which was presumably renewed each day in some sort of ritual.

Sitting before the totemic column in a complicated chair of bone and leather was a hunched and atrophied old woman. Her head was weighed down under the weight of a rat-skull, similar to the one worn by Ruskin, and across her lap she held a sceptre that appeared to be a miniature duplicate of the great pillar behind her. Arrayed around her were perhaps twenty younger men, each standing solidly with what appeared to be shotguns gripped in both hands, as though acting as an honour guard.

Ruskin pushed his arm out in front of Zefer as they entered the square and stopped him from advancing, mumbling something that Krelyn could not understand. He walked forward of the other two, with his staff ringing out metallic notes on the ground. And, as he did so, the old woman prised herself out of her seat and shuffled forward.

'Why have you brought them here, Ruskin?' asked the woman.

Even though Krelyn could not understand a word that she said, her manner was unambiguously displeased.

'He is Kuhnon, bringer of the light, Muridae Roojika,' replied Ruskin, bowing his head as he spoke.

The woman looked shocked and incredulous. 'He is an uphiver! You know what happens when uphivers come into our settlements. Were you followed?'

'No, muridae. We were not followed. The giant sub-hivers called Goliaths gave chase, but they cannot navigate our tunnels,' replied Ruskin, addressing the woman by her ritual title. Roojika the muridae was the settlement's elder, and with her lay responsibility for the community.

'But they are searching for you? They are hunting the ratskin?' challenged Roojika, unconvinced and uncon-soled.

'No, muridae. The hivers did not see Ruskin. Only these two,' he indicated Zefer and Krelyn. 'They will not hunt in the badzones just for two uphivers.'

'I do not like this, Ruskin. You are reckless.'

'But I bring the Kuhnon, muridae. He will lead us into the Garden of the Sump, as it is written,' insisted Ruskin. 'Even had I led the uphiver-predators into the heart of Bandicota, I would have been right.'

'As I said, Ruskin, you are reckless.' Roojika was shuf-fling forward towards Zefer and inspecting him, leaving Ruskin bowed and isolated in the square. As she circled round to Zefer's left, she gasped and staggered back away from him, almost losing her balance. Instinctively, Zefer lunged forward and caught the old woman before she could fall, lowering her gently to the ground for her to recover from her spell. The last time he'd seen an old woman fall, she had been dead by the time he had reached her, and he was pleased that this was not the case now. That old woman had been the first dead body that he had ever seen, and the memory had stuck with him.

'Ask him to show me his arm,' said Roojika breath-lessly, struggling out of Zefer's grasp and appealing to Ruskin.

'You can ask–' began Ruskin, but then he broke off as he saw Zefer release the muridae and hold his arm out for her to see. The glowing green veins pulsed more brightly than ever.

Roojika looked from his arm to his face and back again, incomprehension, dread, and awe competing for positions on her wrinkled face. 'You… you can understand me, uphiver?'

'Of course.' As he spoke, a chorus of mumbled whispers erupted throughout the square, and the crowds that had gathered around the perimeter started to press in closer.

'Tyranus!' yelled Krelyn, snatching a stubgun from her back and racking it. She leapt towards Zefer and then turned her back to him, scanning her weapon along the line of advancing ratskins. 'Tyranus, what's going on here?' She hadn't understood a single word.

'They just want to look at my arm,' said Zefer calmly, turning and pressing down on the barrel of Krelyn's gun to make her drop her sights.

Reluctantly and hesitantly, Krelyn lowered her gun.

'Why don't you listen to what they're saying, instead of leaping to conclusions?' asked Zefer, with an edge of irritation to his voice. 'You're supposed to be looking after me, remember, not the other way round.'

'I am listening, Tyranus.' she snapped, turning on him and shoving him in his chest. She didn't know what was happening to him, but she really didn't need this blithering curator getting out of control. 'I just don't speak ratskin. The real question here is how on Necromunda can you understand them?'

Zefer stumbled backwards and tripped over the muridae, crashing into a heap on the ground. Krelyn watched helplessly as he fell and then turned away in disgust, shaking her head and wondering why she had even bothered with all this. She should have just stayed back in the Spire, spying on curators in the librariums. But as she turned, she stopped short, with dozens of pike-blades and shotgun barrels pointing into her face. She froze.

'Tyranus!'

'IT'S A DEAD END,' said Triar as the others came stooped and stumbling around the corner behind him. The Subversives were finding it hardest, as the constricting and twisting tunnels crushed in on their huge bulks. But their eyes were good, and the dark was not such a problem for them. It was Triar who had bruises and cuts all over his head.

Elria just stared at him, shaking her head in patronising disbelief. 'I should have known better than to follow you.'

'Watch your mouth, witch!' rebutted Triar, striding forward towards her. 'In the bowels of the hive, there are only the eyes of the Undying Emperor to see you die.'

The Coven's leader didn't look scared, but she sunk onto her back leg and let her hand drop to her weapon. In the dark, Triar couldn't really see what she was doing. He could just see the flames in her eyes burning in the blackness.

A sudden explosion rocked the tunnel, throwing the gangers from their feet and dislodging a shower of stone from the ceiling. Before the resonations had even died down, the sound of Subversives whooping and yelling blasted through the passageway, followed by rattles of gunfire and the strafing explosions of munitions.

'No deadend now!' came the call, repeated and chanted like a war-dance.

As Elria and Triar climbed back to their feet, brushing a thick layer of rubble and dust off themselves, they saw the cavorting Subversives ahead in the tunnel, lit by the molten remains of the rock wall that had seemed to block the way. The passage dropped about ten metres down, but then ran off into the darkness. The floor of the passage they were in had slumped, collapsed, and partly melted under the Subversives' onslaught, and a ramp had been formed down to the next level.

Without a word to each other, Elria and Triar pushed past the others to the front of the group and set off down the ramp.

ALL OF THE ratskins from the Bandicota settlement were crammed into the central square. The children had pushed through to the front of the crowd and were sitting in a haphazard circle around the central pillar. Roojika was back in her ramshackle throne, and Ruskin had been accorded a position of honour at her left shoulder, as befitted a totem warrior of his age and standing. Krelyn and Zefer sat next to each other on the steps of the dais on which the two elder ratskins held court.

'The people of Bandicota have always had hope,' began Roojika in a low rumbling voice.

Even though Krelyn could not understand what the ratskin chief was saying, she was still amazed that the people at the back of the crowd could hear her from so far away. Her voice was quiet, and the background clatter of the barges, garbage deposits and the power station almost drowned out the little splutters and coughs, even from where Krelyn was sitting. She had heard that the ratskins had a more intricately evolved sense of hearing, able to track the giant rats that they hunted ceremonially from miles away. It seemed plausible, therefore, that the crowd could filter out the background noise as they listened to their leader. It was also possible, pondered Krelyn, that their speech was only half audible, and that much of the communication was done psychically. Looking around, she noticed that many of the ratskins bore marks of mutation, as she would have expected at this depth in the downhive, and with mutation often came wyrd powers. Despite what the Redemptionists would have people believe, lesser powers such as telepathy were not even that uncommon in Hive City. This was not the first time that Krelyn had wished she was at least slightly wyrd.

'We have always had hope, because we have maintained our memories and lived here in the manifest memories of the Hive Spirit itself,' continued the muridae, her words greeted by murmurs of agreement from the crowd.

'But now, Totem Warrior Ruskin has brought more than hope to his people. He has been wandering the wastes of the badzones for many years, fasting and trekking through the uncharted labyrinths that crawl with rats and foul subhiver-prospectors. Because of his ceaseless industry and constant meditation in praise of the spirits of the hive, our cleric has been rewarded with a prize greater even than his own personal purification. Not only has he earned his own passage to the bright lights of the afterworld, to join his ancestors when his body is finally absorbed back into the foundations of this hive, but he has also been granted a guide to take us all into the Garden of the Sump,' announced Roojika in her understated and slightly breathless way.

As she mentioned the legendary gardens, a chant erupted from the crowd, as though completing a ritual incantation. 'When you look up, there is nothing but the sky.'

'What?' snapped Zefer, reaching up and tugging at

the edge of Ruskin's cloak. 'What did they say?'

The old cleric lent down towards Zefer and whispered, so as not to disturb Roojika, who continued to speak. 'When you look up, there is nothing but the sky,' he repeated. 'It is a line from your own sacred text, Kuhnon.'

For a moment, Ruskin looked concerned. 'Are you testing me, master?'

'The prophesy is passing, and the bringer of the light is amongst us. As it is said in his own book: "*Though he may have been lost, salvation is always found buried in the depths of space and time, where Kuhnon first planted his roots.*" At last he has returned to his roots in the very foundations of the hive – speaking the tongue of his people and bringing evidence of the light in his very being,' continued the muridae, preaching a sermon to the excited ratskins.

As Roojika paused for breath, the crowd once again struck up a ritual chant.

'In the beginning he lay the end into the ground, and his finale was buried beneath the foundations, as though expecting the sky to fall into the abyss in the days when Kuhnon's salvation will come.'

Zefer was on his feet now, the shock of the words being chanted around him leaving him dazed. As he got up, a great cheer rose out from the crowd, expecting him to speak, but he was rummaging inside his clothes, searching for the notebook into which he had so meticulously scribbled his thoughts over the last few years. He really had no need to check those lines – even the youngest school children in the Ko'iron academies would be familiar with those famous opening words – but something in his brain rebelled against the incredible coincidence and he was suddenly unwilling to rely on his memory in case it was deceiving him. So many things had changed over the last few hours and days, including some things in his head; it was not inconceivable that his memories had shifted and mutated into new shapes.

In one of his sleeves, his hand fumbled across a square of paper, which he realised was the envelope that he had eventually been given at the Wall. But that wasn't what he needed now. He stripped off the long coat that he had been given by the women of The Coven and started to pat around his upper body, suddenly panicking that he had lost his book even after coming all this way.

The crowd had fallen into silence, and dozens of black in black eyes were staring up at him with confusion written into the blankness of their gazes as they watched his glowing arm dart around his body. But Zefer had completely forgotten that he was the spectacle, and he struggled against Krelyn's hand when she reached up to try and calm him. In the end, she gripped hold of his arm and yanked him back down onto the steps.

'What are you doing?' she demanded, hissing in a barely controlled whisper, apparently believing that the situation could still be salvaged. 'What's going on?'

Zefer flashed a look at Krelyn, making her recoil slightly under the unexpected venom. For that fraction of a second, it was as though Zefer had been replaced by somebody else entirely.

'It's the words... the words from the book. They said them. All of them... but they're different–' He was back.

'Slow down.' said Krelyn, and she slapped him. The crowd gasped.

'Ah!' exclaimed Zefer, oblivious to the strike but suddenly pulling a soggy and battered notebook out from underneath his vest. 'Here it is.'

Sitting on the edge of the dais, he carefully opened the book onto his knees and pushed his face down into the pages. He sniffed, inhaling deeply and holding the book against his nose as he sat back up again. The musty scent of the seventy-third floor of the Ko'iron librarium still lingered in the paper, but it was swamped now with a blaze of other things, pungent and noxious like the effluent in which it had been soaked.

Sniffing one more time, Zefer opened his eyes and suddenly realised where he was, as though the dank and stinking pages had finally brought it home to him. Looking out over the edge of his notebook, which was still pressed over his nose, he saw the crowd of ratskins staring back at him in incomprehension. Turning, he saw the same shocked look on the faces of the muridae and cleric. Finally, there were the curious eyebrows of Krelyn, whose eyes remained hidden behind her visor.

'Well?' she said.

Placing the book back into his lap, Zefer smoothed out the soaked and buckled pages. 'Yes – see, here,' he said. 'The ratskins just chanted these lines.' He pointed to some smudged text that he had carefully penned into the paper years before and then handed the book to Krelyn. 'This is where we are supposed to be.'

'This is were I am supposed to be,' he repeated, standing and addressing his remark to Ruskin. As he spoke and thought the words to the ratskin, the crowd erupted into cheers, and Ruskin's face relaxed into a smile.

SUDDENLY THE CROWD stopped cheering and scattered. In only a few seconds the town square was virtually empty, with Ruskin and Roojika the only ratskins still there.

'What did you say to them?' asked Krelyn, climbing to her feet next to Zefer to take a better look.

'I just told them what I told you,' he replied, taking his notebook back.

'They are coming. We must go,' said Ruskin, picking up Zefer's coat and handing it to him. 'We must get to the garden gates now, before it is too late.'

'What?' said Zefer, deciding that this was not the time to worry about his diction. 'Who's coming?'

'The hunters are coming. They have found us at last,' said Roojika, showing no signs of getting out of her throne.

'They must have followed our trail after all,' added Ruskin, turning and bowing to the muridae. 'My humblest apologies, muridae.'

'It is too late for apologies, Ruskin, but not too late for Kuhnon to fulfil the prophecy. Take him to the garden gates, and we will hold them off for as long as we can,' hissed the old woman, as though on the verge on unconsciousness. By the time Ruskin had nodded and turned back to Zefer, Roojika was already mumbling the wordless sounds of an incantation and the soft light under the square was beginning to burn a little brighter.

'We must go,' said Ruskin again, grasping Zefer by the sleeve and half-dragging him down the steps.

'What's going on?' asked Krelyn, slipping her finger into the trigger cavity of her stubgun as she skipped lightly down the steps after them.

'Triar and Elria are here,' explained Zefer. 'The ratskins heard them coming out of the tunnels on the perimeter of the settlement. Ruskin is going to take me to the archeotech–'

He was cut off by the clink of a grenade hitting the

metal floor and skidding towards the centre of the square. As it detonated, Krelyn and Ruskin dove at Zefer and squashed him to the ground beneath their combined weights. Sheets of fire sizzled through the air above them and Krelyn realised that Triar must have deployed another plasma bomb. However, as she lay waiting for the superheated sphere of plasma to expand into a miniature star above their heads and incinerate them all, a sudden blast of cool energy coursed through her and the coruscating flames in the air simply blinked out.

Rolling off Ruskin and Zefer and springing to her feet, Krelyn saw Roojika floating on a column of green, liquid light in the middle of the square. Threads and streams of the strange liquid had seeped up from under the scrap-metal floor and extinguished the fiery discharge from the plasma grenade, and a web-like lattice of tendrils had caught the fledgling star before it could form, choking the life out of it and suffocating its flames. Roojika was held entranced, muttering and mumbling wordlessly, orchestrating the hive's very own defence mechanisms.

'She's talking to the hive,' said Krelyn, the realisation striking her like a concussion. But, as she watched, she heard the crisp report of a bolt gun from the edge of the square and saw the muridae's head explode into a fountain of red. As her body flew back off the pillar of light, the energies in the square seemed to lose all focus, and the tendrils of icy green started to lash and whip in every direction at once.

Tracing the line of the shot, Krelyn shouldered her stubber and rattled off a hail of heavy bullets towards the shooter. An ear-piercing scream told her that she'd found her mark, but the dull clanging from her gun also told her that the ammunition had run dry. She cursed the Subversives for leaving near-empty weapons laying around in their cavern and cast the hunk of metal aside, grabbing a grenade launcher in its place.

Ruskin and Zefer were up and running, with the green lightning slashing over their heads and all around them. The ratskin cleric had his staff brandished into the air above him, and the tendrils of hive energy seemed to be sucked into it as he ran, drawing the lashes away from their bodies.

By now the sputter of gunfire and explosions could be heard from all around, and Krelyn realised that the ratskins had engaged the uphive gangers with their shotguns and pikes. It was hardly an even contest considering the kind of firepower that the uphivers would have brought with them. As if to confirm her fears, screams of pain cut through the shadows.

'Good luck!' she yelled at the disappearing figure of Zefer, reaching her decision and dropping a chain of frag-grenades into her weapon's reservoir, leaving only one still clipped to her belt.

'What?' he said, skidding to a halt and spinning around, pulling Ruskin to a standstill alongside him. 'What are you doing?'

She had started walking in the other direction, towards the sounds of battle. 'You're the one who knows about the artefact, you have to recover it – not me. Jurod just told me to make sure that you didn't screw it up. Baby-sitting is really what I do best.' She paused, removed the Ko'iron medallion from round her neck, and threw in over to Zefer. 'Return this to the prince for me.'

'We must go,' urged Ruskin, not really understanding what the woman in the square was saying. 'Leave her.'

Zefer paused. If the truth were known, he thought, he didn't really know anything about the artefact at all. He had just thought that he had made an interesting discovery about some new lines in a book in the Ko'iron librarium. They said something vague and suggestive about the foundations of the hive, and how House Ko'iron was there, but nothing specific. That said, after a slow start, everyone did seem to be making a bit of a fuss about it, and even he was beginning to believe the hype.

Grabbing a shotgun from his back, he racked its stock and turned back to Ruskin. 'Right,' he said, 'let's go.'

BEFORE KRELYN MADE it to the edge of the square, a group of ratskins came flooding in, wailing and shouting with flashes of tracer rounds zipping between them and over their heads. They were being routed. Bracing the launcher against her shoulder and angling it up into the air, Krelyn fired off a clutch of frag grenades. They arced over the top of the charging ratskins in a tight parabola and then rained down into the street behind them, exploding into showers of lethal shrapnel.

The tracer rounds suddenly stopped chasing the ratskin braves, and the braves skidded to an abrupt halt when they saw Krelyn. There was a moment of indecision as they tried to work out whether she was on their side, but then they remembered her from the dais and watched her lob another volley of grenades over their heads into the crowd of gangers at their heels.

Fanning out to take up positions on either side of her, the ratskins threw themselves onto the deck and rolled into firing positions with their shotguns, prising up slabs of metal from the floor to act as cover.

It was no great shock to see Triar leading the charge of gangers into the square. His silver mask sparkled and his eyes flashed as he levelled a plasma pistol and

squeezed off a burst of energy shells. Close behind him
came Elria, her straggled hair flaring out around her
like blue flames, and her red eyes surging with fire. And
then came a storming line of intermixed Salvationists,
Subversives and gangers from The Coven, bristling
with discharging weapons.

Krelyn loosed another barrage from her grenade
launcher and then threw it aside as it clicked to empty.
Triar and Elria charged through the explosions, almost
bathing in the flames, and Krelyn watched Triar fire
another round from his plasma gun. This was her
chance – plasma weapons may wreak havoc on the bat-
tlefield but they took too long to recharge to be
practical at this range.

Breaking into a run, Krelyn pulled her curved daggers
out of her boots and charged towards Triar, turning
flips and springing with her cloak whipping around
her to disrupt the sights of the ganger's weapon. When
she landed, Triar had already drawn his sword and was
poised waiting for her. She hit the ground and charged,
spinning her curved blades into twin frenzies on either
side of her, making Triar retreat under the onslaught,
hopelessly prodding forward with his sword as he staggered backwards.

Without breaking her rhythm, Krelyn suddenly
changed direction, stabbing out to the side with one of
her blades and feeling it slide home before she turned
to see Elria's shocked face falling towards her. Whipping the dagger out of the Escher's stomach, Krelyn
wheeled and swiped back towards Triar, spinning
around behind him as he tried to charge her in the split
second that she was distracted by Elria.

Bringing the inside of her elbow around his neck, she
pulled Triar back into her chest, with one blade held at
his solar-plexus and the other at his ear. She dragged

him round so that he could see the figure of Elria bent double and coughing up blood in front of him, as hails of gunfire ripped through the air all around.

Triar felt a trickle of blood run down his neck and he closed his eyes, waiting for the deathblow, muttering a silent prayer to the Undying Emperor that his soul be saved.

But the slice across his throat never came. Instead, he felt the weight of Krelyn fall against his back. He stepped aside, and she collapsed forward onto her face with two seeping entrance wounds on her back.

With a broad grin hidden behind his mask and a muttered thanks to the Emperor, he picked up his plasma gun and turned back to face the broken figure of Elria.

'Suffer not the witch to live,' he said, and fired a volley of superheated energy into her constantly burning eyes. Then he turned and charged back towards the battle raging against the ratskins. This was turning into a proper Redemptionist crusade, he thought.

'Is SHE DEAD?' hissed Curion, as Orphae stooped down and prodded Krelyn with the barrel of her still-smoking needle rifle.

'No, not yet,' replied Orphae, with her voice tinged with amusement. She rolled Krelyn over onto her back and lifted off her own visor.

'I have always wanted to meet you,' she confessed playfully, pushing up Krelyn's sleeve and admiring her snaking tattoo. 'The last of the genuine Delaque in our part of the hive, an authentic Red Snake. Very impressive.'

'And you have certainly been very helpful to us,' nodded Curion, not bothering to crouch down beside her.

'Yes, the masters will be very pleased to hear how

much havoc you have caused. Our power is now virtually unchallenged, thanks to your efforts,' explained
Orphae with mock gratitude.

'Of course, if the Ko'iron Contract is returned to us,
then you would return with it. Needless to say,' spat
Curion, the little red snake under his eye twitching
with disgust, 'there are many in the Red Snakes and in
House Delaque more generally who would rather not
share their kingdom with you, Krelyn Delaque.'

'Yes, it certainly would not do for you to attempt to
reclaim your birthright. It would cause… problems for
the masters.'

Drowning slowly, with her mouth full of blood, Krelyn could offer no answer to the venators, but she
realised that this was the second time that they had
knocked her to the ground in the last few days. She
also realised that actions speak louder than words, and
she thumbed the detonator on the last frag-grenade on
her belt.

10: SALVATION

AN EXPLOSION CUT through the persistent rattle of gunfire. It wasn't deafeningly loud, and it was way back in the central square, but it brought Zefer skidding to a halt as he ran after Ruskin. He turned just in time to see the smoke and flecks of shrapnel billow up into the air, breaking over the low roofline of the ratskin settlement.

'That was Krelyn,' he said softly, watching the smoke dissipate and mingle with the rest of the sludge in the air.

'Yes,' said Ruskin simply but with an edge of impatience.

Despite the energy of battle and the frantic strangeness of the surroundings in which he found himself, Zefer felt a calm sadness settling into his mind. He had hardly known Krelyn at all. He had met her for the first time only hours before. But, somehow, he felt that there had been a bond between them, the kind of bond that was built only after years of shared experiences. Her death took him by surprise, because he could suddenly not imagine the world without her. His world had been turned upside down over the last few hours and days; inexplicably, he had know that the explosion was her and, in that moment, his life had changed once again.

'How… How did I know?' asked Zefer, turning back to Ruskin and appealing to his wizened face as he might to a cleric or teacher.

'You are Kuhnon,' replied Ruskin, as though it was a simple matter. 'You feel the pulse of the hive.'

'And you, Ruskin?' asked Zefer, willing to believe anything at this point. 'You also feel this pulse?'

'You test me again, Kuhnon?' said Ruskin, slightly offended. Then he collected himself. 'Like all the ratskins, and more so.' He thrust this spirit staff forwards, as though that were proof.

A cloud of dust whipped through the street behind them, carrying the scent of burning fur and the metallic taste of shot. Zefer sniffed as he closed his eyes to prevent the particles from stinging them. As he did so, a burst of images besieged the darkness behind his eyes. He saw ratskin braves in flames, throwing themselves at the ground and rolling over and over, struggling in vain to extinguish them. He saw warriors charging with their pikes lowered being cut down by volleys of fire from the Subversives' autocannons. He saw Triar turning on Elria, and he saw Krelyn bleeding to death on the ground, thumbing a grenade.

His eyes snapped open and he saw that Ruskin was impatient to leave. His staff was glowing more brightly than ever, and he was twitching his head from side to side, checking the little alleys between the structures all around them.

'I can taste the wind,' marvelled Zefer, holding his glowing arm out in front of him and staring at it. Krelyn had been right – he was changing. It wasn't just the journey. It wasn't just that his body was toughening in a new and harsher environment. It wasn't even just that his eyes had been opened to new ways of viewing the hive – that process had begun with the

incongruous picture in Princess Gwentria's palace
weeks before. He was actually changing into something
else – the spirit of the hive, or whatever the effluvial
sludge was in that Subversives' cell, was changing him
from within. No matter what had brought him here, it
was somebody new who was finally arriving.

'For it is better to be well defined at the top than lost
in the paradoxes of foundations – unless it isn't,' he
quoted, looking deeply into Ruskin's black eyes.

'And it isn't,' answered Ruskin, as though Zefer had
spoken the first half of an ancient code.

'Perhaps it isn't,' said Zefer, striding after Ruskin as he
turned and hurried on through the outskirts of the settlement.

'Not far now,' said the totem warrior. 'We are nearly
at the gates.'

THEY WERE HARDLY the Spiral Gates, reflected Zefer as he
looked up at the huge, smooth surface of the nearly
featureless doors. Although he had very limited knowledge of building materials, even Zefer could see that
the dull, grey-blue material from which they had been
constructed was unusual. There were little trickles of
green fluid running down them, but otherwise the
doors seemed perfectly smooth and unmarked.

They were set into the side of a small dome, which
seemed to be made of the same material. It was almost
completely hemispherical and, again, totally
unmarked on its smooth surface. Round the perimeter,
however, Zefer could see mounds of rock that had been
hacked away from the ground where the walls of the
dome dove into it. It was as though somebody – or,
more likely, some teams of people – had tried to dig a
trench around the edge of the structure. The surrounding area was littered with broken tools, snapped

pickaxes and abandoned rams. Here and there, half buried in the rubble, Zefer was sure that he could see skeletal limbs protruding.

Set into the open ground on either side of the doors were two banks of columns that resembled the one Zefer had seen in the central square of Bandicota. Sure enough, as Zefer scanned his eyes over them, there was one more on the right than the left and a shallow pit had been dug into the ground where the missing pillar should have been. Presumably the ratskins had removed it and taken it as the totem for their town.

Like the one in the central plaza, these columns had simple, flat panels cut into them at about their midway points, but on these this was the only decoration. The panels were as grubby and grimy as the rest of the structure, but Zefer could just about make out the hint of a family crest under the layers of dirt. Straining his eyes in the dim light, he was sure that he could discern that crucial word, Kuhnon, etched into the bottom of the crest-panels.

Even leaving aside the lack of decoration and ornamentation on these columns, they still looked slightly different from the ceremonial monument in the heart of the ratskin settlement. For one thing, Zefer noted that they were not held vertically out of the ground, but rather stuck out diagonally in various directions. It was certainly possible that they had slipped over the centuries and millennia, but there was something ineffably deliberate about their formation that made Zefer think that they had been carefully positioned in that manner.

At their bases, where the dais had been around the totem in the town, heavy mounds of rock had been piled, as though to help support the weight of the wayward pillars. However, through the rubble and dirt,

Zefer could clearly see that the mounds were actually part of the columns themselves, like huge ball and socket joints in the ground, simply covered by ages of rockfalls and, perhaps, ceremonies.

As he watched, Ruskin picked a loose rock off the ground and wandered over to one of the pillars. He stuck his staff into ground next to him and muttered a quiet mantra, before carefully placing the rock onto the pile at the base of one of the columns. 'For the ratskin braves who have already fallen today,' he said solemnly as he saw Zefer's questioning look.

Zefer nodded in response, respecting the totem warrior's traditions but his mind racing with more rational, scholarly explanations for this site. Despite all the changes that he had undergone, he was still a curator of House Ko'iron, first class.

PUTRID GREEN FLAMES jetted out of holes in the ruined remains of the square, and the great column in the centre finally keeled over under the onslaught from the gangers of the Subversives. They cheered as the structure crashed down into the scrap-metal of the ground, smashing through the plates of plasteel and splashing sprays of fiery green out into the air. As the pillar fell, the dais around its base crumbled and wrenched out of the deck, exposing a complicated, bulbous metal structure grafted onto the end. Although the shape was melted by the flames and corroded by the toxins in the effluvial flow, there was the clear suggestion of a chair pointing out along the barrel, and a series of levers.

Standing in amidst the flames in the square, bathing in the light with his arms outstretched, his mask shimmering and his eyes flashing with delighted passion, Triar soaked in the atmosphere of righteous destruction. All around him lay the corpses of dead mutants, ratskins and witch-Coven-heretics. His blue cloak was soaked with grime, green effervescent slime, and deep red blood. It was torn and tattered as it fluttered around him with the flames. If he had realised how much fun it would be, he would have been on a crusade into the Underhive years ago.

From one of the burning sidestreets, Koorl, Triar's favoured deputy, came running. There was a clutch of Salvationist gangers behind him, limping and struggling to keep up, but Koorl himself seemed unharmed.

'The curator is heading for an old bunker at the edge of the dome,' called Koorl, skidding to a halt in front of Triar and watching his boss's eyes flare with unearthly blue fire. He had seen the glow of righteousness in those eyes before, but he had never seen them burn so violently. A thread of horror stitched itself into his soul as he realised what it could mean for the Redemptionist firebrand.

'Then we will bring the wrath of the Undying Emperor to the mutant and his disgusting ratskin lackey!' Triar's voice bellowed unnaturally, sending waves of imperatives and commands rippling through the devastated plaza. As he spoke, all of the gangers stopped hacking, slicing and blasting their way through the haphazard structures of the settlement. He had always been a charismatic and persuasive boss, but there was more to his tone than charm now.

Pushing Koorl aside, Triar swept through the square, letting the toxic flames lick at his boots and reach hungrily for the fabric of his fluttering cloak. He held his plasma pistol in his left hand and his long, elegant sword vertically in his right. Like a blazing angel of death he strode forth towards the edge of the blistering remains of Bandicota. The Salvationist gangers fell in behind him, grabbing the heaviest weapons that they could find from the dead grips of the fallen. Then, after a few seconds, the Subversives around the toppled totem in the centre of the square broke into a run, pumping their autocannons and heavy flamers from side to side as they went, finally falling into step with Triar's minions.

'How DO WE get in?' asked Zefer, running his hands over the smooth surface.

Pressing so intimately against the heavy doors, Zefer could see that the layer of grime and sluice that coated the material had been scraped and struck in various different places. The crack that ran down between the double doors was so clean that it looked as though it had been scrubbed everyday. Just below his head height, a shattered fragment of metal stabbed out from the crack, as though some kind of rod had been jammed in and then snapped off under pressure.

'Has anyone ever been in before?' he asked, realising that these were the residual marks of attempts at forced entry.

'Never,' said Ruskin simply. He wasn't watching what Zefer was doing. Instead, his back was to the doors and he was facing along the ramshackle path that had brought them there. Beyond was the settlement of Bandicota that had been his home for his entire life. As far as he knew, it had sat undisturbed for millennia, buried deep in the badzones of the Underhive and undiscovered by the predations of the uphivers. And now it was a blaze of ruination and flame, and the energies that pulsed through the air were replete with the death-agonies of his ratskin kin.

His spirit staff was aglow with energy, and he gripped it firmly in both hands. He was murmuring under his breath, and tendrils of acid-green liquid were trickling and creeping over the rocky ground in little streams, converging at the point where his staff cracked the stone at his feet.

'People have tried, from time to time,' he continued, talking as though it were merely an automatic impulse as he continued to murmur and concentrate on his staff. 'False messiahs have come with explosives and guns, but the gates to the Garden of the Sump remain undamaged, awaiting your return, Kuhnon.'

It was clear to Zefer that Ruskin was right. People had tried to force their way into the little dome, but they had failed. Whatever they had used had simply had no effect on the unusual material of the doors or of the dome itself. Underneath the thick, syrupy layers of grime, the structure must have been just as it had been when it was first built. Whatever that material was, Zefer was reasonably sure that it wasn't used anymore.

'So, how do we get in?' asked Zefer again, stepping back away from the impregnable doors.

'They are coming – you must hurry,' said Ruskin, apparently ignoring his question. 'They are coming, now.'

Zefer turned as the first shell screamed overhead. He saw Ruskin standing in an expanding sphere of green light, against which the ranged shots of the distant gangers bounced and burst. Looking back into the township, he could not yet see the advancing figures of the gangers themselves, but he trusted Ruskin's nose and he could not deny the periodic explosions of ordnance.

He turned back to the doors and stared at them. There must be a way in. There must be. He hadn't come all this way just to be thwarted by a simple puzzle. He solved puzzles everyday – that's what he did. He was a curator in the Historical Research Section – it was his job to solve puzzles and logic problems like this. Surely he hadn't changed so much that he had forgotten how to think.

How do you open doors that cannot be breached?

The most obvious thing about the question was that half of it was redundant, he reasoned. The fact that the material from which the doors were fashioned is unbreakable is irrelevant if the task is to *open* the doors. He was not trying to blow them up or knock them down, he just wanted to open them. The great adamantium Spiral Gates were virtually indestructible, but they creaked open from time to time when the right person gave the right papers to another person with the right key. It was simply a question of procedure.

What is the correct procedure for opening these doors?

A better question, thought Zefer, congratulating himself on his progress as another shell screeched overhead and slammed into the side of the dome. It's detonation was odd, since all of its force was thrown back in the direction from which it had come, spraying heat and light in every direction except into the dome itself. It was as though it were a las shot bouncing off a mirror.

A series of smaller explosions rattled above his head, but the bolter shells ricocheted energetically, bouncing back towards the shooters as though the impacts had had no appreciable effect on their velocities. However, the impacts did have an effect on Zefer, who spun round to see what was going on behind him.

The gangers were plainly visible now, clearing the fringes of the settlement and charging forward towards the archeotech site. Ruskin stood defiantly in their paths, sucking the tendrils of green sluice off the ground through his staff and then radiating an incredible green energy field into a dome that encompassed both him, Zefer, and the lower half of the impregnable doors. The hail of bullets that flashed out of the charging mob just seemed to glance off the field, but each impact made it stutter and flicker, and Zefer was sure that it would not hold forever.

Turning back to the doors, he struggled to discipline his mind once again: what is the correct procedure? He needed some clues. There was not enough information here to him to be able to answer the question. He needed resources, texts, people to interview... anything.

'You must hurry, Kuhnon,' called Ruskin, his voice trembling and weak, as though his strength was slowly deserting him.

Zefer looked from the ratskin totem warrior to the doors and back again, his mind racing but devoid of thoughts. He just didn't know what to do. And why should he, he realised suddenly. He wasn't Kuhnon. He didn't even know who this Kuhnon was supposed to be. He was a curator – a first class curator, but a curator nonetheless – not a ratskin messiah sent to bring light to the Underhive. He had just come on a research trip to see whether there was any evidence that the Ko'iron had been here at the foundations of the hive.

As if to show that it was all the fault of something else, Zefer snatched his notebook from its pouch and slapped it down onto the ground. He could blame the book, at least. But as the book smacked onto the step in front of the doors, it puffed up a cloud of dirt and dust and, from underneath, Zefer saw a familiar glint of blue.

He dropped down onto his knees and started scrambling at the dirt, shovelling aside slime and sludge with the cover of his notebook. In an indentation in the

stone, filled with guck and ancient grime, Zefer frantically uncovered a little crest. Even in the uneven, pale
green light of the Bandicota dome, Zefer could see the
tell-tale blue lines of the Ko'iron seal.

Tearing a page out of his book, Zefer used it like a
cloth to clean out the rest of the sludge, but it was
already clear that this was the mark of Ko'iron. He sat
back in amazement as he realised what this meant. He
had been right about the *Paradoxes of the Spire*; House
Ko'iron had been down at the foundations of the hive.
He could hardly wait to see the expression on the face
of that senioris, whichever one it was, when he told the
Historical Research Section the news.

Peering down into the hole a bit more closely, Zefer
screwed up his eyes in a moment of confusion. The little seal looked just like the Ko'iron seal in every
respect, except that it seemed to have the word 'Kuhnon' etched into the base, where 'Ko'iron' should be.
For a moment he was concerned, but then a flash of
insight struck him and he reached his finger down into
the hole to scrape away the remnants of the sludge that
still partly covered the emblem. He dug his nails into
the dirt, but it was firmly fused to the surface of the seal
and he couldn't budge it; eventually he gave up trying.

Slouching back against the doors, his hands covered
in iridescent grime, Zefer looked out at Ruskin, still
standing heroically with his hands clasped around his
spirit staff. The sphere of green energy was beginning
to fade and the gangers were now besieging him from
three sides, laying withering fire into the pulsing field
from their heavy weapons.

The cacophony of the battle seemed to fade into the
background as Zefer realised that he just had no idea
what to do. He still had the weapons that he had taken
from Krelyn, but he had never fired a gun in his life,

and was relatively sure that he wouldn't be able to confront the evangelic rage of Triar and the brute power of the Subversives all by himself. Even Ruskin's heroism just seemed poignant and depressing, as Zefer played idly with the page he had ripped out of his notebook.

He smoothed the paper out on his lap and sniffed at it automatically. Buried in amongst the smells of toxins and death, he could still just about make out the soot from his candle in the librarium, and he smiled weakly. Tilting the page into the light, he read the famous words for the last time:

In the beginning they lay the end into the ground,
And the finale was buried beneath the foundations,
As though expecting the sky to fall into the abyss
In the days of Ko'iron's salvation to come.

With a start, Zefer jumped to his feet and yelled over to Ruskin.

'I've got it! In the beginning they lay the end into the ground—'

He was cut off by a huge explosion of energy. Ruskin collapsed to his knees in exhaustion, dropping his staff to the ground. As he fell, the protective sphere of green light blinked out of existence and the tirade of fire that had been pounding into it from three sides suddenly burst through. A flurry of superheated plasma smashed into the doors above Zefer's head, but the abrupt and unavoidable crossfire shredded Ruskin instantly, leaving him lacerated, bleeding and dead on the floor where he fell.

'How DELIGHTFUL TO see you again, and in such enchanting surroundings,' said Snakryn, waving one hand around the private lounge in the back of the

Quake Tavern while swirling a glass of rich, red wine in the other.

'Master Snakryn,' nodded Prince Jurod. His guards fanned out around the perimeter of the room before he walked through the door with Gwentria in tow. 'It has certainly been a long time.'

Jurod sat opposite the venator master and picked up the glass of wine that had been poured for him. He handed it to one of his guards, who took a tiny sip – enough to test it for poison, but not enough for him to enjoy. Nodding confidently, the guard returned the glass and stood back against the wall. Jurod wiped the rim before taking a mouthful, wondering whether the Red Snakes of House Delaque were cunning enough to lace his taster's lips with poison.

'Can I have some?' asked Gwentria, reaching for the carafe without waiting for an answer. She propped herself up on her tiptoes and leant across the table with her fingers wriggling to reach the wine, but it was infuriatingly just too far away.

'You may not,' said Jurod bluntly, pushing the carafe even further out of his little sister's reach.

'But you said!' stamped the girl, clearly displeased as she folded her arms into a sulk.

'I said that you could attend this meeting with our old allies, not that you could drink their wine,' explained Jurod patiently.

'We are new allies too, are we not, my prince?' injected Snakryn smoothly, amusement playing over his face. 'Let us say that we are timeless allies.'

'Indeed, venator lord,' confirmed Jurod absently as he motioned for Gwentria to sit. 'Tell me, what news do you have of the crisis in Hive City?' asked Jurod, a look of serious concern returning to his countenance.

'As my messenger must already have informed you, my prince, the virtual collapse of the Snake Charmers – the Orlock gang led by Orthios – created a significant power vacuum in the sectors closest to the Wall, not to mention the inconvenience that this must have caused to your own house's supplies, my prince.' Snakryn smiled sweetly and appeared to be waiting for an appropriate response.

'Yes, indeed, we are all too painfully aware of the shortcomings of Orthios and his Orlock Snake Charmers,' responded Jurod encouragingly. 'It was most generous of you to step into the breach, so to speak.'

'Think nothing of it – the Delaque have long memories, and we remember a great many things about House Ko'iron,' replied Snakyrn, still smiling; it wasn't quite what Jurod had expected him to say.

'As you are aware, my prince,' continued the venator smoothly, 'there have also been other developments in these regions of the Hive City that may have implications for House Delaque. In particular, I am pleased to be able to report that we have succeeded in neutralising the threats posed by The Coven – the Escher gang of that witch Elria – and by those fanatical Cawdor idiots of Triar's Salvationists. In short, my prince, we in the Red Snakes of House Delaque are now unchallenged in our control of that vital sector of Hive City.'

'That is certainly excellent news for you.'

'And, I hope, for you, my prince,' added Snakryn. 'With such solidly consolidated control, House Delaque is in a uniquely strong position to guarantee supplies to the Noble House of Ko'iron through our Red Snakes.'

'Indeed,' mused Jurod, not altogether impressed by the subtlety of Snakryn's speech, but aware that he was speaking the truth.

'It is not that we were willing merely to "step into the breach," as you said. Rather, I am here to represent the collective wills of the masters of House Delaque and all our various gangs throughout Hive Primus: we would be willing to shoulder the full burden of the Ko'iron Contract once again,' concluded Snakryn, finally getting to the point.

Jurod nodded slowly, swirling the remains of his drink. Making a decision, he beckoned to one of his guards, who rushed over with a document pouch and slid it onto the table in front of the prince.

'Very well,' said Jurod, throwing back the rest of his drink and opening the pouch. 'This is the contract. You will find it the same as before. The same as it was for the unfortunate Orlocks. Should you fail to fulfil its terms, it will be unilaterally revoked – not exactly "timeless". Is that understood?' He pushed a sheet of paper across the table towards the venator master.

'Perfectly,' smiled Snakryn, pushing his chair back from the table as though about to leave.

'There is one further thing,' said Jurod, leaning forward.

'Anything, my prince.' His smile was fixed.

'I am sure that you are aware that Krelyn Delaque is currently on a mission for me in the downhive. I understand that you will be anxious to have her back, but I would be grateful if you could permit her to complete her mission for me before recalling her to your house.'

'I'm afraid that Krelyn is dead, my prince,' confessed Snakryn, furrowing his brow into an ostentatious frown. 'My agents in the badzones found her body. I am sorry. However, I am more than happy to provide you with a replacement venator from my own entourage.'

Snakryn beckoned over his shoulder with his hand. 'Curion, come out and show yourself.'

The prince's body-guards levelled their weapons as a cloaked figure emerged from the shadows behind Snakryn. He had been completely invisible until he stepped up to the table, but now Jurod could see the visor set into a deformed, scarred and burnt face. Under the rim of his visor, the remnants of what was once a snake tattoo twitched.

'Does that mean the funny man's not bringing me back my toy?' complained Gwentria, already grumpy about not being allowed any wine.

THE BULLETS RIPPED past his head as he ducked down, fumbling with the medallion that Krelyn had given him. They ricocheted off the door, bouncing back over his head instantaneously. He could barely hear the thudding of charging feet over the pounding of his heart as he stuffed the medallion into the hole in the ground and twisted it around until it clicked into place. In the beginning, he thought, closing his eyes as if in prayer, they lay the end into the ground, and the finale was buried beneath the foundations. Well, this was certainly the finale, and he was laying the pristine seal of his house into the ground.

A creak and a hiss of wind made him open his eyes. The great doors in front of him were opening slowly inwards, and volleys of fire were rattling in the widening angle. He jumped to his feet and pushed at the doors with all his strength, willing them to open faster. After a few seconds, the crack was side enough for him to get through, and he turned sideways to slip into the darkness beyond, with burning bright plasma shells hissing around him.

As he cleared the doors, he tripped, falling flat onto his face on the ground, splitting his lip and smashing his nose. Scrambling wildly to get back to his feet, his eyes fell upon another little hole in the ground, the mirror of the one out front. Without thinking, he plunged his medallion down into the slot and the doors ground instantly to a halt. Another second and they were moving back the other way.

Zefer sat on the ground with blood coursing down his chin, and he watched the huge, impregnable doors drawing back together. The vertical shaft of light that pushed in between them seemed incredibly bright when compared with the utter darkness in the bunker, but it grew rapidly dimmer as the doors started to meet in the middle. A fraction of a second before they finally sealed shut, Zefer saw a flurry of plasma zip through the crack and then a burst of blue fire as Triar crashed into the doors and pressed his face against them, reaching only fingertips into the interior.

Then it was black. Completely and utterly black. The dull thuds of the gangers' futile attempts to get in were barely audible, and Zefer simply sat motionless, listening.

After a while, his eyes became more accustomed to the light, the only source of which was his gently glowing arm, and he looked around. The space was roughly circular, like a small cave. The walls were smooth and curved, matching those he had seen outside. The only feature appeared to be a pedestal in the very centre of the chamber.

Clambering tentatively to his feet, Zefer shuffled over to the little podium, holding out his glowing arm to help light the way. The pedestal was also made of rock, carved and decorated in designs that looked vaguely familiar to him. Lying on top of the plinth was a large envelope. It seemed to glow green in the reflected light of his mutated arm, but it was probably white. Printed neatly on the front of it were five crisp characters: *CCA04*.

Zefer stared in incomprehension. He stared for a long time, although he had no sense of the passage of time in the darkness. Finally, he reached out and picked up the envelope, drawing it close to his face to sniff the paper. The scent was clean and lovely, reminding him of the Spire.

He carefully flicked off the Ko'iron seal on the back of the envelope and laid out the papers within on the pedestal in front of him. He stared again, shaking his head faintly and listening to the blood coursing through his ears. There was a pass to get him back up through the Spiral Gates and a collection of requisition vouchers for him to collect supplies and a guide from a depot on the Hive City side of the Wall. There was also a little certificate, promoting him to the position of first class curator.

A memory struck him and his hands flew all around his abdomen, searching and patting down his clothes. He found the little envelope in the curator's pouch in the sleeve of his undergarments, exactly where he'd left it.

Dropping it onto the pedestal with the other papers, he inspected it closely. The text across the front read: *Zefer Tyranus, Ko'iron Curator – First Class*. Whoever had written that must have known about his promotion already. He turned the envelope over and looked again at the little red icon stamped into the seal on the back. It resembled a tiny snake, but this still meant nothing to him so he flicked it off and opened the envelope.

Inside was a single sheet of paper. Zefer turned it over and over, checking both sides, but there were only three words printed onto one side in a cursive, elegant script: *Thanks, Zefer. Snakryn.*

After staring at the words for an immeasurable time, Zefer slumped down to the ground with his back against the pedestal, shaking his head in bewilderment. He had no idea who this Snakryn was, or what he had done to deserve his thanks. He had no idea what his documentation was doing waiting for him in this bunker and, most of all, he had no idea how he was going to get out of there.

Then he laughed, despite himself. For it is better to be well defined at the top than lost in the paradoxes of foundations – unless it isn't, he thought, understanding the sarcasm for the first time.

ABOUT THE AUTHOR

C S Goto has published short fiction in
Inferno! and elsewhere. In real life he
writes philosophy books, but real life
isn't all that it's cracked up to be. He
lives in Nottingham with four cats,
where he remains very anxious about
being a writer, since he is also a fiction
himself. In his spare time he dreams
about what he would do if he had more
of it. *Salvation* is his second novel following the Warhammer 40,000 epic
Dawn of War.

More action and adventure in the savage underworld of Necromunda:

ISBN 1 84416 188 9

She's the most dangerous woman in the underhive, so who the hell is brave enough to double-cross her?

Download the first chapter FREE at www.blacklibrary.com!

READ TILL YOU BLEED

DO YOU HAVE THEM ALL?

WWW.BLACKLIBRARY.COM